DON'T BELIEVE HIM

MONICA ARYA

To Rio, one of the greatest men I've known. I love you and always knew it was supposed to be woman's best friend. Thank you for keeping my feet extra warm while writing these books, for barking at absolutely nothing to make sure I'm safe, but also growing up with me. You're the best, my furry doodle.

And to those that ended up with the villain but had the courage to realize you never belonged in the darkness and can shine just fine on your own. This is our now.

AUTHOR'S NOTE

Dear readers,

Thank you for choosing my book to spend time with. This is my eighth novel and fifth thriller. As always, please note that I include content warnings at www.monicaarya.com and urge you to check those out if you have any concerns. I hope you enjoy Don't Believe Him!

My best always,

Monica

CHAPTER ONE

The day my husband got a vasectomy made me realize that it was true—women are, in fact, the superior species. I had pushed out his two giant-headed children, one of which I didn't even make it to the hospital for and delivered in the car. A day later, I was on my feet, doing laundry, meal prepping, and breastfeeding with cut nipples and wearing an adult diaper. Meanwhile, he gets snipped and was in bed for four days, moaning about the agonizing pain with bags of iced peas on his crotch, exclaiming that this had to be the worst pain a human being could possibly endure. It took every ounce of willpower and fear of the law to not smack him in the head with a cast-iron skillet.

It's amusing how much marriage shifts over the

years. I went from being crazy about my husband to realizing how every little thing he does drives me crazy. The symphony of his nightly snoring, the smacking of his lips when he chews, and even the sound of his breathing irks me. It wasn't always that way. Perhaps we changed along the way? We went from two carefree individuals to a married couple, cohabitating as exhausted parents and essentially roommates. There's a sweet time when the hardest decision in a relationship is what restaurant to eat at or what movie we'd watch, to suddenly being suffocated by intense decisions like mortgage lengths, college funds, and life insurance policies.

Life changes and, as a result, so do people. Who you married then is no longer the same person you're married to now. It's the simple truth, but a hard truth to stomach. Especially when you look over at the person next to you as they snore obnoxiously, and you realize you don't even know them. They've become a stranger. Oh, the irony. We grow up to be fearful of strangers, avoid them, and now, here we are, living with one.

My husband, Warren Cooper, is one of the most beloved and reputable professors at the University of North Carolina at Johan. He's admired, he's respected, he's fawned over. He's the perfect and annoying example of a man who only grows more attractive with age. While I'm toppling over my ten-step skin-care regimen as gravity does its best to hunt me down daily, he washes his entire body with a bar of Dove soap and goes to bed the second his salt and peppered head hits the pillow.

Sometimes I lay awake at night with the shimmering moon peeking through the pointless, aesthetically-pleasing sheer curtains and wonder what he's dreaming of as his lips twitch into a slight smile. It bothers me that he's sleeping completely worry-free as I run through the never-ending to-do list. But our children, Max and Ava, were both officially in college now, and we were embracing the empty-nester life. This would be our first-year prioritizing being husband and wife over being mom and dad.

Ava, our daughter, was going into her junior year, studying abroad in London. Meanwhile, our son, Max, was going to stay on campus for classes and baseball. Since Warren was a tenured professor at UNC, and both our children did extremely well in high school, they were accepted and were able to get discounted tuition. We really were blessed with the all-American family. A daughter, a son, a marriage of twenty-one years, a gorgeous home filled with laughter and memories. A photo gallery filled with black-and-white images that spanned from when Warren and I had just met, to when Max and Ava were infants, to recent family vacations and graduations.

It was the life I suppose so many dreamt of. Stability is such a gift in life. Warren and I didn't have a traditional way of meeting one another; it was actually quite controversial at the time. The nature of our relationship was a scandal of sorts, but every scandal eventually withers away, replaced with something new and exciting.

That's what his haggard, now dead mother referred to me as: something new and exciting. Looking into the mirror now, I wasn't new nor exciting; I was actually quite boring, and... well, stable. We had sex twice a week—Tuesdays and Thursdays, and on birthdays. We ate dinner at the same time, I met with my close friends who lived on the lake near us for drinks, and besides that, most of my days were spent shuttling the kids around. But now that my baby birds were flying free, my free time was starting to make me nervous.

My reflection showed creases around my eyes and forehead that weren't always there, my breasts needed a quality bra to resemble a reasonable shape, my lower abdomen held on to the weight from two pregnancies and deliveries. Stretch marks splashed across my once smooth hips, and new sunspots were making their way on my once clear skin. Stretching my face upward, I tilted my head. Maybe a little Botox would boost my self-esteem. Standing to the side, I sucked in the small curve of my abdomen. It was the overzealous bounce-back culture that inflicted deep-rooted body dysmorphia in women and mothers. After having a baby, society didn't care how quickly or well you recovered or healed; no, they applauded you for how fast you could fit into those pre-pregnancy jeans, or the old lady at the grocery shop pestering you to make sure you breastfeed because it'll "melt the fat right off." Here I was, seventeen years postpartum, still eyeing my body with hints of judgment. Relaxing, I recognized that, as a forty-year-old woman, I'd never felt freer from the weight and burdens society had continually pegged onto me. I was starting to realize that I had a husband who loved and adored me... who desired me. I had two beautiful children who appreciated me, and wonderful friends who enjoyed my company. That's why life was good.

"Hey, sweetheart, I'm going to be late tonight." Warren came around the corner into the foyer where I stood, staring at the girl in the reflection I no longer recognized.

Turning around, I clutched the console table, pressing my butt against it. "I can't believe you're still going to teach a full schedule." I pursed my lips. "You promised we'd spend this next chapter of our lives traveling and doing all the things we've put off."

Warren, my handsome husband, wrapped his arms around me, tugging me closer. "I'm sorry, love. We still are going to take the beach trip, and I promise this weekend we will go on a date or something. Why don't you go for a swim? The weather is perfect, and I bet the water is heavenly. Besides, the kids will both be at college all year. We have plenty of time together." He nodded toward the backyard. "Go for that swim."

We had put in a gorgeous, heated swimming pool when Ava and Max were in middle school and, of course, Warren and I hardly used it.

"Yeah, I think I might." I shrugged and fixed his sports coat lapel, patting his tie down carefully.

"I love you, sunshine." He lifted the dainty necklace with a pendant engraved with a compass around my neck before kissing me. "You've always led me in the right direction."

Sunshine was the nickname he gave me in college. He always said I brought light back into his otherwise darkened life.

"I love you, too, professor." I rolled my lips together

in a small smile as he grabbed an umbrella and began to walk out.

"It's not supposed to rain today, is it?" I questioned.

"You never know when a summer shower will happen. It's best to be prepared for the storm, Nina. Storms always come when you least expect it." Warren's forehead crinkled as he looked at me standing in between our opened front door.

The way he was staring at me sent a shudder through my body. Swallowing, I parted my lips to speak, but before the words came out, he smiled at me.

"It'll be a late evening. I'll see you when I see you." Shutting the door behind him, I stumbled back and looked around the oversized foyer.

The scariest sound in the world taunted me.

Silence.

CHAPTER TWO

"You need a hobby, Ni." Paige eyed me over her glass of prosecco as we sat around the blazing firepit in the backyard. With the lake rippling behind us, the scent of freshly cut grass around us, and a stunning sunset above us all made for the perfect evening.

"Why don't you come to Pilates with us?" Joselin reached for crackers and cheese from the charcuterie board she brought over. Paige and Joselin, or Joss, were my two best friends. Not only were they my best friends, but they were also my neighbors. The three of us had lived on Ivory Lane for the past decade.

"I don't need a hobby, I just… I mean, is it that bad to want to spend quality time with my husband? He's never home, and at this point, we've basically become

8

roommates." I took a long sip of my wine, swirling it around, looking into the dense trees that circled the lake.

"Maybe he's having an affair." Paige stretched her arms over her head and yawned. Her beautiful blonde mermaid hair toppled over her shoulders as Joselin gasped and shot her daggers with her eyes.

Swallowing the lump in my throat, I looked between them both. Suddenly, I felt something crawl on my arm. I looked down and my eyes widened before I swatted the giant insect off my arm. Shuddering, I looked up as the darkened lake blended into the towering trees surrounding us.

"Why would you think that?" I tried to keep my voice steady, but it was shaking. The thought had crossed my mind before. I questioned why my husband went to work, wearing cologne and dressed to the nines. Why my husband came home happier than he was when he left? Why he eagerly taught year-round when money wasn't a problem, and this was the point many professors slowed down and headed toward retirement. But we had stability; we loved our family, and...

"What kind of professor comes home when it's dark out? And I thought he wasn't going to teach a full schedule..." Paige popped a chocolate-covered strawberry into her mouth. Out of the three of us, Paige spoke her mind with zero filters. We loved her for that; she was the friend you went to for the truth, even if it hurt to hear it.

"Warren would never cheat on me. Besides, I know most of his coworkers, who are all boring, grumpy professors," I scoffed, quickly finishing off my drink.

Joselin nodded and poured more wine into my glass. "I don't think he's having an affair; he's probably just sitting in his office with all of his books and just…"

Warren loved to read, and write, for that matter. He was working on a thriller novel, and it made sense that he'd stay in his office to write. He had secured his dream literary agent and recently signed a two-book deal with a publisher. Writing this novel had consumed all of his free time. If he wasn't teaching, he was writing. He said he refused for his first novel to be anything less than perfection.

"He has to grade countless papers, and then he has office hours. Then, it's the writing deadlines for his book. Some people love their work, Paige." I stabbed a marshmallow onto the skewer and aggressively shoved it over the flame, watching it burn quickly.

"That's fine. Just make sure you're not trying to

convince yourself more than me." Paige stood and swatted in front of her face.

"Fucking mosquitoes. I'm out, ladies. Cash is waiting for me." She winked at us and blew a kiss before turning away, her flowing white dress spinning behind her.

"Goodnight, Paige!" Joss and I chimed behind her. When we knew she was gone, Joselin immediately dropped in closer. The crickets chirped in the tall, murky grass as the fire crackled.

"Listen, Nina, I don't think he's having affair, but I do think you have to maybe, I dunno, just find out why he's gone so much." Joss paused and looked up at the darkened sky. "Having kids changes a marriage, being married to the same person for years on end gets... well, lackluster."

"I don't think it gets lackluster," I said sadly. But I agreed, once we had kids and got into the rat race of life, we grew farther and farther apart. It was as if once we let the gaping hole widen, we couldn't stop it from expanding rapidly.

"And I think Warren is really lucky to have you for that reason, and so many others. But men are natural hunters." She reached for the bag of marshmallows and popped one into her mouth.

"I don't understand?"

"When things get calm and steady, they crave the hunt… the chase. They need the next—"

"Ladies?" Warren's voice cut through the warm evening air as we both flung to look toward our deck.

Joss cleared her throat and immediately stood. "Hey, Warren."

"Well, I'm heading out, but I'll call you tomorrow. Love you." She hurriedly grabbed her shawl and waved at Warren, avoiding his eyes.

What was that about?

I looked over at my husband, who was standing with a smile on his face. He was glowing. Who came home from work that happy?

Most of all, as I tilted my head and looked at him, I realized maybe someone else was making him that happy while he was at work? Or *supposed* to be at work.

CHAPTER THREE

"*I* wish you'd come home more often. I miss you, Max." I pushed my sunglasses on top of my head and looked across the table at the on-campus café. Warren was here, too, but in lecture, and I knew better than to be a desperate wife, staking out in front of his office.

"Mom, I have practice, classes, and…" His eyes flicked behind me, causing me to follow his line of vision.

My son stood up excitedly as a beautiful young woman bashfully came up to our table.

"Mom, I want you to meet someone." He quickly grabbed a chair from another table, and the young woman sat in it and looked at me with a small smile. My heart began to race from being caught off-guard.

"Hi, Mrs. Cooper, I'm Scarlett. It's so nice to meet you." She stuck her hand out as I glanced back at my son with widened eyes.

Taking her hand, I smiled politely. "It's nice to meet you, too, Scarlett."

"Scarlett and I started dating a while ago, but I figured we'd keep it to ourselves a bit. She transferred to UNC in the spring semester, and we became fast friends." Max leaned back in his chair.

"Scarlett, where did you transfer from?" I don't know why this felt awkward to me. Maybe because this was officially my son's first college girlfriend. He had dated casually in high school, and I had met all his girlfriends, but college relationships had a higher chance of turning into something serious and long-term. It's how my marriage had started.

"I transferred from UCLA." She started to fidget with her fingers anxiously.

"Oh wow, California to North Carolina is quite the journey. Are your parents…" I began, but was quickly cut-off by Max.

"Mom!" His voice raised as he squinted at me with annoyance.

Startled by his reaction, I parted my lips with my hand on my rapidly beating heart, "Oh… I'm…"

"No, it's okay. It's okay, Maxie," Scarlett started.

Oh, dear God. Maxie?

"My parents died in a car accident when I started school... it's why I transferred. I couldn't heal being there. They died on the way to visit me, right outside of campus." Scarlett's icy blue eyes looked straight into mine. The way her face was emotionless was concerning, but then she smiled. That simple, yet quick shift in emotion startled me.

"It's fine, though. I've got my Maxie now, and I've never been happier." Slicing her eyes back over to my infatuated son, I looked down at my coffee.

Something didn't feel right. I had my first child when I wasn't even able to legally drink, and Max right after. From the moment I became a mother, I realized the concept of a mother's intuition is factual. I could feel something off or wrong before it even happened. It's an innate need to protect our children. I remember once learning in college about elephants being some of the most protective animals—they make sure the youngest member of their herd stays on the inside of the group in order to best protect them from predators. Human mothers, well... we didn't have the same privilege. While it takes a village to raise a child, most of the time there is no village. No one shows up when you're deliriously exhausted, no one shows up to give you a break, no one holds your hand as you second-guess what you're doing and how you're raising your children.

No one does that because it's an assumption that this is your job as their mother.

Protect them, at all costs.

From predators. And for some reason, as I stared at my giddy son and his beautiful, fiery-red-headed girl-friend, I couldn't help but feel the predator had already arrived.

She was sitting next to my child in a sundress, and I knew destruction was coming.

But the thing no one warns you about mother-hood, is that when you feel that gut-instinct sensation coursing through you faster than your own blood, you're warned to push it aside. You're coaxed to remember your baby bird can fly on their own...

And that's what I did. I just didn't realize how fast my baby bird would lose his wings because the predator sliced him down.

"Mom?" Max cut through my thoughts.

Shaking my head and forcing a smile out, I cleared my throat and grabbed my purse. Brushing my hand against the bright green dress I wore, I stood. "I've got to get home and start dinner. Your dad said he'll be home on time… which, have you seen him on campus today?" I asked as I grew closer to Max with open arms.

Scarlett quickly wrapped her arms around him. Furrowing my brows, I looked at her with agitation.

Max awkwardly released one of his arms to give me a semi-hug in order to keep his sloth of a girlfriend on him.

"No, I haven't seen him in a while. It's a huge campus and honestly, I'm not really looking to hang out with my dad here, Mom." Max shrugged as Scarlett stared at me with no reaction or detectable expression.

"Well, come home soon for dinner. The house feels so empty without you and Ava. You're thirty minutes away, but you haven't been home more than once a month." I knew I needed to stop nagging him; it wasn't fair just because he stayed close to home to hover over him.

"Mom, I miss you and home, but Dad's always riding my ass about medical school and cutting back on baseball… yada, yada, yada." Max made his hand into a talking mouth and rolled his eyes.

I should have felt sad for my husband; I should

have defended him. But in some sick way, I felt relieved to know it wasn't me being the overly annoying, hovering parent.

I was the good parent... the more loved parent.

No parent would ever admit it, but being the favorite parent is one of the most satisfying feelings in the world when you have children.

"I love you, Max. I'll drop off some food for you soon. But I'm not taking any of your laundry home with me." I wiggled my finger at him as he squinted at me and subtly nodded toward Scarlett.

"I'm just kidding. He is such an independent young man, Scarlett." I feigned seriousness.

She didn't laugh, and she didn't smile.

"Don't worry, Mrs. Cooper. I love Max more than you ever could. He doesn't need anyone else now that he has me," she said without a hitch. There wasn't a playful grin or joking smile on her face.

No, she was dead serious.

There was a lingering, awkward silence between us as I gripped my necklace and cleared my throat.

Max nudged her slightly, and as if he were turning on a robot, she blinked. "It was nice to meet you, Mrs. Cooper."

Nodding, I waved goodbye to them both and quickly left.

But even as I walked away from Max, my stomach twisted into knots.

I knew I was right.

I knew I had just left my son with a predator.

What kind of mother does that?

CHAPTER FOUR

*P*acing back and forth on the deck, I looked out at the lake. Our infinity pool dropped into it, and part of me wanted to just jump in one or the other and drown out my racing thoughts. Glancing at my watch, the hands ticked away.

"Where the fuck are you, Warren?" I murmured and called him for a tenth time.

The ringing taunted me, but when I heard his calm tone in his voicemail, I clutched my phone and shrieked at the screen.

My hands shook with anger as I sank into a lounge chair and laid back. The comforting cool breeze rippled through the air, and from a distance, I could hear neighboring children laughing and the scent of charcoal burning. I had texted Paige and

Joselin to see if they wanted to come eat the giant pot full of chicken tikka masala I had made, thinking my husband would actually be home on time.

But here I was, sitting alone, and he hadn't texted or called me in hours. My friends were busy with their own lives, and my children no longer lived at home. That's something no one tells you about your forties. It's that you can go your whole life full of noise and chaos and someone always needing you to suddenly being completely alone in the quiet.

"Hi, sweetheart." Warren's footsteps grew closer and I closed my eyes, pretending I had fallen asleep out by the pool.

The scent of his cologne was more pungent, and I knew he was leaning in toward me. Brushing a straggling piece of hair from my face, he whispered, "You used to be more beautiful…"

My skin crawled as the man I loved and respected shattered my heart with six words.

A moment later, he draped a blanket over my body and planted a kiss on my forehead.

I was frozen in place, forcing myself to steady my breathing. His footsteps retreated, and the scent of sandalwood and cedar dissipated. A single tear escaped from my eye and rolled down my cheek.

As soon as the door shut behind him, I sat up and slapped my hands across my mouth, gasping on an impending sob that choked me. The sky had darkened completely and not even a star was in sight. Standing, I peeled my clothes off and looked out at the pool and lake it fell into.

I had never actually swam in our lake before, and truthfully, I was terrified of it. It was because I was terrified of the unknown. I couldn't see through the murky water; therefore, I didn't know what could be lurking underneath. Laughing at myself, I slapped my hand against my forehead.

Oh, the irony. I was always living life in fear and on the safe side, but here I was, living with a complete stranger. My husband was drowning himself in work, just so he could avoid me. Walking down, I dipped my toes into the dark water and looked up at the shadows of trees that hugged it. Maybe swimming in the lake for the first time at night with no one around wasn't the best idea. Walking backward, I turned toward our pool and watched my reflection.

Shuddering for a moment in my nude bra and panties, I dragged my toes through the pool water, watching as the small lights mirrored inside. Raising my hands up high, I positioned my feet together and glanced down at my body.

My hips fell slightly over my panties, embedded with stretch marks and bloating. My T-shirt bra wasn't doing any favors for my breasts, but I unsnapped it and threw it down.

This body grew and nurtured two babies, this body fought through countless illnesses, this body...

I was proud of this body.

"Fuck you, Warren." I dove into the pool and crashed into the cold water below, feeling free for the first time in a long time.

Staying under the water, I held my breath longer than I should have. I opened my eyes and immediately, my lips instinctively parted.

Choking on mouthfuls of water, I saw her face.

Scarlett.

My son's girlfriend's red hair was flailing around as her pale, translucent skin and her icy-blue eyes popped, even through the water. Her thin fingers reached out toward me and a small smile tipped across her lips.

Shoving myself upward, I gasped and coughed violently. Pushing my hair out of my face with both hands, my chest heaved rapidly and I tossed my head back and blinked, my breathing completely erratic.

Placing my hand over my heart, I counted my breaths. "Please, no," I whispered to myself, closing my eyes that burned from the chlorine. I waded around in a circle to check for her. Where was she? Squinting, I froze.

Something was wrapped around my fingers.

Lifting my hand slowly, my fingertips were wrinkled and strands of red hair were tightly wound around them.

I felt lightheaded.

Since I was a child, I've had these premonitions. Not visions, nor hallucinations; I was completely sound of mind. Some may call it déjà vu, while others just say it's intuition. They rarely happened, but when they did occur, there was a one-hundred percent rate that they would come true.

Looking into the pool, I shook with the breeze slapping against my drenched bra and panties and damp skin. Grabbing the blanket from the chair, I wrapped it around myself.

No one was in the water.

CHAPTER FIVE

*D*elicate fingertips padded against my face in the middle of the night. Clenching my eyes tight, I didn't want to see him. Fingers ran through my hair and suddenly, a cold breath blew into my face. My chest tightened. I realized something.

It wasn't Warren's hands.

My chest rose and fell faster as I heard footsteps retreating. I was too scared. If I saw who it was, they may kill me. I waited until only the distant sound of wind brushing through the trees echoed. Slowly opening my eyes, I blinked away the darkness.

Sitting up, I watched as our curtain danced wildly with the wind.

It was open, and I knew, without a shadow of a doubt, that we never slept with it open. Glancing at my oblivious husband next to me, I shuddered. Was it just a dream? Sliding out of bed, I tiptoed to the window.

Nothing but the darkened lake, rippling slowly as the moon glimmered against the endless water. Brushing my hand across my face, I grabbed the bottle of melatonin and swallowed two.

"Warren, I think someone was in the house…" I whispered so quietly, I knew he wouldn't hear me—it just felt reassuring to say it out loud. But I didn't know if I even believed myself.

I woke and heard the shower running. I really didn't want to face Warren. How could I? He had admitted that I was once beautiful, meaning he wasn't attracted to me anymore. Worst of all, I was now mad at my husband, and he didn't even know it. He thought he was confessing something so cruel to his sleeping wife.

I knew I couldn't pretend to sleep the morning away. I always made him breakfast, and I always packed his lunch… I was always the perfect wife and mother, and now I was laying here, realizing I didn't even know who I am anymore.

Who is Nina?

"Good morning, sleepyhead." Warren stood at the end of the bed with his towel hanging off his perfectly defined hip bones.

Pushing myself upright, I offered a tight-line smile.

"It's Thursday." He smirked at me, and ran his hand through his unnaturally thick hair. Where was male-pattern baldness or something, anything to make him less attractive?

"It's Thursday morning." I shoved the comforter off, repulsed by the thought of having sex with my husband who had just called me unattractive to my face only a few hours ago.

"Baby, what's wrong?" His tone changed, and he quickly walked over to my side of the bed, caging me in with his opened arms.

He reeked of his expensive cologne.

"Why do you need to wear so much cologne when you're teaching a bunch of teenagers?" I fired at him.

His forehead creased as his eyebrows knitted together. "I've worn the same cologne for the past twenty-five years of teaching, Nina. What kind of accusation are you trying to make?" He took a step closer to me, filling in the space between us.

"I just don't understand why you're working so late every single night. I…"

"I just don't understand why you're being so damn needy. Maybe you just need to stop analyzing what I'm doing and figure out something *you* should be doing." Warren's fist clenched and his jaw ticked. Taking a step back, my legs hit the bed and I looked down at his hand.

Scoffing, I rolled my eyes. "What, you're going to hit me now?" I glanced back at my husband, knowing I was playing with fire.

Blowing out a breath of air, Warren unclenched his fist and turned away. "Get a fucking hobby, Ni."

Sinking down into the bed, I clenched my teeth. *I guess we aren't going to have our usual Thursday sex after all.*

Warren left for work wearing a white button-down and a fitted gray suit. His hair was slicked back, and he looked like he belonged in an ad for the damn cologne he swam in.

I ended up going back to bed and falling asleep for another three hours. I woke up to my phone buzzing, and I felt overjoyed to see my daughter, Ava, was calling me.

"Hi baby," my voice broke.

"Hey Mom! How are you?" I could hear the bustling of the city behind her. Closing my eyes, I couldn't help but smile, picturing my beautiful, smart daughter living the life I had always envisioned for myself.

She was studying fine arts and was traveling through Europe this summer. Before I had met Warren, I had always dreamt of doing the same. Painting, dancing, and drinking my way through gorgeous countries around the world.

That's what I loved, painting. That was a hobby I enjoyed but had abruptly stopped when I became a mother. How could I paint with a husband who was always gone, no family in town, and trying my best to stay afloat through postpartum depression and anxiety while everyone around me pretended I was just fine?

There wasn't much awareness; hell, there still isn't. As mothers, we don't realize we are drowning while trying to be everyone else's anchor. I didn't enjoy giving up my identity. Warren and my friends keep telling me I need a hobby, but where were they, telling me that, as I was in the thick of motherhood alone? Did anyone say, "Let us take the baby so you can paint?" No, no one did. Even when the children got

29

older, I was racing around between carlines and extracurriculars. I was wiping noses and holding vomit buckets at three a.m.; I was cooking dinner, maintaining a clean home, and keeping up on the groceries. I was consumed by being a wife and a mother, and there was no room left to be me.

And no one cared. Because I was filling everyone else's cups, and when everyone else was hydrated and happy, they didn't care that I was withering away. You're just a stay-at-home mom, after all.

"Mom?" Ava repeated.

"Hey, baby, I'm sorry. I… I'm doing good. Missing you, of course. How are you? How's London? I hope you're taking your vitamins and carrying your pepper spray everywhere." I smiled, fighting back the emotions that were overcoming me.

Ava let out a laugh. "I miss you, too, Mom. I'm fine, everything's fine. Don't worry so much."

"It's my job to worry." I sighed and pulled myself out of bed. Walking over to the curtains, I tugged them open, revealing the bright sunshine pouring in.

"I know, but I hope you're having your epic year of fun. Besides, you finally got annoying Max out of the house, so you need to live it up."

"Oh yes, it's been fun, for sure. I'm going to head

out and get a mani and pedi with Paige, and then..." I started, but my phone signaled another call.

It was Max, and he never called me unless it was important. "Hey, sweetie, I'm going to call you back; your brother is calling." I swear, everyone always called simultaneously.

"No, no, it's fine, Mom. I'm heading in to get happy-hour drinks with friends. I love you, and I will call you over the weekend."

"Okay, honey. I love you, too!" I quickly switched the call over to Max.

"Hey, Mom." Max was out of breath, and my heart quickened and panic set in.

"Max! What's wrong?" I raced to the closet to grab clothes to change into.

"Mom, calm down. I just got done with a workout. I'm just letting you know that me and Scarlett are coming to the house this weekend for the cookout." I could hear him chugging water.

"Oh... wow, okay. Yeah, that would be so much fun," I quickly replied, trying to push the thoughts of my son's new girlfriend drowning in the lake from my mind.

Max began talking to a friend in the background and laughed. "Great, Mom. I'll see you Saturday." He hung up immediately.

Maybe this is what I needed—something to look forward to. I suppose I envisioned the year full of travel and romantic evenings with Warren. It was okay to feel disappointed. Something I had realized as a wife and mother is you can't blame people for disappointing you when maybe, you were expecting too much from them. It was the sad truth, but sometimes that's what people did; they'd disappoint you.

So instead, in this moment, I decided to take control over this year of change. I could find myself and figure out who I was beyond what I'd always been expected to prioritize.

Forcing myself to push the irking feeling that my husband was hiding something while my premonitions about Scarlett continued to haunt me, I knew I needed to do something else.

With a pep in my step, I played Shaggy on my Alexa and danced around while getting ready. I could push it all aside, put makeup on, and slide into a pretty dress to tune out the noise for a bit.

CHAPTER SIX

"Oh God, this feels so good. Mmm..." I moaned, tossing my head back as my nails dug into the armrest.

"Damn girl, you really do need to get laid." Paige looked over her glass of champagne at me.

Widening my eyes, I dropped my jaw. "Paige!" She spat out a bit of champagne and laughed at my reaction.

"You're getting off by a nail salon massage chair. I'm just speaking the truth." My feet were being scrubbed, my back was being beat up by a leather chair, and my entire mood had shifted.

"Isn't it Thursday? Shouldn't Warren be spanking you tonight?" Paige asked with mischief dancing in her beautiful green eyes.

"Shh!" I waved my hand at her. Paige and I were polar opposites. She was a free spirit, who spoke her mind and lived each day doing whatever she loved. I was the logical, rational, over-thinker who was much more modest.

"You're reading too many smut books again, aren't you?"

Paige erupted into laughter while my face heated in embarrassment.

Pressing my head into the chair, I turned to face my ridiculous friend. "We got into a fight this morning. I confronted him about the cologne overdose and late hours..."

Paige immediately stopped laughing, her eyes slanted as she looked at me for a moment. "What did he say?" She took a long sip of her drink and finished the glass.

"He got upset. Turned it around to me essentially not having a life and fixating on him." I licked my lips before setting my glass down.

"Cash uses a PI for his business. Maybe..."

"No, no... Oh my God, I'm not going to hire a PI to investigate my husband and father of my children, Paige." Shaking my head, I looked back down at my toes. I had picked a bright blue shade—something fun and different from my usual go-to, which was a blush, pale pink.

"Oh-kay, if you say so. But you know what they say…" Paige wiggled her freshly painted hot-pink toes.

"I don't know what they say, but I'm sure you're going to tell me." I lifted my brow.

"If you see people by their actions, then you'll never be fooled by their words." Paige stretched her hands over her head.

"Right now, he's wrapping you up in his words, trying to make you think you're crazy or being irrational. Gaslighting, my friend." Paige tugged out a tube of bright red lipstick and handed it to me. "Take it, wear it… It'll change you, and then you'll be smarter. Smarter like me."

Taking the tube of lipstick from Paige, I shook my head. "What does that even mean?"

"You're too trusting and nice. Women like you get taken advantage of. So, it's time that you change a bit. Use the lipstick as a crutch to start that journey. You're forty-years old, Ni. It's now or never. Do you want to be married to someone you aren't even sure if he's out there, fucking some sexy, nerdy professor colleague?"

Opening the lipstick, I looked at the creamy red

and glided it over my lips. "I think I'm going to sneak into his office," I whispered.

Paige had a look of excitement and intrigue on her face. As much as I loved my friends, it was true. People loved when you had drama happening in your life. You became the new source of entertainment.

"Want me to come with?" She tapped her freshly done nails together.

"No, no… he's got a meeting across town tonight. So, I'm just going to drop by campus and look around. I mean, really, he might just be holed up writing his book or just trying to impress his students. My husband is a walking example of a mid-life crisis." Sliding my feet into the cheap, foam slippers, I trekked to the drying station with Paige beside me.

"Well, just remember how he met you." Paige sank into the chair next to me.

That's what scared me the most. Did my husband have a type? He was thirty-six when he met me, back when I was sitting in his class as his student. Nothing was different then.

Closing my eyes, I thought about the gold band that sat on his finger when he'd stand in front of my class of eager students, sucking us in with his charm and charisma. I was a good girl, who would have never, in a million years, thought I'd fall for him.

Did karma finally come around?

But he was separated when we met, and I wasn't the cause or reason of his first marriage ending.

Yet, there I was, a beautiful, overly-eager young woman, falling for a much older man who already had a tainted relationship.

What if there was another girl out there just like me?

"What if she's not a colleague?" I looked over at Paige.

"Do you think Warren, a fifty-seven-year-old professor, is seeing a student?" Her eyebrows lifted.

"I don't know... That would be crazy, right? He's... he's old enough to be their dad. I mean, Max and Ava are literally students at the university he teaches at. He'd never... No."

"Sounds like you're trying to convince yourself more than me, honey." Paige stood and checked her nails.

Nodding, I knew she was right. My stomach twisted in knots as I stood.

"And just remember, when you go looking for something, you're definitely going to find something.

And that something is often the cause of heartbreak. Just... make sure you can handle it, okay, Ni?"

Leaving the nail salon, we walked into the bright rays of sunshine blaring down from the stunning, vivid Carolina-blue skies. The clouds resembled fluffy white marshmallows, and I turned to hug Paige.

"It'll be okay," she whispered into my ear. "No matter what, you've got your kids, Joselin, and me." She squeezed me tightly.

"Yeah, I know." I slid my sunglasses on and walked to my car.

The thing was, friends and kids weren't enough for me. I wanted to be married. I wanted my husband to be mine. I wanted Warren. I loved him... but did he still love me?

CHAPTER SEVEN

$\mathcal{T}$ightening my trench coat around myself, my heels clicked against the cobblestone path of campus. There was an unusual gloom that clung to the sky, while droplets of rain began to splatter against the stone, making it slick with each step. My hair was in a neat bun, I had sunglasses on, and realized I looked absolutely outrageous.

Why did I think I needed to dress as a detective? I had spoken to Warren earlier and knew he was already at a meeting off campus. Turning into his building, I looked over my shoulder and walked past chatty students. Walking down the narrow hallway, another set of footsteps seemed to echo behind me. My mouth grew dry as I turned and slowed down. Turning around, I looked over my shoulder.

Someone was lurking right by the corner, and as soon as I turned, all I saw was a flash of hair and petite body race away.

Brushing my hand across my face, I clenched my teeth together. I didn't have much time and knew I was hyperaware of everything around me. Quickly walking up the narrow staircase, I made a sharp right to his office. Rolling my lips together, I stood in front of the door. It was the same door I'd walked into as a fervent nineteen-year-old to debate the B- grade he'd given me when I knew I'd earned an A. That's all it took for a charming professor to melt in front of me. He said he loved my wit, my feistiness, and the fact that I had typed an entire document of points on why my essay was an A-plus paper.

His gold band adorned on his left-hand ring finger had me keep a distance. But then, the ring came off, and we…

Shaking my head, I pushed the spare key Warren kept hidden in his sock drawer and unlocked it.

Stepping inside, the scent of sandalwood and cedar was intoxicating. Lingering coffee mugs were strewn on one side of his desk. A few photo frames were neatly displayed and a jar of his favorite Lifesaver mints were opened, with wrappers scattered about.

His diplomas were hung on the wall and books lined the massive oak bookshelves.

His office hadn't changed in the past two decades. But he had.

Brushing my fingers against his desk, I made my way to the oversized leather chair behind it and sank into it. Spinning around once, I leaned back.

"Okay, what am I even looking for?" I said to myself as I pulled the top drawer open. Paperclips, a stapler, scattered pens, and lotion were in it.

Harmless knick-knacks. Granted, the bottle of lotion vexed me—my husband never used lotion. I didn't want to jump to conclusions of what he was doing in his office with that, but a sinking pit in my stomach taunted me.

I rummaged through multiple drawers until I reached the bottom. Jamming my fingers into the groove, I tried to tug it open, but it was locked. "Shit." I lifted the door key and knew there was no way it was the same. Looking around for a small key that fit, I quickly realized I was out of luck.

Tapping my head, I tugged the bobby pin out of my bun and eyed it carefully. Biting it, I widened it and slowly pushed it into the keyhole. Twisting it around, I took a few deep breaths until I heard the *click*.

"Yes!" I quickly opened the drawer, but immediately cringed.

"Oh my God," I gasped. Pulling out the stack of pornographic magazines, I bit my bottom lip as I grabbed the bottle of lubricant and tissues, setting it together on Warren's desk.

The magazines were plastered with young college girls and women kissing and groping one another.

Sniffling, I dropped to the ground and dug deeper into the drawer. The manila envelope in my hands had my heart pounding in my chest.

Looking up at the ceiling, I knew I had to open it. It could just be nothing… or it could be something.

Something that could change everything.

Opening it carefully to not rip the envelope, I held it upside down over the desk, and small, black and white Polaroid pictures toppled out. Lifting one up between my fingers, I tilted my head. It was a woman, with long hair tousled down her back that exposed her thin frame and protruding spine. She was flawless, but I couldn't see her face. Squinting at it carefully, I saw she was in bed with a sheet covering her bottom half. Fingering through the other images, I lifted them up one by one. Another image of a woman standing by a window, with similar frame, but definitely not same one from the first photo—this woman had a tattoo. She was in the same room as the first photo, and holding a bedsheet around her bottom half, too.

Tears grew in my eyes, but I fought them back. These didn't necessarily prove Warren was having an affair or perhaps, affairs. I didn't know if he even took them. I…

I was making excuses for my husband.

Forcing myself to look through each one and snapping photos with my phone before carefully putting them back and resealing the envelope, my breathing hitched as my eyes caught a small USB drive.

Warren's laptop wasn't here, and I couldn't risk using his desktop the university gave him.

But I had to know what was on it. Shoving it into my purse, I froze when my phone rang.

My heart raced as my fingers trembled, and I reached to grab it. Before even saying 'hello,' he began to speak.

"Hi sweetheart, I'm turning in to the house now. I'm so sorry about this morning. I know… I know I've been distant. It's the stress of working and writing this book. I…" Warren started as I quickly jumped up and made sure everything was back in place.

"Wait, where are you?" I could hear Warren's gear shift as he parked.

"Oh, um… I went to get my nails done and just

went out for a bit to shop." I was flustered. I was never good at lying.

"Okay, sweetheart. I'm going to start making us dinner. I'll see you when I see you?" Warren's car lock chimed in the background.

"Yeah, I'll see you." I quickly left his office and gripped my purse to my chest.

I had to see what was on that USB.

CHAPTER EIGHT

I walked inside the house to the scent of olive oil, garlic, and onion. Classical music radiated through our home as I dropped my keys into the small glass bowl on the console table. "Hi, beautiful." Warren spun around in the kitchen and beamed at me.

"You think I'm beautiful?" I grabbed a cherry tomato from the salad he had made and popped it into my mouth.

Letting out a dry laugh, he put his hands on his hips. "Are you being serious right now?" Warren carefully put the spoon down and walked toward the kitchen island.

"Baby, you are the most beautiful woman I've ever

laid my eyes on." Dropping his hands to my hips, he tugged me into him. His lips grazed my neck and his hand wrapped a handful of my hair in his palm. Letting out an aroused moan in my ear, I felt repulsed, but I stood there, frozen in the arms of the man I promised a lifetime to.

"Are you cheating on me?" I planted my hands against his chest and pushed enough to duck under his arm.

"Here we go again…" Warren muttered under his breath with annoyance.

"What do you mean by that?" I spat, turning the bubbling sauce off on the stove.

Warren grabbed a bottle of wine and aggressively uncorked it before pouring himself a hefty glass.

"You've always been so damn insecure, Nina. You need constant reassurance, and it's exhausting." I hated how calm his voice was. I hated how easily he said a simple, insulting sentence without a hitch.

Slamming my hands against the quartz island, I looked at him angrily. "Really? You're going to gaslight me? I asked you a question, and I want an answer, Warren." I squinted at him with my heart racing. It was completely out of character for me to raise my voice. We hardly ever fought; sure, we bickered like every married couple does, but rage like this... I always controlled it, because, of course, I was expected to.

"No. I am not having an affair, Nina." Warren poured a second glass of wine and sipped it, completely calm. I hated that about him. He never showed spikes in emotion. It was true, behind every overthinking, anxious wife was a husband who had zero worries in the world.

"Sweetheart, what's going on with you? Just tell me what you need from me, and I'll do it." Warren placed his glass down and walked toward me. Wrapping his arms around my waist, he drew me in. What was I supposed to do? Tell him I'd snuck into his office and found several pornographic magazines and images of women in a locked drawer of his desk? How I was counting down the seconds to see what was on the USB drive?

What did that even prove? The images could have been just that, images. He wasn't in them, so what evidence did I have that showed he was an adulterer? People on the outside of marriages are so quick to judge. They'll tell you to leave him, to start fresh or question why you're complaining and not doing something about what it is that bothers you. But the truth of the matter is that marriage is like a security blanket. It's warm and cozy, familiar. At forty, I didn't want to lose my comfort and stability and be forced to start over. This was the time in my life I wanted to be on cruise control, not having to speed down a crowded highway.

"I just feel like you've been so distant." I pressed my forehead to his chest as he rested his chin on the top of my head.

"Oh, baby... I'm so sorry. You're right. You know I've been so caught up in my career and now, writing this novel. You know how badly I've wanted this—to be a published author after all these years of trying to write this book." Warren's fingers brushed the nape of my neck before tracing a line along my collarbone.

Swallowing, I looked away. I felt like the girl Warren fell in love with was a completely different person from the woman in front of him. I was care-free, daring... beautiful.

"Do you think I'm still... attractive?"

There is a vast difference between nineteen and forty. Gravity was a bitch.

"You're more beautiful now, my love."

That was it. Another lie seeping from his lips.

We ate dinner in an awkward silence. I swirled my

fork through the pasta noodles and thought about the photos in Warren's drawers.

Looking up across the dining table, Warren was chewing slowly but watching me with a frown. The lines between his brows deepened, and just as I parted my lips, he smiled at me.

But the smile wasn't warm... the smile was sinister.

I made my way downstairs as soon as Warren had fallen asleep. Gripping the black, industrial-style railing, I held my breath as my footsteps caused the wooden stairs to creak.

I got downstairs, dug inside my purse, and lifted the USB drive out. Looking over my shoulder, the house felt even quieter. No crickets were chirping, the trees were still, and the small quirks of our home didn't come to life like they usually did.

Sliding my feet against the cool floor, I made my way to Warren's office. Crouching, I opened the drawer that held my old laptop and charger. Quickly plugging it in, I flipped the USB open and waited for my laptop to flick on.

Blowing out a breath, I waited for the small loading

bar to fully finish and saw a small blue folder on my screen.

My fingers hovered over the mouse pad as I hesitated.

"Fuck it." I clicked it.

The scream that left my mouth startled me as I stared at the screen.

It was a doll... A child's doll. Her head was shaved, leaving nothing but a few braided locks of hair glued or taped down. I felt like I recognized it from somewhere... but where? Her face was stained, and one eye was missing. What even was this?

My entire body was covered in goosebumps as I tried to figure out the background.

Swallowing, I noticed a second file. Clicking it, I immediately squinted as my entire body felt numb.

It was a row of shallow holes in the dirt. Furrowing my brows, I didn't recognize the site. I didn't understand what any of this was. Just as I attempted to save it all on my laptop...

"Nina?" My eyes shot up as I slammed my laptop closed.

"What are you doing in here?" Warren rubbed his eyes as he dragged his feet closer to me. I was sitting on the floor, looking up at him as he squinted down at me.

"I couldn't... I couldn't sleep," I stammered as I looked at him. The image of the creepy doll was branded into my mind.

"It's time for bed," he said, and just as he was about to look back at my computer, I quickly pressed my hand over the USB drive.

"Okay," I whispered.

CHAPTER NINE

The week flew by. I dragged myself to a Pilates class, volunteered at the animal shelter, purged the linen closet, and finally, after watching two hours' worth of videos on home organization, spent three hundred dollars on acrylic bins and baskets, I decided to put in my earbuds and go out back to listen to some music.

It's amazing how busy we feel most of our lives. The stigma of a stay-at-home mom is still so prevalent. No one realizes just how busy you really are when you're the sole caretaker of children. I went from counting down the seconds to bedtime somedays, to having rowdy teenagers slamming doors in my face, to kissing them both goodbye, knowing they'd never ever need me the way they had always needed me.

I had to rediscover myself beyond mom. Who the hell was Nina Cooper? Closing my eyes, I laid back on the pool lounger. We did live in the most picturesque place. Lake Johan boasted emerald-green water and was mostly clear beyond the shadows of the trees. Warren bought this house decades ago, when Lake Johan was a quiet, intimate community. Luckily for us, the part of the lake our home sat on was still secluded from over-zealous college students and locals seeking solace from the scorching sun in the cold depths of the lake.

Leaning back, I clasped one hand behind my head and slid the other through my playlist.

Bopping my head to the beat of the music, I began humming. Thirty-minutes or so flew by as I sipped fresh lemonade and enjoyed the even fresher air. Closing my eyes, I began drifting into a light nap, but was jerked from a peaceful trance when I heard a voice.

Looking around with a cloud of confusion hanging over me, I pressed my palms into the thin linen.

It was a woman, maybe a girl? But then I heard him.

My husband.

And I realized the conversation was not near me… it was emitting through my earbuds.

"You are perfect." Warren laughed between words.

What did the woman say before? I hadn't processed it.

"Dr. Cooper, I feel so terribly sorry that I knocked all the essays off of your desk." The woman—no, definitely a *girl*—giggled.

My heart raced as I pushed the earbud deeper in.

"I don't mind making a mess with you, beautiful," my husband replied, his voice low and forcefully sultry. Standing on trembling legs, I walked back through the house as realization sunk in.

Looking through the oversized window, I watched as the sun was setting in a sherbet-tinged sky. There he was.

My husband was sitting in my car with a giant smile on his face. My Bluetooth had connected to my earbuds. I couldn't decipher the remainder of the conversation because my head felt light and hazy. My hands went cold, and I gripped the edge of our formal dining table to steady myself.

"I've got to go, sunshine. I'll see you next week." Laughter emitted.

"You hang up," she teased.

"No, you hang up," he crooned.

I watched Warren grin as he turned the ignition off and grabbed his satchel. He took my car so he could get its oil changed after work. My bottom lip quivered as I watched him grin to himself, clutching the strap of his bag before coming up the steps.

What is he doing?

Pushing myself off the dining table, I squinted. Sucking in a breath of air, tears stung my eyes.

He was checking the zipper of his pants. I suppose when he assumed everything was in order, he started to make his way up to our house.

Swiping underneath my eyes, I sniffled and quickly blew a puff of air out. Jamming my thumb into my palm, I forced myself to stay composed.

"Ni? Sweetheart?" Warren called out, completely blasé. I clenched my teeth as he repeatedly called, "Sweetheart."

"In here." My voice was hoarse but I quickly cleared it and moved toward the kitchen. He was glowing, basking in his own happiness. My husband was having an affair, spending his free time with another woman while I sat here, alone, thinking about this chapter in our story being one of connection.

"Well, don't you look lovely?" He opened his arms

as I stood there with my head slightly tilted, staring at the man who was by my side through every major life milestone.

The man I had loved since I was nineteen years old. The father of my children. Smiling slowly, I walked around to the wine rack and tugged out a new bottle. Jamming the sharp end of the wine opener into the cork, I aggressively twisted it outward until the satisfying *pop* released, and I grabbed two glasses. I wanted to jam the corkscrew into his jugular and twist it 'round and 'round.

"You know, I've been thinking…" I began to pour.

The deep-red liquid sloshed around the crystal until Warren exclaimed, "Nina! It's about to spill!"

Swooping the bottle upright, I dabbed my finger at the brim of the glass, swiping a bit of the expensive liquid onto my finger before tasting it.

"You are just like this wine, my darling husband. Vintage, dry, but… intoxicating." I lifted the glass and took a muddled sip.

"Ni, what's going on?" Warren took his satchel off and placed it on the stool.

"I'm starting to realize that I've been really fucking bored with our marriage." I took another long sip, then smacked my lips before making an obnoxious, satiated sound.

Warren's eyebrows cinched together as he looked at me in shock.

"I mean... all my friends and their husbands go out on dates, vacations, even walks around the park in the evening. But you... you just live in your own little bubble. Our sex is vanilla, something I didn't even know existed until I met you..."

I knew that would sting. When Warren met me as a bright-eyed young college student, I was confident in wild sex. I mean, it's what you did. You fucked behind dorm buildings, in the car, at a sticky-floored frat house. That's why he fell for me, I'm assuming. I shook up his otherwise vanilla and lackluster life.

A life he wasn't willing to settle into.

"Nina!" Warren, although for the most part was soft-spoken and an intellect, was also an egomaniac... Well, also synonymous for man.

Rushing over to me, he clutched my neck and grew so close to my face that the scent of winter mint gum brushed against my lips.

"You want it rough, baby?" he spat out.

Clenching my jaw, I looked into his eyes. "It's a good thing you're good with your tongue, because aging is making your dick limp." I cocked my brow at him and shoved his hand off of me. Lifting my glass and the bottle, I walked to the back door, opening it slightly. "Our son and his new girlfriend are coming over tomorrow for a cookout. I hope you still know how to work the grill." I shook my head and left through the back door.

Joss and Paige were heading over for a nightcap, even though my head was spinning and I wasn't sure if I wanted to scream, cry, or sucker-punch the asshole inside my home.

I lit the fire-pit and watched as the flames crackled and burned the wood with intention. Slowly, but impactfully.

There wasn't a rush to the path of destruction, it was strategic and slow. The flames used the wood to linger and be cared for until they were ready to let go.

"Hey, love," Paige and Joss called out.

"Hi." I forced a smile out as my best friends came up the creaky wooden steps to sit with me.

"It's so freaky," Joss said. Following her line of vision, I looked at the lake, which looked completely black in the darkness.

"What?" I asked curiously as Paige opened the wicker picnic basket she always brought over.

"The lake. It's like you could legit hide a body in there, and no one would ever know. Shit, for all we know, there's already some in there..." Joss rubbed her arms as if her words sent chills down her body.

"Okay... Why so gruesome?" Paige scrunched her nose and shrugged at me.

Looking back at the lake, I lifted my locket up and brushed the smooth metal.

"She's right, though..." I licked my lips and looked over at my friends. "I could really make someone disappear right in my own backyard." Raising my glass, I smiled to myself and took a nice, long, slow sip.

CHAPTER TEN

*G*ood girlfriends can make or break your life. Something I've definitely learned as I've gotten older was quality over quantity was the best kind of friendships. I liked to think of myself as an extrovert in my twenties, but then I had kids and developed anxiety. I became a different person, and that's okay, because as humans, we evolve. We must. But the worst part of changing yourself is realizing not everyone may be okay with that.

I tossed and turned next to my oblivious, snoring husband. Warren wasn't a confrontational man; whenever we'd get into arguments, I'd usually be the one yelling while he was usually the one who stayed quiet and pretended nothing had happened by the next day. Quiet men were always the most dangerous, though.

I couldn't stop watching him—the way his dark lashes fluttered or the way his chest rose and fell. It's strange really, in the past five hours, I've replayed that young woman's voice as my heart shattered when she insinuated having some form of a physical relationship with my husband on his office desk. Something I once did with him…

I felt suffocated when I replayed my husband calling another woman 'sunshine.' That was the same term of endearment he had called me from the moment our relationship turned into one of desire.

Who was she? Did she not see the gold wedding band he wore? But I knew that sometimes Warren took his band off. He was one of those men who wore his wedding band only when necessary. For appearances, really. I never thought I'd be married to one of those kinds of men, but then again, I didn't think I'd be married to a lying adulterer, either.

Was she a new teaching assistant? A new professor? Pausing, I looked at the streaks of silver shining in his otherwise dark hair.

There's no way he'd have an affair with a student at this age. When I met him, he was thirty-six. He's fifty-seven now, with children in college.

Biting my bottom lip anxiously, I shoved the goose down comforter off of my body, scratching at my neck. The clicking of our ceiling fan puttering and all the small noises seemed louder as my mind went into overdrive.

"Fuck!" I hissed. I was exhausted, and I didn't want to deal with this. I had finally reached a part of my life where my kids were grown, we were financially stable, I was working on a healthier and happier version of myself, and now…

Swiftly turning my head, I looked at Warren, but a light from his nightstand caught my eye.

His phone was charging. Slowly sitting up, I spun my legs over the bed and tiptoed to his side. My heart was pounding against my chest as I squatted and lifted his phone in my palms.

A passcode. I typed in our wedding anniversary, his birthday, my birthday, the kids' birthdays, our home address…

Nothing worked.

Suddenly, his face turned toward me, and I froze with my eyes widened. Holding my breath, I slowly tried to place his phone back down, but when I knew for sure he was still deep asleep, I looked at the screen and turned it to his face to unlock it.

But as I held it and prayed the light wouldn't wake him, his lips curved into a small smile.

Gasping, I dropped his phone and stumbled back

into the moonlight streaming in, slapping my hands over my mouth as I swallowed.

He started to snore again. Chills decorated my arms as I shook my head and walked back to my side.

This was reckless. Sliding back under the thick comforter, I reached into my nightstand drawer and took two melatonin pills before closing my eyes and hoping sleep would come so I could escape what had become my new living nightmare.

My entire world and life as I knew it was on fire, and the scariest part of it all was that I knew the one holding the match. *It was the man I loved.*

Faint chirping of birds, along with the golden rays of sunshine flooding into our bedroom, had me yawning and glancing at the alarm.

It was six-forty-five. Another thing that I couldn't help but laugh at. I remember rocking my children in the glider with bleary-eyes, a messy bun, and watching the days blur into nights, feeling completely isolated, thinking and dreaming of what is now my present day.

A day where no one came barging in, telling me they had wet the bed, had a monster in their closet, or threw up on the rug. A day where I could sleep in until ten a.m. Scoffing at myself, I looked at the empty spot next to me.

Warren was always up at five a.m. for his morning run around the lake. The entire loop was six miles, and the man never missed a day. I didn't know what to do and where to even begin with Warren and his mistress, but today was not that day. Today, my son and his girlfriend were going to be over, spending the weekend with us, and my home would once again be filled with noise.

I got in the shower, letting the hot pellets beat away the tension in my shoulders and neck from being uncomfortable all night. Pressing my hands against the glass door, I closed my eyes as I let the stream target my hip and leg where my sciatica often flared. I felt a momentary blanket of peace wrap around me.

But then, something crashed, and had me opening my eyes, causing shampoo to trickle down and burn them.

It was her.

Scarlett, my son's girlfriend, was standing there, watching me shower. Her red hair straggled around her pale, gaunt face, and her arms hung awkwardly as she slumped forward, as if something was causing her pain.

Falling back, I slapped my arms over my breasts

and stared back. Blinking rapidly, I shook my head and opened them again.

"Scarlett?" I questioned.

"Hi... Nina." A small, demented smile curved her lips.

"Would you mind guiding me to Max's bedroom?" she whispered calmly with her eyes locked on mine.

She was really here. This wasn't a premonition or hallucination.

"Oh my gosh, Scarlett. Just... His room is down the hall to the left." I waved her away, thankful that the shower glass was mostly steamed up.

"Okay." She nodded quickly with her boney cheeks completely flushed and pink. Coming closer, she pressed her hands against the steam that covered the mirror as I took an additional step back.

Lifting her index finger, she tilted her head and drew a small smiley face.

"Scarlett, please leave," I forced out as I covered my body, and the water went cold as she slowly walked backward.

Wiggling her fingers at me, she nodded. "Bye, Nins."

Covering my mouth with my hands, I shuddered and spun the knob off.

What the hell was that?

CHAPTER ELEVEN

I sat at my vanity and lifted my hairbrush, but just as I went to brush my hair, I paused. Lifting it closer to my face, I straightened my spine and slowly looked behind me.

It felt like someone was watching me. The sound of footsteps retreated. "Hello?" I called out with uncertainty lacing my words. Turning back, I stared at the red hair tangled in my brush.

She used my hairbrush? Carefully plucking the strands from the brush, I hung them over the small trash bin but hesitated.

Opening the small drawer, I placed them on a napkin and tucked them away.

I quickly put on a full face of makeup and made my way to change my clothes.

"Mom!" Max's voice called out. With a smile, I turned and saw him, his goofy grin spreading as soon as he saw me.

No matter how irrelevant I felt sometimes, spending my life as a stay-at-home mom, these were the moments that reminded me I had the greatest job in the world. I *was* relevant and important, and looking at my son now, I knew I still was.

"Hey, sweets." I brushed my hand against his cheek. "Growing out a beard?" I scrunched my nose as he let out a laugh.

"No, just laziness." He wrapped his arms around me in a hug. How did that small baby wrapped in a sky-blue blanket turn into a man who towered over me?

"Scarlett left her bikini at her apartment and felt too awkward to ask you if you had anything she could borrow?" Max asked uncomfortably. "And I already rampaged Ava's room. She took everything with her." He shoved his hands into his pockets and glanced behind me.

"Um… I might have an old bikini for her, but isn't that a bit strange for her to wear your mom's bathing suit?" *It was more than a bit strange.*

"I know, I know, but I want to take the boat out and swim in the lake while you guys grill up my favorite burgers." Max batted his eyes at me dramatically.

I couldn't help but laugh. "Okay, okay, I'll find something for her. By the way..." I was about to tell Max how I thought Scarlett may have—well, definitely —used my hair brush and came into the bathroom while I was showering, but I decided that wasn't a necessary conversation to have. This weekend was about fun and family.

"Here." I popped open a tote box hidden in the far corner of my closet. We all know the tote bin, everyone has it. The one packed to the brim with cute clothes from a past version of ourselves. Favorite dresses we went clubbing in, the best pair of jeans that were now either too low or too tight or maybe too baggy. Digging in, I grabbed a couple of swimsuits.

Stretching it out in front of me, I thought of the fond memories jumping into this very lake when Warren and I first started dating, and then got engaged and married. Teeny pieces of material that I strutted myself in, knowing he couldn't resist me and was counting the seconds until he could tear it off my taut, young body.

Clutching them in my hands, I didn't want to give them to Max. It was odd. My son's girlfriend, who already had me wary, was going to wear them.

"Thanks, Mom!" Max grabbed a bright red bikini off the floor.

"Oh, wai—" I began. That red bikini was my favorite; it was the one I wore the very first night I ever spent with Warren.

But before I could make up some pathetic excuse on why I needed it back, Max rushed out. Shoving the rest of the bathing suits back in, I paused and held a black one in my hands. "You know what? Screw it." It was a two-piece black bikini, and sure, it might be a size or so smaller, but with the ties on the side I could loosen it, and I wasn't going to act like forty meant I had to wear some modest one-piece I didn't even like wearing.

Peeling my clothes off, I looked at myself in the mirror as I tied it on. "Your boobs are significantly better now." I smiled and adjusted the straps. Grabbing a pair of denim shorts, I tugged them on and threw on a straw fedora.

I heard a few voices as soon as I walked out. One in particular stood out. "Ava?" I slapped my hands over my mouth and ran over to my daughter.

"Mom!" she shrieked and left Max and Scarlett. Grabbing me in her arms, she squeezed me tightly.

Pressing her face into my hair, I couldn't believe she was here. She had left to study abroad in London for her spring semester and chose to stay for the next semester. I only saw her for four days in between, which was mostly shopping and packing for her.

Max cupped his hands around his mouth and bellowed, "Mom's favorite child has returned." Glancing over Ava's shoulder, I shook my head and rolled my eyes at Max.

"How are you here?" I brushed a strand of her shiny black hair behind her ear.

"I missed home. I can do my class virtually until I go back in two weeks."

"You're here for two weeks?" I couldn't believe it.

"Yeah, I just... Well, Lars and I broke up, and I'm just... you know, homesick. Most of all, I missed you." She smiled at me with her beautiful, brown, almond-shaped eyes glimmering.

Lars was her French boyfriend she had jumped into a whirlwind romance with. While Warren was panicked and went into full blown-dad mode, I knew she was just experiencing life and wanted to let her write the narrative of her own story, rather than choosing to rearrange the words for her.

"I'm sorry. Time to find a hot British guy." I winked at her as she threw her head back and laughed.

I had Ava when I was twenty-years old—a junior in college who went from the party-girl to the married mom. Ava and I essentially grew up together in many ways, and admittedly, I was almost living vicariously through her.

"Have you guys seen your dad?" I looked between my kids.

"Nope, he's probably out there doing planks mid-run," Max teased.

Walking to Scarlett, I did a quick sweep of her outfit. My red bikini fit her perfectly, too perfectly. She had a thin white sarong wrapped around her waist.

She brought a sarong but forgot her bikini?

"It's good to see you, Scarlett." I smiled at her.

"Thank you for loaning me this. It feels so good…" She looked at herself and immediately looped her arm into Max's, tugging him closer.

The way she said everything felt distorted and unsettling.

"Ava, have you met Scarlett?" I waved my daughter over.

"Yep," she said, popping the 'p,' and came up beside me.

"I didn't know he was capable of getting a girl." Ava mocked and laced her arm into mine.

"Says the girl who can't keep a guy around for more than a month," Max fought back.

"It's not my fault that most men act like little boys." She shrugged as I smacked my head at my teenagers fighting.

"Amen to that," I whispered under my breath. "Okay, you all play nice. I'll make some breakfast and bring it out back. Max, you can go down and get the boat ready if you wanted to take Scarlett down there."

They all left as I made my way to the kitchen. My heart felt fuller with everyone home. I knew it was temporary, and by the end of the weekend, Max would leave and Ava would probably spend most of her free time catching up with old friends. But I was fine. Suddenly, my husband's affair seemingly made me want to not only figure out what I'd do with him, but also realize how ridiculous I had been. I had continuously put everyone before me, and as a mother, yes, it's the right thing to do, but as a wife, it's not. I am supposed to be an equal, and I was realizing that I was exhausted from pouring from an empty cup.

Making these rash decisions with my life had undermined my long-term goals. And suddenly, my long-term goal was understanding how I'd make sure my husband knew he wouldn't just replace me with the next best thing. No, not after everything I'd given him.

CHAPTER TWELVE

"*H*ey sunshine." His voice rasped from behind me. I held my breath as his hands wrapped around my waist from behind, hoping the natural shudder my body emitted wouldn't be obvious.

"I'm sorry, baby..." he whispered into my ear before nipping at my earlobe.

"About?" I questioned. What did I expect, that Warren would magically drop to his knees with clutched hands and confess how badly he had screwed up?

"About being a complete distant asshole." He slowly spun me around and tilted my chin up with his index finger. "Here." With his other hand, he showed me two pieces of paper.

"What is this?" I tugged them from him, and my eyes widened. "Hawaii?"

Warren had always promised we'd go.

"Really?" I took the second ticket out. Two first-class tickets to Hawaii. Lifting my eyes to Warren, I couldn't help but laugh, and to him, I'm sure he thought the laughter was emitting from happiness and excitement.

"We'll leave in three months. I've already put the time in, and we can kick back in our private villa, just you and me," Warren boomed with open palms.

Sweat beads were pooling at his hairline and his tight gym shirt clung to the moisture of his skin post-run. He reeked with a mix of sweat, grass, and a tinge of his aftershave that was masked by his natural body odors.

Yet, he still looked sexy—and that was agitating and unnerving in itself. The man never didn't look insatiable.

His pale blue eyes held an arrogance in them as he realized my eyes trailing his entire body.

"Ava is home." I blinked rapidly. The lines between Warren's eyebrows deepened and instead of looking elated, he seemed annoyed.

Warren always had a bit of the misogynistic personality embedded in him. He'd pretend he was all for feminine rights and equality, but simple manner-isms or things he'd say would prove otherwise. He wasn't thrilled with Ava choosing to study abroad in London—he thought a young girl shouldn't be galli-vanting through foreign countries without a man accompanying her. I convinced him to let her go, even threatening him that I'd drop her off at the airport alone if I had to, but she'd never turn down amazing opportunities. Ones I had turned down for him.

"Great!" Warren clapped his hands together, quickly changing his tone. "Are you excited for our trip? Think of this as a second honeymoon." He cupped my face in his palms.

"Mm-hmm... I'm so excited." I forced out. What my husband didn't know was that a lot could happen in three months.

"I'm going to take a quick shower and meet you outside, babe." Running his hand through his damp hair, he winked at me before turning quickly.

Looking down at the tickets to Hawaii in my hand, I put them into the mail holder and looked at the pancake that had been cooking on low for the past ten minutes. Lifting it into my hands, I looked at the bottom.

Completely black. "Just like your fucking heart, Warren." Opening the trash bin, I shoved it in there, along with the entire bowl of batter... bowl included. Grabbing my keys, I shook my hands and forced myself to suppress the scream budding inside me.

Sinking into my car, I decided to drive to pick up some donuts. What was I? Some personal chef who catered while everyone else was frolicking in the lake or boating? Or running miles around the lake to retain a body that clearly attracted the attention of others?

As I drove, I strummed my fingers against the already warm leather steering wheel. Faint rain pellets began beating down on my windshield. Turning my windshield wipers on, I watched as they squeaked against the barely wet glass. Suddenly, the maintenance required sign lit up on my dashboard.

I thought Warren went and got my oil changed? Puffing my cheeks, I looked around my car. I drove a pearl-white SUV with third-row seating. Meanwhile, Professor Cooper bought himself an overpriced two-seater Porche convertible, as what I assumed was his mid-life crisis mobile. Clearly, he didn't stop there. Pulling into the drive-thru, I ordered a large iced coffee and a dozen donuts.

"Here you are, ma'am!" the young, beautiful drive-thru employee chirped. Squinting at her, I thought her voice sounded awfully familiar, like recently familiar.

"Um… do you happen to have…" I became flustered as I bit into my bottom lip.

"Did you need anything else?" The young girl popped her head out, glancing at the building line of cars behind me.

"No, it's fine," I stammered as I tried to cling onto her voice, her tone… her.

Driving off, I couldn't believe it. Is this what an affair did to the spouse who was being cheated on? Did they leave you hungry for details and thirsty for explanations?

I pulled over, opened the box of donuts, lifted the sticky, sweet circle in front of my face, and took a massive bite.

I did the keto diet, I tried restricting calories, I took countless gym classes, and Pilates all to maintain my body for him. I couldn't help but laugh. I tried to maintain my body so he wouldn't look elsewhere.

I was going to eat this fucking donut, and then I was going to start a healthy diet and plan to look even better—and not for his sorry ass. No, it was for the day I left him and could show him what he'd be missing.

"Mom!" Ava waved at me as soon as I got to the deck. She was wearing a yellow swimsuit and was smiling brightly.

Warren was laying back on a lounger while reading the paper. "Hey, sunshine. I would have picked that up…" He shielded his eyes and smiled at me.

"Where's your brother?" I glanced around and looked back at Ava.

"Oh, he took his new girlfriend out for a lake tour."

"Did you meet her yet?" I handed Warren the opened box of donuts.

He picked the plain, unglazed donut. Scrunching my nose, I turned to leave the box on the table. Apparently, Ava didn't eat carbs, so she was drinking some kind of overpriced green juice.

"Met who?" Warren asked as I sank into the lounge chair next to Ava.

"Your son's girlfriend." I stretched my arms over my head and rubbed my face.

"Oh, no, not yet." Warren didn't take his eyes off the newspaper.

"So, honey, what's going on?" I asked my daughter, who was fixing her oversized straw hat.

"What do you mean?" Ava lowered her sunglasses down the bridge of her nose. Her eyes were just like mine, unlike Max's. Dark chocolate eyes that occa-

sionally looked lighter if she was on the verge of
crying.

"I mean... baby, you came home so abruptly."

Warren crumpled the newspaper in his hands
behind us.

"I'm fine. I just... missed home and you." She
cleared her throat before looking back at her dad.

"Oh-kay. Well, I'm so happy... we are so happy
you're here. Right, Warren?" I shot him a look of
daggers.

"Yes, of course. You know I hated to see you leave,
sweetie," he added flatly.

"Dad!" The echoing of footsteps against the wood
had us all turning to see Max with his damp hair, no
shirt, and bright red swim trunks. He smiled goofily
before pausing at the top and reaching his hand out.

Scarlett appeared behind him, proudly grabbing
his hand and biting her thick bottom lip with her eyes
locked onto his.

Her bikini—*my* bikini—clung to her wet body,
revealing her nipples through the thin material.

"Son." Warren finally put the paper down and took
a sip of his coffee before turning to Max and Scarlett.

As soon as he turned and saw them, he choked on
his drink, coughing violently.

Rolling my eyes, I felt disgusted. My husband was

gagging on his coffee because he was probably so taken aback by the swimsuit model in front of him.

"You okay, Dad?" Ava looked at him, completely unaware what her father was probably thinking about the girl who was close to his own daughter's age.

"Yeah... yeah. Max, hey." Warren was flustered. His cheeks reddened, and not by the summer sun or heat.

"Dad, this is my girlfriend, Scarlett. Scarlett, this is my dad. He's actually a professor at Johan."

Scarlett smiled shyly before wiggling her fingers at Warren. "Hello, Professor Cooper."

Clearing his throat, Warren rubbed his palm against his face. "Hi," he paused, "Scar-lett." The way he hung her name into two parts had fury pooling inside me.

"I'm going to go get a bit of work done inside, but I'll get the grill fired up for lunch." He quickly looked at me and nodded.

"Okay," I replied and averted my eyes from his.

As soon as Warren went back inside, Ava shrugged and laid back into her lounge chair. "Ava, have you talked to Scarlett?" I asked her as Max took Scarlett to grab towels from the outdoor storage.

"No, I have no interest in getting to know who will

be Max's college fling, one of ten," she scoffed and flung her dark hair over her shoulder.

Ava was always my logical, calm child. She was the typical first child—responsible, compassionate, and understanding. Max was always my carefree, act first, think later second child.

"She's going to break his heart," Ava mumbled under her breath as she paged through a book.

Just as I made myself comfortable against the lounger, I looked over at her. "Why would you assume that?"

"Mom, the girl just blushed while greeting her boyfriend's dad. She's obviously a tramp."

Parting my lips, I was stunned by Ava's crass words, but looked over to Scarlett and sucked in a breath of air.

Her eyes were locked on mine as Max dried her off. And then, as my son bent down to wipe her legs off for her, she tilted her head and smiled at me in a way that sent chills up my spine. Lifting a brow and rubbing her hand across her breast, she kept staring at me.

"I don't like her," I whispered to myself.

"That doesn't matter, because he does." Ava sighed and pointed at Max.

CHAPTER THIRTEEN

Scarlett was screeching excitedly on the back of our jet ski, tightly grasping Max's sunburned back.

I was trying to focus on the romance book I had randomly seen an ad for on my Kindle. I much preferred paperbacks, but there was no way I'd live it down if Warren or my children saw me reading a book with a cover of a male model's abs.

"Hey, babe!" Joselin's voice echoed. *Yes, she came.* I had texted Paige and Joselin to come over in our group text but I hadn't heard back. After Warren disappeared and texted me that he had to grab groceries for the cookout, I decided this whole family weekend was awkward within the first hour, and I needed some serious backup. Backup being my girl-friends. When I stood excitedly, I immediately froze in my spot.

Joss wasn't alone. Instead, she had her arm wrapped around a muscular arm, covered in tattoos. My eyes widened as I shamelessly scanned him from head to toe. The lens of his blue reflective aviator sunglasses matched the fitted swim trunks he had on. He wore a completely unbuttoned white, short sleeve button-down that exposed his perfectly carved abs.

Joss cleared her throat with a giggle. "Adam, this is my friend, Nina, the artist I told you about." She flicked her eyes between us before tilting her head at me with broad eyes.

"Hi, Adam…" I choked out like an embarrassed teenager. "I'm Nina… which you already know because Joss just introduced me." I stuck my hand out awkwardly as his lips ticked up slightly, like he could read my emotions with ease.

I couldn't believe Joss had told this random man about me, and besides, calling me an artist was a stretch. I hadn't picked up a paintbrush in years. She had been on me for a while, telling me I should get back into it, but I had felt so uninspired and art was something that absolutely required inspiration.

Passion and fire used to fuel me, and now nothing but the embers were drifting around me.

"It's nice to meet you, Nina." Adam gripped my hand gently and shook it. His touch had my cheeks fill with warmth as Joss feigned a cough to pull me out of the trance I was in.

"Yeah. Welcome yourself. I mean… make yourself welcome," I stammered.

Joss cringed as I fumbled my words, but noticing Ava behind me, she let go of Adam and immediately darted over, plucking an earbud out from her ear. Ava shrieked, "Aunt Joss!" before she jumped up and they embraced tightly.

I smiled as I watched their interaction. There were many times while Ava was growing up that I sometimes envied the relationship she had with Joss. She'd call her first about a breakup or drama with a friend. But then, on the flip side, I was grateful she even had those bonds and trusted another female adult so deeply.

"What a perfect view," Adam said, and I turned back to face him, quickly hugging myself and cursing the fact that I left my cover-up inside.

My shoulders were scrunched upward as I rubbed my body, trying to pretend I was cold—and not trying to hide the imperfections.

"Yeah, well, my husband… He lucked out when Lake Johan wasn't as residential and scored the best lot and view." I smiled.

"So, I didn't even know Joss was dating someone." I shrugged.

Adam moved closer to me, filling the space between us with zero hesitation.

"We're not dating, we're just fucking." Lifting his fingers, he tucked a loose strand of my hair behind my hair as my breathing hitched. "And, I wasn't talking about the lake view…" He pushed his sunglasses off his face, revealing stunning whiskey-colored eyes.

I could smell the tinge of mint on his breath as he smirked and pulled away, leaving my heartbeat completely erratic and my entire body covered in goosebumps, even on an otherwise sweltering morning.

Walking to the railing of the deck, he looked over as if he'd been here countless times. "Just making myself welcome." He peered over his ridiculously buff shoulders and winked at me.

. . .

I wiggled my fingers at him and quickly turned, running straight into another man.

My husband.

CHAPTER FOURTEEN

"Hey, sorry." I stumbled back with my palms raised.

Warren was wearing the goofy apron I got him last Christmas that said, "grill-master" in bright red letters, and he balanced two plates in his hands.

"Where have you been?" I asked, annoyed. He was gone for hours after Ava had finally come home and Max was visiting.

"I told you I had to get groceries for the cookout. Nina, you invited half the town, and we needed food." He eyed the burgers and hotdogs. "The rest of the food is on the kitchen counter; I could use a hand."

"You went grocery shopping for *two hours?*" I shook my head and rolled my eyes as I pushed past him.

"Where's Paige?" he called out before I walked through the doors.

Looking over my shoulder, I squinted as the sun cut through the bright blue clouds and directly into my eyes. "She hasn't come yet." I opened my hands with confusion.

"She was here two hours ago in the house," Warren said quickly.

"What?" She didn't come out here or text me.

I rushed over to the side table and lifted my phone. No missed calls or texts.

"You actually saw her in the house?" I arched my brow and glanced back at my dumb-founded husband.

Warren's cheeks turned red as he looked away. "No, maybe I thought I heard her voice or something in the house…" he trailed before heading to the grill.

"Grab the condiments and sides, Nina," he said crassly.

Sometimes you need your spouse to do something terrible in order for you to see them in the correct light. My husband never *asked* me to do things; he told me to do them. Twenty-plus years of marriage later, and I'm now realizing I don't like being told what to do by a man who can't get me off, even if I handed him a road map of my body.

"You know, I'm actually going for a swim." I

stretched my hands over my head and strutted past Warren, who had his jaw slightly dropped.

Joss, Adam, and Ava were at the dock, while Scarlett and Max were splashing around in the lake.

Pressing my phone against my ear, I called Paige. It kept ringing until her voicemail started. Puffing out a breath of air, I hung up.

"You good?" Joss came toward me with a seltzer in her hand.

"Yeah, yeah…" I waved her off and forced a smile. Why would Paige have been in our house and not have come out to see me?

Worst of all, what had she seen that made her leave so abruptly?

"It's so good to see Ava and the family all together." Joss wrapped her arm around my waist.

"Mm-hmm… and your eye-candy isn't so bad, either." I took her seltzer and sipped it.

"You know he's been talking about you…" Her eyes filled with excitement as they flicked to Adam, who was climbing down into one of the kayaks.

"What? Why? We just met, and you are…"

"We aren't anything. We screwed once, and I was over it after that." Joss yawned.

I looked over at her. "So, he's a bad lay?" I laughed.

"No… the best actually. But, you know, he's so

insightful and wants to cuddle and talk about history or current events and life… and well, you know I don't do that." Joselin shrugged.

It was true. Joss was the epitome of an independent woman.

She didn't want a man to weigh her down, and that was okay. It was honorable, actually. After all, even in today's day and age, society pinned us to think that, as women, if we didn't have it all—a career, a husband, two kids, and a white picket fence, then we were lacking.

But if a man had nothing beyond an amazing, established career, well, then he was ambitious and goal-oriented.

Joss and Paige both broke the barriers; they didn't give a damn what people thought. I wish I could be that woman, but I never was—I always cared what people thought. I was a people-pleasing, anxiety-ridden, over-thinker who wanted more than an adulterous husband and sex schedule.

"Warren is cheating on me," I said as soon as Adam and Ava were out in the water with Max and Scarlett.

"I know." Joss didn't look at me, keeping her gaze forward.

"What?" I pushed her arm off me, instantly feeling betrayed.

"I mean, I didn't know for sure... but I mean, come on, Ni. He's gone all the time, you're having no sex, and he's walking out dressed like he's going to a photoshoot when he's a, quote on quote, professor." Joss brushed her hand against my elbow, giving me the look, I hated the most.

My mother once told me when I was younger that there's two types of men; good men and men who pretend they are good. The scary part is, you take a gamble and never know which one you've got until you're too far deep in with them.

"Do you know who it is?" Joss asked calmly.

Looking at her, I couldn't help but feel a wave of sadness crash over me. My best friend was asking me if I knew who my husband was sleeping with. Who my husband was cheating on me with.

Swallowing the lump in my throat, I was thankful the dark shades were covering my eyes. "No." I bit my bottom lip as I looked over my shoulder, watching Warren grill the burgers and hot dogs.

"Then how'd you find out?" Joss whispered.

"Hey, besties!" Paige came jogging down the dock with her husband close behind her. Gripping two bottles of wine, she wiggled them excitedly at us.

Her stunning blonde hair was into two mermaid-style braids and her eyes were covered with rose-gold sunglasses.

"Hey, Paige. Hey, Cash." I gave Joss a look that she knew meant to not say a word of our conversation.

Cash wrapped his arms around me and gave me a kiss on top of my head. "Hey, girl, it's been a minute," Cash said in his Southern drawl. Paige and Cash were the epitome of the perfect couple. Cash was the Southern gentleman everyone loved, but he traveled frequently for work. The catch was, Paige always went with him. She was smart, she knew men couldn't be trusted to roam wildly. Clearly.

"I'm going to give Warren a hand, make sure the professor over there ain't burnin' my meat." Cash winked at me before giving Joss a hug and leaving to help my husband.

Once he left, Paige immediately gasped, "Who is that?" She waved one of her wine bottles at Adam, who was hanging out in the lake, completely unbothered by my kids pestering him in their canoes.

"Joss's new boy-toy." I shrugged and chewed on my bottom lip, recollecting what he had said to me earlier.

"Nope, just my plus-one for this family cookout. I'm done with him." Joss lowered her sunglasses and winked at me.

Immediately tightening my shoulders, I grinded my teeth.

Paige looked between us. "Wait, what's happening?"

Joss put her index finger against her lips and leaned in. "I'm not saying."

"Okay." Paige's cheeks were tinged pink as she popped the wine bottle and took a long swig before handing it over to me.

Squinting at her, I felt something wasn't right. She'd never let it go without knowing every little detail of any form of drama or gossip.

"Hey, Warren said you were in the house earlier?" I asked mid-sip.

Paige's jaw tensed slightly. "Well, Warren should get his eyes checked. Cash and I just got back from his sister's house." She peeled her coverup off, kicked her flip-flops to the side, and skipped down the dock.

"That was weird." Joss grabbed the wine bottle from my hands and took a sip.

My stomach flipped as I tried to recollect the voice that radiated into my earbuds. Looking between my two best friends, I brushed my hand across my neck.

What if the woman he was having an affair with was someone I knew? The woman's voice wasn't clear through the car Bluetooth connecting to my headphones.

But what if…

"Mom!" Ava came running down the dock, laughing hysterically as Max came behind her with an old water gun, shooting lake water at her as she shrieked. Scarlett trekked behind him with her hands crossed over her small frame and a completely desolate expression.

Her straggling red hair dripped as she looked between Ava and Max with irritation.

Ava grabbed me and hid behind me as she erupted into laughter, while Max shot the water gun directly at us, hitting me with a cold stream of water.

"Max!" I shot my hands up, protecting myself from his water gun as everyone laughed around us. Spinning around, I hugged Ava tightly and looked over her shoulder.

Warren was standing at the top of the deck, looking down at his phone with a smile on his face.

The joy I felt dissipated so quickly, I didn't even know if it was real. Who was he talking to?

"Come on, babe, I'm starving." Max dropped the water gun to the side and grabbed his bored girlfriend's hand. Joss, Paige, Ava, Max, and Scarlett all trekked up the deck, where Cash was flipping burgers while my husband was completely engrossed in his phone.

I stayed back and turned to walk toward the end of the dock, rubbing my arms as a warm breeze fluttered through the air, making my semi-damp bikini cling to my body.

Adam was climbing back onto the dock and shaking his hair out as pellets of water flicked around him.

Smirking at me, a dimple I hadn't noticed deepened.

"This is the most stunning lake I've been to." He ran his hand through his thick, dark blonde hair.

Wrapping my arms around my waist, I offered a small smile. "Do you live around here?" I shivered.

"I live about twenty minutes away. I just met Joss at a work conference." He reached down and lifted the white button-down from the dock.

Handing it over to me, he arched a brow. "Oh no, I'm fine." I waved him off.

"If you're going to keep trying to cover yourself up, at least humor me and let it be something of mine wrapped around you..." He opened his shirt and draped it behind me, tugging it over my chest as I slid my arms through the sleeves. My heart was pounding aggressively against my chest as he flashed his bright, white teeth at me.

"For the record, I prefer you..." his eyes dropped down my entire body, "uncovered."

Sucking in a breath of air, I shook my head. "That's wildly inappropriate seeing that I am married." I looked at my husband, who couldn't have cared less where I was.

"Sure, you are... but is he?" Adam asked coolly, but the simple statement was a punch to the gut.

Because it was the absolute truth.

In our marriage, only one of us was keeping our vows. Only one of us valued our marriage.

"Why... Why would you even say that?" I stammered and looked up at this complete stranger, shielding my eyes from the trickles of sunlight crafting a halo over his head.

"Because if you were mine, there's no way in hell I'd leave you alone with a man better looking than me..."

My lips parted as I looked at this completely confident, somewhat arrogant man in front of me. Maybe a good wife would have defended her husband in this moment. Instead, I decided I was tired of being a good wife so I did what I really felt like doing, which was laugh so hard, I clutched my abdomen as Adam's perfect pink lips turned into a devilish smile.

"Mom!" Ava yelled out from the deck at me.

"I'm comin'!" I waved back through the laughter.

Turning away I started to walk up the dock and paused mid-way. "Wanna eat?" I asked Adam over my shoulder.

Running his hand through his hair once more, he walked toward me. "Yeah, I do. But what I want to eat isn't being served on the deck."

My cheeks were hotter than the ever-warming sun that had left a cast of a tan on Adam's upper body. I could see the slight difference in his skin color by the band of his swim trunks. My thighs clenched together as I took a deep breath and blew it out.

"Nina!" Warren yelled out to me, and that's when the haze I was in shattered and I remembered—although my husband had forgotten, I had not—that I was a married woman. A mother of two.

Walking beside Adam, I looked up at him. "How old are you?"

"Thirty." He tucked his sunglasses into the band of his swim trunks and looked at me.

Pausing momentarily with a sigh, I shook my head. "I'm forty. See those teenagers up there?" I pointed at my kids as we made our way to them. "Mine." I exhaled.

"I'm an uninteresting, married, mom of two

teenagers. Trust me when I say, you don't want to eat what I'm serving."

Behind me, Adam gripped the stair railing. "You couldn't be more wrong."

Looking over my shoulder, I found his eyes were shamelessly on my ass. Shaking my head and brushing my hand over my mouth, I picked up my pace and jogged up the rest of the stairs.

"This is Adam, Joss's friend." I pointed with my thumb behind me as Warren handed me a plate with clear agitation.

"I needed you to serve the food." He glanced at Adam briefly before looking at me angrily.

"Well, I wanted to go spend time with my kids," I fired back and took a bite of the chicken burger.

Warren's jaw clenched slightly. "*Our.*"

"What?" I asked, wiping the corners of my mouth.

"Our kids."

Cash looked between us as he piled hot dogs onto a full plate.

"Well, Cash seemed to be doing all the leg work here." I waved my hands at him.

Warren stared at me for a moment before grabbing his phone and pushing past us with his plate.

"He seems fun." Adam came around and popped a hot dog into a bun before taking a massive bite.

"Adam." He stuck his hand out to Cash, who smiled cheerily and greeted him like a normal human being, unlike my rabid husband.

"So much fun." I took another bite of my burger. Paige and Joss were huddled in the opposite corner, whispering to one another. Where did Warren go? Ava and Max were scrolling through social media, basking in the sunshine.

"Hey." As soon as I walked closer to Paige and Joss, they immediately stopped talking. "What?" I pushed my sunglasses up on top of my head and looked between them. Joss took a sip of the wine cooler in her hand, and Paige placed her plate down.

"Did you know Warren's first wife killed herself?" she whispered almost inaudibly.

Blinking rapidly, I swallowed. My mind took a moment to process something that caught me completely off guard. "No... she lives in Texas." I rubbed my lips together, annoyed that my friends were at my house, gossiping about me.

"Why are you..." I started, clutching the rim of my plate tightly.

"She lives in Texas." I repeated.

"No, she doesn't. She died. Apparently, she killed herself, and well, let's just say there was no body to do an autopsy on. There was a suicide note that she, apparently, left in the mailbox."

"What... Where did you even hear something so outlandish?" I hissed at my best friends.

Paige pursed her lips. "I had a guy from work look into it today."

Joss immediately looked at the ground. "Why?" My palms grew moist with a slight tremble coursing through my veins.

"I *was* here early this morning." Paige's shoulders tightened as she straightened her back.

"Oh-kay," I breathed out slowly, my pulse pounding.

Paige took a sip of her wine cooler and looked at Joss, who nodded at her. "I walked into the library room, you know. I figured you'd be in there... but you weren't." She looked back at Joss, who was fidgeting with the can in her hands.

"Stop looking at her and just tell me, Paige. I..." I hated how rude I was being.

"There was a cell phone sitting on the end table, and I know I shouldn't have, but I... well, I picked it up and there was a video of some woman, but you couldn't see her. It was dark, so you just saw her silhouette, but she was touching herself... and moaning Warren's name." Paige stopped and scratched her head anxiously.

"There was a bottle of lotion and dirtied Kleenex scattered, but then… Warren, well, he came out of the bathroom and had his pants sagged below, and his… well—"

"What?" I slapped my hand over my mouth. He was getting himself off in our home to a video of some other woman?

"Well, I ran, and he immediately called me. I ignored it countless times, but he kept calling. He made me promise not to tell you. He was saying how you guys are in a rough patch right now, and that woman is you in the video and you're just flirting. But I knew it wasn't you." Paige opened her arms for me to come into.

Blinking away tears, I shook my head. "Why did you look into his first wife then?" I asked as a tear straggled out.

"I'm trying to find out who the woman is. My guy couldn't find anything beyond his first wife. I'd need more…"

"He told me she had remarried and lived in Texas. They were only married for two years… I… I didn't really care to dig into her." I looked up.

"Well, she's dead. And, truthfully, I'm not convinced she killed herself," Paige said.

Wiping my tears away and sliding my sunglasses back on, I whispered, "What are you getting at?"

Joss tugged me into her arms and squeezed me. "I think you already know."

CHAPTER FIFTEEN

*I*t's bizarre, really, the concept of marriage. You quite literally meet someone who is a complete stranger, open up to them, hide your flaws, while displaying the positive, and then, in the snap of your fingers, you get into this legal arrangement, promising an eternity to one another.

When I sat in the lecture hall at UNC-Johan, I remember seeing Professor Warren Cooper walk through the doors. He was late. His hair was slightly splayed across his forehead, like he had broken into a light jog just to make it to class. He had this navy-blue sports coat, a somewhat wrinkled button-down, and a glisten of sweat across his forehead.

I remember chewing the tip of my pen watching

him, along with every other female student in the lecture hall.

I couldn't believe this man was going to be my professor. I always thought of professors donning plaid jackets, with gray hair and deep wrinkles, but Warren Cooper could have been a graduate student—and a stunning one at that.

Eager students flocked around him after each class, feigning extra interest in his lectures, pleading for any opportunity to sign up for a research study. Meanwhile, I always lingered in my empty row, watching him as his eyes flicked toward me. A small, sexy smirk would always grow on his face whenever he caught my gaze on him.

My heart would race, my palms would grow moist. But then, I'd remind myself that he was married.

That thin, gold band that was still shiny with a new marriage was proudly displayed on his finger.

Hindsight is even more inexplicable. I remember the day my husband was wearing a wedding band that another woman had slid on his finger.

Yet, I still wanted him. Out of all the men in the world, not to mention a campus overflowing with horny college students, I just had to want him.

That's human nature, though, wanting what we can't have, no matter the immense destruction our actions will inflict. We get ourselves into situations and allow it to spin us around and around, gaining a high from the adrenaline of the excitement, but then what we see once we are expelled from the rush is nothing more than shrapnel and chaos.

"Nina?" Adam's voice cut through my thoughts. I couldn't hear the laughter, I couldn't hear the gossip, or the voices clattering together around me as everyone happily ate. I just laid on a sun-chair pretending to be asleep. But really, I was replaying every single moment from the beginning of my relationship with my husband.

I started out as the other woman. Sure, he was separated, and sure, they got a divorce soon after—and not because of me, but because of 'irreconcilable differences.'

Which, what the fuck did that even mean?

A bougie term to say, well, we hate each other and can't stand one another and we need an out.

"Yeah?" I pushed myself upward, looking up at the man in front of me, holding a glass of whiskey.

Scanning the deck, I realized everyone was gone, but I could hear shrieks of laughter from below. They must be swimming or kayaking, happily.

"Here." Adam sank in the chair next to me and handed the caramel liquid to me.

I held up a hand. "I don't drink whiskey."

"That's like a woman saying she doesn't suck dick. You never know until you try it and let it hit the back of your throat."

I choked on my saliva as my eyes widened under my sunglasses. "Where the hell did Joss find you?" I rolled my lips, trying to suppress my laughter at this man's immensely crude language.

"I'm not a stray dog, Nina. Your friend didn't find me on the side of the road." Adam lifted his glass with a smile.

"Could have fooled me." I let out a small laugh before lifting my glass, matching his.

"Cheers to forgetting those who deserve to be forgotten." Adam's eyes locked onto mine as chills raced across my arms.

"What did Joss tell you about me?" I glanced down at the dock, where Paige and Joss were floating in the lake. Ava was kayaking with Warren, but I couldn't see Max and Scarlett.

"Nothing. But I can see it all over your face... how badly you wish you could forget him the way he's forgotten you." Our glasses clinked together and the liquid sloshed before Adam tossed his back with ease and I paused with hesitation.

"Cheers," I mumbled and drank the bitter whiskey in one long sip.

"Ah, fuck. That's good shit." Adam placed his glass down, then stretched his arms up. He had a white button-down on, but his tattoo peeked out of his shirt.

"Where'd you buy it?" I asked just to make small talk.

"Buy it? Nah, I stole it from your husband's office." The devilish smirk reappeared and this time, I couldn't hold back. I laughed so hard I snorted. I froze with embarrassment, but Adam leaned in, squinting and lifting my chin as he smiled. "Don't ever stop that gorgeous laugh." I could smell the whiskey lingering on his breath and I suddenly felt intoxicated.

"Nina?" Warren's voice sliced through the moment, and I jerked back.

"Hey, War—" I said with my voice shaking. Standing, I looked up at my husband, whose eyes were on Adam.

"I have to run back to campus."

Annoyance immediately built inside me as I looked at him. My best friend just caught him masturbating to some other woman's video in our home, and now, he magically needed to go to campus?

"Why?" I asked flatly.

"I left my laptop and need to put grades in this

weekend. I'll be back in an hour." He gave me a look—the look that meant, stop pestering me, especially in front of someone else.

"Okay." I nodded as Warren stepped around me.

I hated the way he looked at me, so unlike the way he used to look at me. Fire used to blaze in his dilated pupils whenever he'd see me naked or undressing.

All of that was gone.

Moments of silence passed as I began to clean up straggling plates, lingering beer bottles, and soda cans. Adam made his way and grabbed the trash bag out of my hands.

"Oh, you don't have to." I shook my head and waved my hand at him to give the bag back.

"I got you, girl." He lifted his hat from a chair and put it on backward.

Oh no. I was flustered. Turning away, I grabbed more trash and peeked at everyone laying on towels or still hanging out by the water.

"He's lying, you know." Adam came closer to me, taking the trash from my hands and putting it into the trash bag.

"What?" I asked, even though I knew what he was talking about. I couldn't help but feel embarrassed.

"His laptop was on his desk when I went looking for the good liquor."

Pushing my sunglasses up to my hair, I tilted my head. "What would you do if you were me?"

He didn't answer.

"What would you do if the person you loved more than anything was lying to your face?" I asked again.

Adam tied the trash bag and placed it in the bin. "I wouldn't react; I'd play it cool and find out every single thing I needed to. You can't pull the trigger with an empty gun."

His words seared into me, and those were the words I needed to hear. It was true, while I wanted to slap him, scream at him, pack a bag, and storm out in the middle of the night, or maybe throw all his clothes out the window and put on an entire drama, I knew that wouldn't be enough.

No, I needed to know. I needed to know everything about the stranger I had married.

I needed to know how many bullets I'd need to fire.

CHAPTER SIXTEEN

I was about to pull out of the driveway when I saw Ava come running out. "Mom! Mom!" she screamed with her hands put up.

My tires screeched as I braked quickly and rolled the window down. "What's wrong?" I yelled.

"I want to come with you!" Ava jogged to the passenger seat.

"No, honey, I'm just grabbing some... You know what, Dad forgot his office keys so I need to take them to campus."

"I'll come with." Ava slid inside and fastened her seatbelt. Her long hair was now in beautiful waves from swimming and the sun drying it.

I looked at her. "Where's your brother?"

"I don't know. They both left, probably to have sex." Ava pretended to gag herself.

I shook my head, and Ava let out a laugh. "I'll text Lindsey and see if she's around. She said she was doing research this summer. You can drop the keys to Dad, and I'll see her for a bit?"

I hesitated, but realized I didn't have time to weave some elaborate lie up. That was my husband's expertise.

"Okay, let's go." We drove to campus and spent the drive catching up about London, boys, and life. It eased the dread that was lingering in my lower abdomen. As I strummed my fingers against the steering wheel, I glanced at Ava, but her eyes widened.

"Mom! Watch out! You're going to hit her!" Ava shrieked.

I jerked my head forward and slammed on my brakes. The tires screeched loudly against the pavement.

My heart thudded against my chest as my mouth dropped.

I didn't see anyone.

Turning the car off, I opened my door and looked around.

Sliding back in a moment later, I looked at my daughter, who was staring ahead blankly.

"Ava?"

She turned her head slowly and finally blinked. "I'm sorry, Mom. I..." She began laughing, tossing her head back and laughing harder. "Mom, I'm sorry, it was a joke!"

"Ava! That is not funny!" I shouted and jammed my key back into the ignition.

After lecturing her for the rest of the drive, I dropped it. But glancing over at her, the smile and laughter on her face seemed so... forced.

Turning into campus, I couldn't help but feel nostalgic every time I was here.

"I'm going to the coffee shop on east campus, Mom. Just text me when you want to head back home." Ava pecked my cheek with a soft kiss, and I brushed my hand against hers.

"Sounds good, baby." I watched as she got out and walked away. Unfolding the visor, I looked at myself in the small mirror. Tugging a tube of lipstick out, I spread the bright red across my lips before brushing my fingers underneath my eyes.

My sandals hit the concrete as I made my way to

Warren's office. Campus felt empty and eerie with only sprinkles of students lingering on the weekend.

The sun was hidden through the thick canopy of hundred-year-old oak trees as I stood in the center of the quad and closed my eyes.

20 years ago

"Hello, Miss. Paxton." I was sitting barefoot in the lush green grass, leaning against the rigid trunk of an old oak tree, reading a book for my English literature class.

My eyes flicked upward, from the cognac brown leather shoes, khaki dress pants, a button-down, and then him.

Clearing my throat, I quickly pushed my feet back into my sandals and stood, cursing how short my denim cut-offs were.

"Professor Cooper," I stammered, feeling my cheeks flush as his gorgeous pale blue eyes locked onto mine.

"Your paper really stood out to me... it was exceptional. I have never seen such a thought-provoking take on the effects of trauma on a female versus male with societal pressures." Professor Cooper adjusted his satchel and brushed his hand across the light scruff on his jawline.

"Wow, really?" My brows cinched together as excitement grew inside me. "I'd love to eventually become a psychologist." I smiled back proudly.

"And you will, as long as some charming college guy doesn't swoop up such a smart and beautiful girl first."

My lips parted in disbelief as my heart pounded against my chest.

"How long have you and your wife been married?" I asked while stuffing my books into my backpack.

"A couple of years, but she'll be gone soon," Professor Cooper said without a second thought.

"Oh my gosh, I'm sorry. Is she... Is she ill?" My hand flung to my chest as I looked at him, feeling embarrassed for even asking my professor about his wife. I was just irked on how he said something somewhat suggestive to me while wearing a wedding ring.

"No, she had an affair with my brother. They're going to get married and move to Texas. So now, I'm losing my wife and my brother." Professor Cooper seemed flustered as the words came out of his mouth.

Gasping, I shook my head. "I can't believe it. I'm so sorry." I had to force myself to not show my true emotions. Why would he tell me this? His phone chimed, and I was grateful. Truly, I had no clue how to react to what he was saying.

"Hey. Yeah, the shed." Warren's eyes lifted to mine before he turned and took a few steps away, quietly finishing the rest of his conversation.

"She begged?" Professor Cooper laughed and turned back toward me, running his hand through his hair before filling the space between us.

Ending the call, his face was glowing as if the phone call washed away an entire chapter of stress.

"My best friend got a new dog and..." He waved his hand and laughed.

I couldn't help but smile. My mind was wandering to darker places for a moment.

"I've always wanted a dog." I chewed my bottom lip.

And just like that, Professor Warren Cooper and I went to get a cup of coffee together, and I realized it would be the start of something that should never have happened. They say youth is wasted on the young, and this is the moment I wish I could have erased. I wish I could have erased the man that would eventually change the entire course of my life for the worse.

CHAPTER SEVENTEEN

I gripped the banister and climbed each step slowly. My breathing grew shallow as I approached Warren's office. Standing in front of his closed door, I closed my eyes and pressed my ear to the door.

Did I hear moans? My husband's name being called out? Did I hear creaking of his leather chair or his wooden desk?

The desk he had been intimate with me on countless times when we first started seeing one another.

Gripping the cool steel handle, I turned it. It wasn't locked.

Walking in, my jaw dropped and I froze in my spot.

Warren was there, with his pants down.

But he was alone. His hand was wrapped around

his hardened penis, his head sunk back, and he was pumping his hand up and down. But the worst part was that the doll I had seen in the photo was sitting on his desk in front of him—the doll that was shaved bald, except for a few random colored braids of hair sticking out in all directions.

"Nina!" he called out in shock as soon as the door screeched against the old, tiled floors.

"War..." I covered my mouth with my shaking hand as I stared at my husband.

Tugging his pants on, he looked completely flustered as he stuffed the doll into the drawer and ran toward me. Lifting my hands up with disgust, I backed away as he tried to embrace me.

"No, no!"

His cheeks flushed to a bright red as I cradled my arms around me. "You left our family cookout and weekend with our children so you could drive to campus and..." I looked away, unsure of what I should feel.

"Paige said she caught you this morning, too. What the fuck, Warren?" My voice grew hoarse as I fought back tears.

I thought I'd feel relief if I didn't walk in on the man I loved having sex with someone in his office. But now, I realized I still felt betrayed. Completely betrayed, and most of all...

"What was that creepy doll you were staring at? It doesn't even have a face... and why is the hair shaved off?" My tone turned from pain to anger as Warren kept his eyes on the floor.

A long pause filled the office where the silence felt safe before Warren finally looked me in the eyes. "It's just a... weird kink doll I ordered from the internet. I'm so sorry, my love." His eyes dipped down to the locket hanging from my neck.

"You need help, Warren. A kink doll? What does that even mean? You have to get help, now." I clenched my teeth and looked at him for a moment longer. I knew he was lying.

I knew he was a filthy liar.

But the thing was, I couldn't let him know I knew he had lied to me about what happened to his first wife. I couldn't let him know that I knew he was lying about the disturbing doll.

I knew I couldn't let him know I knew things— things I had to dig up. Because if he knew, then he'd make sure to be three steps ahead of me and cover the messy tracks he was leaving behind.

"I promise," he whispered with a small nod.

Shaking my head, I knew that was just another thing I'd never believe. *His promises.*

"Paige?" I said as soon as the call was answered.

"Hey, babe, where the hell did you go?" Paige said mid-laugh.

"I need you to give me the information of your friend who found out about Warren's first wife." I sank my teeth into my bottom lip to stop it from shaking from the mix of emotions I felt.

"Oh-okay." Paige's voice dropped, and I heard the back-door creak and slam shut behind her.

"What's going on, Nina?" she asked me. But before I could answer, I felt cold fingers tap my shoulder.

Flinging around, I turned.

Warren.

His jaw was clenched, just like his fist.

"Why the curiosity in that low-life bitch?" He grinded his teeth as I slid my phone from my ear and quickly ended the call.

"Warren…"

He stepped closer and had me standing in his shadow.

Tilting his head from side to side, he gripped my

arm. "Sunshine, let me explain something to you..." His breath was stale and warm.

I tried so hard to pretend I was unphased and calm, that my own husband wasn't causing my heart to race, and not in a good way.

"You have lived a beautiful life. You've lived a life all women dream about. When have I ever said no to you?" Lifting his other hand, he tucked a loose strand of hair behind my ear.

"Do you want to know the difference between a shitty life and a good life, my love?" Warren's tone became dangerously low.

Swallowing, I slowly shook my head as he tilted my chin up with his index finger. "If you want to have a good life, then you'll want to make sure I continue to talk about my wife in present tense."

"What... what do you mean?" My voice was low and shaky.

"I don't want to talk about my wife in past tense, but if I need to..." he trailed and paused immediately.

A big smile curved across his lips, and before I could even ask what he meant, his face lit up.

"There's my girl!" Warren spun me around and quickly planted a wet kiss against my cheek.

Ava was walking up to us, but she dragged her feet, as if she could sense something was off.

"Mom... Dad..." she glanced between us.

"How about I take my girls for some ice cream. Did you know I'm three-fourths of the way done with my final edits for the new book, kiddo?"

"That's cool. I can't wait to hear about it," she said, looping her arm into Warren's as they walked.

Trailing behind them, I couldn't stop replaying Warren's words in my head. What a threatening and shocking statement to say to me. I shuddered as my daughter clutched onto his arm with so much trust.

CHAPTER EIGHTEEN

"She was nineteen when they met. He was the teaching assistant to her psychology professor." Paige tapped her long, pink nails across a file folder.

My chest tightened as I stared at the single sheet of paper that had an image of Warren's first wife and the details about her in organized boxes. *Willow Cooper.*

We looked nothing alike. She had platinum-blonde hair, pale blue eyes, and thin pink lips. Her face was full of makeup, and the grin on her face looked forced.

"They got married, then Willow eventually filed for separation. Apparently, they reconciled, but then six months later, she disappeared. Warren was the primary suspect and was questioned, but they had zero evidence. She didn't really have a family, so there was no one to worry about the case. It went cold and everyone moved on. But then..." Paige paused and lifted her eyes to mine. She took a slow sip of her sparkling water and blew out a breath.

"But then, what?" Agitation was clear in my tone.

"Willow Cooper was seen here, in Lake Johan, years ago." Paige proceeded to slide a photograph over to me that she tugged out from her purse. "But not only was she in Lake Johan... she was at your house, Ni."

My lips parted as I blinked repeatedly while looking down at the image. Willow was sitting on our dock with Warren. Lifting the image up with my quivering hands, I shook my head.

"I don't... I don't understand." My forehead crinkled as I looked at Paige. Her eyes filled with pity and remorse for me.

"After this day," Paige pointed at the photo that was shaking between my thumb and index finger, "Willow was never seen again."

Chills splattered against my forearms as I stared at my best friend. The realization of what she had just told me was that the last person my husband's first wife was seen with was him.

"How did you find all this out? Who took this photo?" I placed the photo down on the file and grabbed my water. My throat felt scaly and dry as a budding panic attack was rearing its ugly head inside my body.

"The private investigator who works for us did me a favor. As for the photo it seems someone who was there took it. I don't know, Ni... I have just always felt off about Warren. Then, when I saw him that way in his home office, pleasuring himself as we all were only a few feet away, I just..." She paused, her cheeks flushing pink. This had to be the worst conversation to have with a girlfriend.

Not only did she just imply my husband killed his first wife, but she also reminded me of his... disturbing habits. The doll? The photos? What was happening?

"I'm telling you this kind of stuff because I want you to be safe. Men like Warren... once they find someone new or something to chase, they will do anything to cut the dead weight off them."

"I'm dead weight?" My eyes started to burn as I held back tears and slid my sunglasses on.

Paige reached out for my hands and squeezed them. "Not yet, but you will be if you don't get steps ahead of him. I'm not saying Warren definitely killed Willow; I'm just saying there's a chance. And do you really want to take a chance when it's your life, and maybe even the kids at stake?" she added before slowly pushing the paper and photographs into the manila envelope.

Nodding, I looked around at the bustling restaurant. Lake Johan had three diners close by, and during the summer, they were always packed. Most of the locals despised the summer tourists who flocked in excitedly, but I loved it. It helped drown out the otherwise quiet and stillness that living in a secluded lake town often was.

"I don't think Warren would kill someone, Paige." I turned back and swirled my straw around my drink, watching the ice and sweet tea crash against the glass. This was the man I fell in love with, slept next to for the last twenty-plus years, and brought babies into the world with. I scoffed at the mere thought of Warren, an esteemed professor of psychology, and man who was penning a psychological thriller novel in his free time, as someone who'd kill someone, let alone his first wife. The thought in my mind was that I wanted to know if he'd slept with her while she was here.

What if, after all this time, they were still together? Was she still alive? Was my husband cheating on me with his first wife?

"We are all capable of murder, Nina. The difference is who gets pushed far enough in just the right moment to act upon those urges." Paige took cash out of her wallet and stacked it neatly in the middle of the table.

"All I'm saying is to be cautious." She tapped my hand once more before standing. "I've got to show a house now, but I'll see you later. Love you." She cocked her head to the side as her long, blonde hair toppled to one side. "Are you going to be okay?"

"Yeah, I will. It's still summer. Everything's better in the summer." I blinked away the tears that started to grow in my eyes and wiggled my fingers at her.

"Before you know it, it will be fall. And once the leaves start falling, everything starts dying, my friend." Paige sighed.

Turning away, Paige left, and I sank back into my chair, lifting the envelope in my hands. When Warren and I started dating, he made it very clear that he and his first wife had no contact, nor would they ever care to, especially since they didn't have children together.

It was a clear break from one another, and in all honesty, I loved that. I loved that there wasn't this lingering cloud above my head, where I had to see the first woman my husband loved.

He said she had remarried and moved on, and so

had he. It was simple. I didn't care to ask questions or dig deeper. Partially, because, as a nineteen-year-old, I didn't want to bring up another woman to the man I was enthralled with. That's the problem with young love, though; we are blinded to the logical aspect of the relationship because, in that moment, it is as if nothing else could matter.

But it does matter. It could be the difference in marrying someone who might have killed his first wife or not. It could be the difference in marrying a serial cheater and a man destined to ruin your life.

CHAPTER NINETEEN

I always thought it was a bit eerie living in a house on the lake—I preferred water that I could see through. While Lake Johan was known for its crystal-clear water, especially in the summer, there were still quite a bit of patches where the water was completely opaque and the hundred-year-old oak trees shadowed it. By the fall and winter, it turned even darker, and the leaves all fell into piles and scattered across the reflective water.

Clutching the stem of my wineglass, I looked out into the water while standing in the exact same spot Warren stood with Willow years ago.

The sweetness of the prosecco didn't conceal the bitter taste that lingered on my tongue from leaving lunch with Paige, and then profusely vomiting on the side of the road, thinking the man I'd loved all these years and had children with could potentially be a human capable of taking someone's life. A man with a sick obsession with some creepy doll and a web of lies had had me entangled in.

"Sunshine…" The voice that once sent chills up my spine in a completely different light radiated behind me. Keeping my eyes forward, I watched the ripples of the lake and sunset craft a gorgeous sky full of orange, pink, and yellow. His reflection towered behind me.

One arm snaked around my waist while the other made its way higher toward my breasts. But he didn't stop there; he moved his hand upward, caressing my neck in a way that caused my breathing to grow erratic.

Intrusive thoughts circled my head as I inhaled the humid summer scent, and he cupped my neck with his palm. Leaning in, his cold breath brushed against my cheek from behind, causing my head to tilt to the side.

His fingertips dug into my skin slowly, but enough to know that it was starting to become a poignant touch.

"Are you coming to bed?" he asked softly as I released the breath I was holding.

Shaking out from his arms, my feet teetered too close to the edge of the dock. "Mm-hmm…" I whispered before slowly turning around. His arms steadied me under my elbows, and I looked up at him.

He was shirtless, with slouched gray pajama bottoms on. A small, sensual smirk grew across his lips as he tilted my chin up with his index finger.

"I know things have been bad between us, but I want to change that. This is our first year without the kids living at home full-time with us, and I think we both are simply unsure of how we should react. We just need to well... learn about each other all over again. Don't you think, my love?"

The rustle of the trees, the crickets chirping, and distant voices of people still out boating floated around us.

Clenching my teeth, I looked into Warren's beautiful blue eyes.

"I completely agree. I miss us." I forced out the most believable smile I could muster and laced my fingers with his.

He smiled at our intertwined hands, and together, we made our way back up the dock. Looking over my shoulder, I couldn't help but think of Willow. Where did she go after being on this dock?

Was she the woman in contact with my husband? Was she the woman in the photographs?

Was she still the love of his life? Maybe none of this

was some true crime mystery and realistically, just a story of a woman and man who found their way back to one another.

Either way, my heart was breaking, and I knew I didn't have much time to piece everything together.

Warren was tucked into bed, typing fervently on his laptop as I stood in the doorframe that connected our bedroom and bathroom. Rubbing the thick hand cream through each of my fingers, I watched him.

"How's the book coming along?" I asked. I thought about what Warren had said, and it was true, I don't really know anything that was going on with Warren. I'd become a sponge to my children's lives—constantly thinking, worrying, and listening to them. It was true, marriage and being a wife took the backseat, but so did being a husband. He always put his career first, even above being a father. Society accepted that though. There wasn't "dad-guilt". If Warren took the kids out so I could catch up on laundry or housework, he was applauded as such an amazing and devoted father. Meanwhile, mothers did it all daily, with zero to little appreciation. This was expected from us as women. To be it all. To do it all.

"I think I'll have it wrapped up very soon. My agent thinks it'll be the book of the year." Warren began closing his laptop slowly, removing his blue-light blocking glasses.

Tugging my silk robe closed, I walked around to my side of the bed.

"That's amazing, wow. I... I can't believe it. You're really doing it." I smiled at him as I climbed into the bed and pulled the blanket over me.

"I remember you telling me on our first date that you'd love to be an author." This time the smile wasn't feigned. This time it was one that was genuine, because reminiscing on the days where emotion over-took logic stung in a way I couldn't explain.

"And I remember you wearing this beautiful, emer-ald-green gown. It was so perfectly fitted to your toned body." He sighed as his fingers raked across my forearm.

Looking down at my body, I felt self-conscious. I wasn't even close to the same weight as I was back then. I still had that dress—the dress I always wore to feel extra beautiful. Even all these years later, I couldn't part with it because deep down, I couldn't let go of *her*.

The woman I once was. The girl I once was. Glancing up at Warren, I wondered if he thought the same thing.

"I'm going to get some shut-eye now, babe. I'm too

tired." He put his laptop on his end table and immediately turned his back to me. It was Thursday, a day we always had sex. But he didn't need me anymore for anything; he had someone else. Maybe that someone else was the first Mrs. Cooper. Maybe after all this time, I was just a substitute. Maybe I was just the fling that should have never been more.

CHAPTER TWENTY

"Max, you just disappeared after the cook-out." I balanced the phone between my shoulder and ear as I brushed my paint-brush against a blank canvas.

"Yeah, Scarlett didn't feel good, so we headed out early." I could hear a ball hit a wall back and forth.

Max always threw a tennis ball at the wall and would catch it whenever he was stressed or anxious. He started doing the pesky habit when he was only ten years old, and while it drove me crazy with the repetitive sound, I knew it helped him calm his nerves.

"What's wrong, honey?" I asked, putting the paint-brush back into the cup and wiping my fingers against the towel.

A long pause had my heart race because I knew my

son better than anyone. I knew he was trying to think of some elaborate excuse on why he was just fine.

"I think Scarlett is going to break up with me," he let out with exasperation.

Tilting my head to the sky, I shook my head. I knew I couldn't tell him I thought that would be a blessing in disguise, or how she scared the living daylights out of me with her eerie presence.

"Oh, no. I'm sorry, baby. That's her loss." I feigned. "Why do you think that?" I added, simply to keep the conversation going, because ultimately, my heart hurt for my son. I knew the impact of young love all too well. Young love was beautifully blinding.

"I think she's seeing someone else. Some older guy." The ball hit the wall again.

"What makes you think that?" I walked back into the house and glanced at the time. It was almost six p.m.

I had no interest in making dinner, so I opened the drawer and tugged out our favorite Thai restaurant brochure.

"I saw some text messages..." The ball stopped echoing in the background.

Tracing the granite countertops with my finger, I closed my eyes. "I'm sorry, son." I sighed.

"I love her, Mom. Like, really love her. I know that

sounds crazy, but I would have done anything for her." The vulnerability of his voice had my entire being crumble inside. As a mother, you want to be able to put a band aid on every wound, but some wounds can't be patched up. Some wounds inflict more pain because they aren't external, but internal.

"It doesn't sound crazy..." I pinched my lips and hesitated before I asked, "What did the texts say?"

"It was definitely some man. He said something about being too old for her, and then he kept calling her sunshine. The way Dad calls you..."

I didn't realize I was still tracing the design in our countertops with my finger; I didn't realize my chest started to constrict and how my body didn't feel like mine.

"What?" It was the only word I could muster.

"Yeah, he said in his text, like I'll see you when I..." Max must have finished the sentence but I didn't hear him. I didn't have, to. I already knew what the rest of it was.

I'll see you when I see you, sunshine.

The sentence Warren Cooper, my husband, said to me countless times when we began to see one another secretly.

My stomach twisted as Max kept talking, but I couldn't make sense out of the rest of our conversation. My body was breaking into a cold sweat and my head felt lighter.

"Mom? Mom…" he repeated.

"Baby, I have to go. I… I… Your dad is calling me. I promise to call you back. Love you." I pieced a broken sentence together and hated myself for not being stronger for my son. My phone slipped from my hand as I gasped and clutched the counter. Breathing in and out rapidly, my body shook.

It was as if a movie reel was running through my mind.

The photographs in his desk, the call, the daydreaming…

My husband was having an affair with our son's girlfriend.

Tears streamed down my cheeks, and I broke down in a sob I didn't even recognize coming from my body.

My heart physically hurt, my mind was spinning, and, in that moment, my entire world shattered around me.

Not only because of what Warren had done to me, but most of all, what he'd chosen to do to our son.

"Want another blanket?" Joselin asked as I hugged my knees, already draped in an overpriced, fuzzy cheetah print blanket.

I was on my third glass of wine and curled up by the crackling fire in Joselin's living room. "No, I'm fine." I was shuddering still, basically convulsing from the sheer shock of what I had pieced together while on the phone with my son.

I couldn't tell Paige. I knew she was already knee-deep playing investigator about Warren and his first wife, but how could I face her with this now? It was humiliating.

"It could all be a coincidence. You and Paige always catastrophize everything." Joss handed me a slice of lemon cake. I knew she was trying to get me to eat something since I was already pouring my fourth glass of prosecco.

Slicing my fork into the cake, I looked up at Joss. "My husband texted my son's nineteen-year-old girl-friend and called her the nickname he used to call me when I was nineteen. The fact that my hands aren't covered in his blood shows the clear fact that I'm not catastrophizing."

Joss looked at me with concerned eyes. "Don't joke like that, Ni. No matter how bad something gets, don't be stupid enough to—"

"I'm not going to kill him," I snapped.

"That's what every wife who I've ever represented says before they did, in fact, slaughter their husbands." Joss grabbed my glass of wine and put it out of reach.

"Mm-hmm." I rolled my eyes at her as I sank back and took another bite of the lemon cake.

"Listen, Nina, I'm being serious." Joss paused as I wiggled my eyebrows at her. I wasn't drunk, but I sure as hell was tipsy.

"Nina…" she said sternly.

Straightening my shoulders, I puffed out a breath of air and put the cake down. "Yes, attorney Joselin?" I said with a small giggle.

"Nina, listen, you just need to focus. You can't return a damaged item without receipts. You need to start compiling anything and everything you can if Warren is really having an affair with that girl."

I realized I might have been overdramatizing the effects of the alcohol because when my best friend said those words, it was loud and clear. The thing was, I hated how, deep down, I didn't necessarily want a refund. I didn't want to find receipts. I wanted to be comfortable.

Because that's what marriage provides us, comfort. That steady, secure, comfortable safety net.

Blinking away tears, I nodded in agreement.

"We just have to be careful, Nina. He might have something that can loom over your head," she added.

Squinting up at her, I shrugged. "What? What would he have over me? I've spent my life being the wife he wanted me to be, and the mother the kids needed me to be. I've…" I couldn't hold them back any longer, and tears rolled down my cheeks as I covered my mouth and began to sob again.

Joss handed me tissues and cradled me in her arms as my cries grew louder.

"The man is allegedly sleeping with his son's girlfriend. If that's true, then the man doesn't have much of a moral compass." She stroked my hair as acid teased my esophagus. The sheer thought of my husband sleeping with the girl my son… our son was in love with made me want to vomit.

"We will take him down if it's all true. Just don't kill him. Besides, if it ever came down to that…" Joss looked over her shoulder and around her stunning designer home. She dropped her voice so low it was almost inaudible. "There's ways we can make sure no repercussions would be on you."

"Joss." I slapped my hand over my mouth.

"I've got the shovels." We flung around and saw Paige standing there with a smile, holding up two more bottles of wine.

"And I've got the alibi," Joss added, patting my hand.

But I didn't protest; I didn't run out the door and tell them I couldn't believe they implied I'd even want him dead.

Because at the end of the day, I may have been an unlucky wife, but when it came to best friends…

I was clearly lucky. I had best friends who were thinking ten steps ahead of me about how to cover the murder of the man who betrayed me.

CHAPTER TWENTY-ONE

*P*eople joke about anxiety and depression. It's easy to say you're depressed or anxious when you're really just feeling the normal range of human emotions.

It's okay to be unhappy or nervous and not be clinically labeled. It's okay to not be okay. As mothers and wives, that's a concept that quickly becomes foreign to us. Really, as women, we are groomed to never show those feelings of being completely overwhelmed or miserable. Many times, throughout my life, I had experienced the range of them all. Finishing college, getting married, and then getting pregnant. Postpartum hormones rampaged throughout my body, causing my entire mental state to be altered while no one even noticed. Well, even if they noticed, they didn't care. Because I was expected to care for a baby, I was expected to push through the sleep deprivation, debilitating anxiety, depression, and exhaustion.

Sometimes, I would be excessively overwhelmed, and everyone would tell me that the way I felt was normal. So, I started to believe them. I believed that it was normal to feel like the world crashing around you was normal.

Now, at forty, I knew better. I knew this dense, heavy storm-cloud about my head wasn't normal. And most of all, the person who put it there was the man who should have only brought light into my life.

I walked around the next day completely numb. I didn't know what I should have been doing. Was I supposed to be digging around for evidence against my husband? Was I supposed to confront him?

Relationships are complex at every level. When you're dating, it's all about putting your best foot forward to secure something long-term; when you're married, it's all about creating this life together you both dreamed of, and then... the most complicated aspect is the demise of the relationship that took years of your life to grow and nurture.

Clutching my cup of coffee between my palms, I stood by the glass windows that encapsulated the entire back wall of our lake house.

Warren was rowing out on the lake with his shirt off. His arm muscles flexed repeatedly as he moved his arms in sync. The scent of cinnamon and espresso wafted upward as I pressed my lips against the warm mug.

I sighed as I turned away and curled up on the small chaise, tugging my book out. Warren loved writing, and I loved reading, so I guess we still had something in common. We both loved the epic escape that literature provided us—we could be anyone we wanted to. Half an hour easily raced by as I read an angsty romance story, even though I was really in the mood of a violent horror story where a woman slashes her husband's tires and neck.

"Hey, Mom." I jerked around and saw Ava in an oversized UNC-Johan T-shirt and shorts. Her long hair was tied up, and she smiled at me.

"Hi sweetie, I feel like I've hardly seen you." She sank onto a barstool and grabbed an orange from the bowl.

I clutched the kitchen island that separated us and looked at my daughter. "Can I make you something? An omelet? Pancakes?"

She had grown up so much, yet she was still so young. She was twenty, only a year older than I was when I had met her dad. Only a year older than the girl her dad was potentially having sex with. Suddenly, I felt light-headed.

"No, I'm fine, Mom. I'll just have coffee and this orange." Ava lifted the orange in her hands.

A light creaking sounded above our heads, and simultaneously, we looked up at the ceiling. There it was again. "Isn't Dad out on the lake?" Ava looked back at me.

"Yeah," I breathed out in a hushed whisper. Backing away, I glanced out the kitchen window that faced the lake.

He wasn't there. "Mom, is he out there?" Ava's voice was laced with concern as I turned back toward her.

"No, baby. I think he must have come in." I forced a smile out as my heart pounded against my chest.

"Why don't you sit tight, and I'll go check on him upstairs." Rolling my lips together, I moved away and glanced over my shoulder at Ava. She was peeling her orange, completely carefree.

Gripping the banister, I made my way up each step as the creaking grew louder. But then, as I turned and made my way to the sound, I froze. The door was open a sliver, just enough for the morning sunlight to trickle out.

Light laughter mixed with satisfied moans.

"Professor Warren, you are so..." a crackled groan echoed.

"Shh! She's right downstairs. Fuck, I can't believe you snuck in, but this was the best surprise." I could hear flesh slapping together, choked sounds, and muffled laughter.

They were in the room I painted in. My special place I had lost myself in but allowed to collect dust in order to prioritize him. Them. Us.

I was paralyzed. Holding my breath, I looked down at my feet. There was a disconnect between my mind and body as I watched my body move forward. Why was I so nervous when I wasn't the one doing something wrong?

Closing my eyes, I took two more steps before opening them slowly. I wish I had kept them closed.

My husband was standing in between thin, pale legs as fingers that weren't mine were digging into his back. I could see the long, red hair from around his frame. Slowly breathing out, my jaw clenched as my eyes stung with tears. She was sitting on my desk, moaning against Warren's body.

I don't know why I continued to watch—I think it's because, deep down, as humans, we thrive on feeling pain.

Just as Warren tossed his head back with a laugh

and a satisfied moan, I began to back away, but my eyes didn't move off them.

And as Warren leaned down to grab an article of clothing, her eyes met mine.

My lips parted as she tilted her head and widened her icy blue eyes. I couldn't move; I wasn't prepared to confront them. I didn't want to, not now, not like this.

But just as I thought Scarlett, the girl our son was infatuated with, would shout or scream out with shame, she didn't.

Instead, she swooped up her hair in her hands, showing her entire body, and smiled at me.

"Babe, that was the best sex I've ever had." She kept her eyes on me as Warren got dressed, completely unaware of the fact that his wife was only a few feet away.

"Sunshine, you are the best I've ever had." He dipped down and tilted her chin up to kiss her.

My stomach flipped as she kept her eyes open and smiled under my husband's lips.

Sunshine. The nickname Warren called me when we started seeing one another. Then when I turned twenty, after we were married with a baby already on the way, he completely stopped up until recently. He never let the kids hear him call me the sweet nickname and now I knew why. He didn't want Max to piece it together.

"I have to head down, but I'll pick you up tonight. Be careful when you climb down." He planted another kiss on her forehead while his hands ran through her pin-straight red hair.

"Can't wait," she said seductively as he began to move away, and I quickly spun around to hide in my own home. Standing behind my bedroom door, I waited until I heard the door creak and Warren's footsteps ricochet as he jogged down the stairs.

Collapsing on the bench in front of our bed, my body folded in half as I pressed my face into my palms.

In the movies, you see someone catching their spouse cheating and it's the huge, loud, dramatic scene. The wife throws the clothes out of the window, and she may even jump on the woman and pull her hair. She slaps her husband across the face and the entire neighborhood hears the fight.

But here I was, in complete shock. No cries or protests came out of my mouth; no, instead, I just thought about my husband lying in a pool of his own blood.

I wanted him to feel this pain he willingly inflicted on me. I wanted him to understand how he wrecked me and killed a part of me. I'd never get these years back. But most of all, this showed how much he didn't love his own children. How could he hurt our son to an unforgivable magnitude? I walked into our bathroom, grabbed Warren's overpriced shampoo, and opened it. Putting it onto the counter, I reached for my hair removal cream and squeezed a hefty amount into his shampoo. Tightening it back up, I shook it wildly. This was going to be a little preview of how Warren Cooper was going to pay.

And just as I thought about wrapping my hands around Warren's neck in the middle of the night, my door creaked open. Moving my hands off my face, I quickly thought of an excuse to tell him when he asked me what was wrong.

But it wasn't Warren... it was *her*.

Scarlett was standing in the doorframe, looking at me blankly.

CHAPTER TWENTY-TWO

I stood, my entire body shaking, but suddenly, it wasn't from the heartbreak. Pure rage was coursing through my veins. Yes, it's easy to blame "the other woman" when your husband is having an affair, but he should know better. Our society loves to give endless hall passes to men and immediately chastise women. And while I wanted to kill my husband, I was now looking into the ruthless eyes of a teenage girl.

Sure, she was young, but so was I. I was pregnant with Ava around her age, I became a mother and wife at her age.

I walked to her and looked into her stone-cold eyes. "What the hell do you think you're doing, little girl?" I kept my voice low as I looked at the opened door.

Half of her thin lips tipped upward into a smirk as she crossed her almost translucent arms across her tank top. It was clear she didn't have any remorse.

"How could you?" I started.

Scarlett shrugged and clicked her tongue. "Professor Cooper is so irresistible."

Shaking my head, I let out a dry laugh and grew closer to her. "No, you senseless bitch. I meant, how could you do that to my *son*?"

Lifting my finger, I poked the center of her chest. "Get the hell out of my house before I tie your legs up with weights and throw you into the lake, watching the short life you've lived deplete from your eyes."

The condescending smirk on her face melted off and she stepped back. "Sure thing, Nina." She feigned confidence.

Taking a step toward her, I looked her up and down. "It's Mrs. Cooper to you. Now, crawl out of my house like the rat you are." I watched her lips purse as her cheeks filled with pink and she turned around.

I followed behind her to ensure Warren and, most of all, Ava, weren't around.

I could hear them talking downstairs, which had

my heart slowing from the excessive blend of emotions.

She strutted through my art room and, without a second thought, crawled through my window. My eyes shot open as I held my hands up. "Wait!" I hated how the mother in me couldn't imagine a nineteen-year-old jumping off my second story and scaling the roof.

"Don't worry, Mrs. Cooper, your husband set me up with a sturdy ladder. It's how I fuck him easily when you're asleep."

My fists clenched and the only reason I didn't push the ladder off the window with her on it was because I knew one thing...

I looked terrible in orange.

After Scarlett left—after I had watched my husband have sex with our son's girlfriend—I went downstairs and looked at my daughter and husband chatting over coffee without slicing his throat.

He was unusually happier and actually showing interest in Ava. I guess that's what happens when you have a mistress. You're happier.

I kept my eyes off Warren and focused on Ava.

"Mom, I'm going to head to campus and visit Max. He's been mopping around ever since his girlfriend has been acting sus."

Warren immediately cleared his throat. "Sus?"

"Like suspicious. God, you're so old." Ava rolled her eyes.

Warren took a long sip of his coffee and shook his head.

"Apparently, he said she might have genital herpes or even crabs," I said casually while slicing a bagel in half with the sharpest knife I could dig out.

My darling husband began to violently choke on his coffee and looked up at me as Ava dropped her jaw.

"What?" The poor bastard was so flustered.

"Mm-hmm." I lathered on a thick layer of cream cheese and held the knife up, pointing it at Warren.

"We failed our son. We didn't teach him how to differentiate blaring red flags." Warren was barely catching his breath, glancing down at his crotch with sheer panic across his face.

"I'm going to force him out of his dorm and take him out. I'll be spending a lot of money for damage control." Ava stood and came around, opening her arms she wrapped me in a hug. I held her tightly and clenched my eyes shut. I didn't want to be strong, but I had to be. For her and Max. But what I knew in this moment was that I had to be strong for myself, too.

"Spend as much as you need to." I shot Warren a glance as his eyes widened, and Ava galloped away excitedly.

Slapping both halves of my bagel together, I threw the knife into the sink, the clatter of the steel hitting it echoed loudly.

"What the hell, Nina?" Warren stood and wiped away the budding sweat beads across his hairline.

"I've got to go. I'm meeting up with Adam. You remember him from our family cookout, right?" I lied.

"Adam? Why are you meeting up with him?" Oh, the sheer irony of such a simple question.

"He's a contractor, honey. I'm going to see what he thinks about adding the library onto the living room. I really want to have the one with the ladder attached. You remember? I always said I wanted something like the one from Beauty and the Beast?" I paused and chewed my bottom lip, unable to look at him longer. I grabbed a dishrag to pretend I needed to wipe down the already cleaned counters.

Beauty and the Beast set the stage for unrealistic expectations on love. It convinced us as little girls to believe that a beast could turn into prince charming, but that couldn't be farther from the truth. We should have been taught to know that people don't change, and the ones who are beasts will forever be just that. And there is nothing charming about that.

CHAPTER TWENTY-THREE

*W*arren cried out loudly in an almost unrecognizable voice full of panic. His footsteps thudded down the stairs as I stood in front of the steaming cup of coffee.

"Nina!" he screamed out, and I slowly turned. My eyes widened and I slapped my hand across my mouth, quickly concealing the laughter that immediately shot out.

There stood my handsome husband, with patches of his hair completely missing.

"Nina! My head... my hair! It was falling out as soon as I was drying it with the towel." His eyes were wild, his face reddened, and his hands shaking.

"Warren... what did you do to your gorgeous hair?" I feigned shock.

Humiliation seeped into his face as he gripped the counter. "I didn't do anything, Nina! Dammit! I have to call my doctor. I hope it's not some underlying medical condition." Slamming his fist against the smooth granite, he turned away and brushed his hands across his remaining hair—though a few pieces drifted to the ground once he moved his hand.

"You look like hell. You're going to have to buzz it all." I shook my head in disgust. "Anyway, I've got to go…" I grabbed my keys, tossed my hair back as I walked past my husband, and left the house.

I erupted into laughter as soon as I got into my car, gripping the leather steering wheel.

They say be the bigger person. But I'm now realizing that when they go low, it's so much more fun to go lower.

I got lost in mundane tasks around the house just to divert my mind from the crushing weight of what I was supposed to do. I had never felt so alone and isolated before. Joss and Paige had called me fifty times, but I didn't have the energy to listen to my best friends convince me everything would be okay when I knew, without a doubt, it wouldn't be. It's a lie when people say everything will be okay. How could they possibly predict that? My life was about to go up into flames. It wouldn't be okay.

Opening Max's door, I dragged the vacuum into his room. His walls were navy blue and light gray. There were sports trophies, medals, and scattered books strewn across his desk. Dust lined old video game consoles, and his bed still had wrinkles in it from the last time he slept in his childhood room.

I started picking up athletic shorts that were crammed under the bed and paused. Tugging a small, wooden keepsake box out, I crossed my legs and opened it carefully. I paused to look over my shoulder, even though I knew the house was quiet and empty. I swore I could hear creaking echo behind me. Stilling my breath, I chewed at my bottom lip. His curtain danced in the wind as the overcast outside teased heavy rain. Why was his window open? Looking back down, I stared at the box in front of me.

It felt wrong looking through his personal items, but at this point, I felt like I didn't even recognize my own family.

Lifting the lid, I smiled at the concert tickets, childhood pocketknife, and most of all, the compass.

Tilting my head, I lifted it up and brushed my hand across the smooth, engraved metal.

Warren gifted this family heirloom to Max when he turned eighteen, just the same way Warren's father had done for him, and his great-grandfather had done before. I will never forget the look on Max's face when he knew his dad trusted him enough with his most prized possession. Opening the compass, I traced my fingers against the inscription.

Quae seminaverit homo haex et metet.

I remember Warren telling me it was a biblical phrase in Latin that essentially meant a man reaps what he sows. But also, emphasizing reaping corruption, which I didn't quite understand. I suppose it was some form of toxic masculinity?

I watched as the arrow of the compass swayed. It was tarnished all around, but it was truly beautiful. I brushed my hand across the compass-like pendant around my neck that Warren had gifted me.

Sighing, I placed the antique compass back in the box with care, tucking it back under his bed, but while laying on my side, I froze. Tugging out another box, I grabbed it and opened it.

My eyes widened as I looked at the different sizes of lace thongs, panties, and even a women's bra. Why would Max keep these? I stuffed the lid back on the box and wiped my hands against my shirt.

"Mom!" Ava called, and I jerked out from the bed and shoved the box back quickly.

Her footsteps echoed as she jogged up the stairs, and I quickly grabbed the dirty clothes into my arms and stood.

"Hi," I said with my heart racing and face flushed. She squinted and her eyes roamed behind me.

"Did you need something? I thought you were going to see Max?" I fumbled with the laundry in my hands and pushed the vacuum to the wall.

"Yeah, he asked for something. I need to just grab it." Ava ran her hands against her high ponytail.

I stepped to the side and watched her go to his closet, open it, and grab his old varsity jacket from high school.

I knew he wanted it to because it was that article of clothing that comforted him. "I'm going to visit him tomorrow." I told Ava as she folded the jacket over her arm. She had always been an excessively protective sister to Max, something I never took for granted.

"I don't think that's a good idea, Mom. You're going to worry yourself and then he's going to see you all sad." She came closer to me and kissed my cheek. "Let him just get over the skank, and then I'll tell him to come home and hang out with me before I head back to London."

"When are you going back to London?" She just got here and was already talking about leaving?

"Calm down, Mom, I still have another two weeks. I'm just saying it'll fly by. I'm ready to go back." As much as it made me sad to think about her leaving, it was a relief to know she wanted to go and live her life and chase the dreams she'd always dreamt of.

"Okay, well just text me and let me know if he needs me." I hesitated a moment but then said, "Hey, have you seen her? Scarlett? On campus or anything?"

Ava's forehead creased. "Hell no. I don't think she's even taking classes. I think she's just lurking around campus being the school slut."

I didn't say anything else; I just grabbed everything I could balance in two hands and called out behind me, "I love you, Ava, always. Drive safe, baby."

"Love you too, Mom. Forever," she replied as I left Max's room. I walked down the hallway, passing by rows and rows of black framed photos of our family.

Clenching my eyes shut, I made my way past the images that once triggered happiness but now triggered pain. Turning into our room, I looked at our bed.

Nausea tormented me as I bit my bottom lip. If Warren had sex with Scarlett in my art room, what's to say he didn't have sex with her in our bed?

Looking over my shoulder, I licked my lips and brushed my fingers against the foot of our neatly made bed. Walking around, I stood in front of Warren's nightstand. Sliding the drawer open, I found the usual miscellaneous items—nothing unusual or alarming. I pushed it shut and repeated the action with the second drawer, but it wouldn't budge. Squinting, I ran my fingers against the smooth wood and crossed my legs.

Jamming my nails into the sides, I found a small divot that wasn't on my nightstand. Warren had to have had this drawer altered. Forcefully jamming my nails in the sides, I tried to pull it open, but it wouldn't budge. I needed the key.

Looking around our room for a key to my husband's locked drawer—the way an animal scavenges through trash—felt like another blow to any ounce of dignity I had remaining.

Our room was meticulous, we didn't have clutter, yet it felt even harder looking for something that was specifically made impossible for me to find. I rummaged through every single drawer until I realized something.

He'd never hide it in his own drawers; he'd hide it in mine. He always thought three steps ahead, and no

one looks through their own belongings for something someone else has hidden.

So, I opened my drawers one by one. I began
throwing my socks over my shoulders, my leggings,
and then finally, I slid opened my drawer full of
lingerie—a drawer that probably had a light layer of
dust lingering on it from never being used. It wasn't
that I didn't want to wear the sexy lace and silky satin
pieces, it was simply that I felt silly donning them in
front of my husband who felt like a stranger to me.

Brushing my hands through the various styles of
lingerie, I got to the very bottom, where my wedding
night negligee was buried and just like that, a glimmer
from our light hit the small piece of metal.

Bastard.

My heart pounded against my chest as I untangled
it from the delicate lace. He knew I'd never open this
drawer, let alone dig to the bottom where something
that was now three sizes to small was kept.

Lifting the tiny golden key in between my fingers, I
dragged my feet through the plush carpet and dropped
to my knees in front of the hand-crafted nightstand we
had picked out together years ago at a family-owned
shop. I loved the blue paint detailing and the way the
old oak was barely sanded down for a rough finish.

Jamming the key into the small hidden divot, I turned it easily and a *click* echoed. Staring at the drawer, I hesitated a moment, thinking of how easily I could shut it and not burden myself with whatever was secretive enough to lock away from me.

Anger began running through me as I pulled the drawer aggressively, but as soon as I did, I gasped out loud. My breath screeched at the end as my eyes shot wide open and chills raced up my spine.

Rows and rows of tiny plastic bags with necklaces in each one. Lifting one up, I squinted. It was the same necklace Warren gave me all those years ago—a dainty silver necklace with a small compass pendant.

Cupping my face with my moist palms, I couldn't get my body to stop shaking as tears started to line my eyes.

Why would he have so many of the same necklace he once gave me? I thought mine was special... I thought I was special.

"What are you doing, Warren?" I rubbed my hands across my mouth, blankly staring at the wall before a creak reverberated behind me. Shoving the drawer shut, I forced myself up and grabbed the key. Rushing over to our dresser, I tangled it back into my wedding negligee while pain seared through me.

"Hi, baby." I quickly opened my sock drawer and began sifting through it.

"Hey." I replied flatly without making eye contact. He grew closer to me, moving behind me and dropping his hands to my waist. Tugging me into him, he leaned in close while slowly tucking a straggling piece of hair behind my ear.

I could feel him become aroused as he kissed my neck while I clenched my eyes shut. Except, that wasn't a safe place. No, instead of darkness, I saw him in between Scarlett's legs, I could hear her moans and see her sinister smirk when she knew I was watching.

Before I knew it, Warren was pulling my pants down and rubbing his fingers against me.

My heart was racing, and I hated that my body felt stimulated.

"No," I whispered unconvincingly.

"My beautiful wife..." He bit my neck before plunging into me, causing me to scream out in both pleasure and shock.

Gripping the dresser, my body moved over his as his warm breath grazed my shoulder.

I cleared my throat. "Warren, no."

"You are my wife; you can't say no." Digging his fingers into my flesh, he bit into my shoulder as I froze in my place.

I said... no.

Two minutes later, he was done and I stood there shaking.

Turning toward him, I looked up into his eyes. "I need to go." I tugged at my hair and pulled it into a ponytail.

Warren brushed his thumb against my jawline. "To see Adam?"

Nodding, I blinked, praying the tears that were burning my eyes wouldn't come out. What I really wanted to do was chop off this asshole's—

"I don't like you being around some man we don't even know alone. I can come with you," Warren offered.

I laughed. I laughed again, and then laughed some more. Gasping for air in between as my husband stared down at me completely confused.

Slapping his arm, I wiped away the tears that did come out, but weren't ones of heartache; no, these were tears that came from humor.

"What is so funny, Nina?"

Blowing out a breath of air, I turned away from him and grabbed my tube of bright red lipstick. Carefully lining my lips, I smacked them together and looked at him once more. "Your fucking face. You just raped me. I don't need protecting from anyone but you."

Warren's mouth parted as he watched me leave our bedroom.

What he didn't know was I was going to be doing a lot of things now that would make his mouth drop.

And eventually, I'd have his tongue hanging out, watching his life leave his body.

CHAPTER TWENTY-FOUR

"*Y*ou both always leave me out of everything!" Paige protested as we sat outside of Dean's diner, sipping mimosas.

"I think the best course of action is a divorce. Just stop digging for things." Joss cracked her neck to the side and looked at me with concern.

"She just saw her husband having sex with her son's girlfriend, and then found a drawer full of neck-laces—the same necklace he gave her *decades* ago." Paige had her glossy pink lips parted in disbelief. Her long acrylic nails tapped against her champagne glass, and the waiter ran over for refills.

"Keep them comin'! See my friend here?" Paige

pointed at me. "She just found out she's married to the world's biggest douchebag."

Covering my face with my hands, I shook my head as the waiter hurried around to my glass. I hadn't told my best friends about Warren forcing himself on me.

"What if he's some sick criminal? I mean, who is he giving out those necklaces to, and shouldn't she call the cops?" Paige was talking so fast; my anxiety was in overdrive.

Joss looked between us. "The police in a small town like Lake Johan aren't going to take it seriously. Besides, Warren Cooper is one of the most beloved men in this town, and what's she going to do? Tell them about the affair and destroy Max and their family? You don't recover from this kind of scandal in this kind of town." Joss opened her hands across the table to me. Clenching my teeth together, I knew that what she was saying was the absolute truth. That's why I was calculating my plan to the very last minute.

"He has an iron-clad prenup, and I've always been a stay-at-home mom. I would have nothing, and who would hire a forty-year-old woman with no work experience?" I ran my fingers across my pulsing temple.

My friends looked at me with pity and I sighed, taking another long sip of my drink. "I just need to get through the next few months. The kids will be in and out of the house, and they love visiting the lake house. This is going to be our last of everything as a family. These memories are tainted and tarnished for me, but they'll be shiny and memorable for them." The words hurt me to say. This was the end of an entire era of my life. This was a death of a marriage, of truth, of love, and a lifetime.

"Are you going to address the Scarlett affair with Warren?" Paige pretended to gag.

"I will, but I need to get as much evidence compiled. And, most of all, there is no way I want Max to find out. I've spent my life protecting my children… You know, checking under their beds for monsters, and yet, all along, the only monster in their life was their father. But I can't traumatize them." Tears dribbled down my cheeks thinking about them.

No more Christmas traditions, no more family photos with the four of us, no more boat rides and lake swims.

Everything was about to change, and change terrified me. Change was uncomfortable, unsettling, yet undeniable.

"Switching gears for a minute, my friend Adam has been asking about you." Joss smiled over the lipstick-stained rim.

Paige cried out excitedly as I chugged the rest of my drink.

"I thought you guys were a thing?" I tried to be as calm as possible.

"Ugh, no. I'm in my one-night stand era again." Joss shrugged and broke off a piece of bread before dipping it into the olive oil mixture.

"I have no interest in going from one man to the other. I have no idea what I'm doing in my marriage right now, let alone thinking about dating." I sank back into the wicker chair and rocked.

"No one is saying to get into a relationship. But if Warren can have fun, then why can't you? Maybe you could play his game. Why is it that men always get to screw the young, hot mistress? Maybe you should have fun with a younger, sexier man?" Paige raised a brow, and I parted my lips to protest. Except, I didn't.

Marriage has unwritten rules, every single one. But our marriage only had rules that applied to me. Meanwhile, Warren was living however he wanted, without any concern on how it'd impact his wife, his marriage, and most of all, his children.

He betrayed his own son.

He was scum.

"Give him my number." I nodded at Joss as Paige high-fived me.

After wrapping lunch up, Paige headed back to work and Joss hovered next to my car.

"Bring me one of the bags with a necklace in it." Joss shoved her hands into her pockets as I shielded my eyes from the sun.

"How, Joss? What if he notices?" I knew she didn't want to speak about these things in too much detail around Paige. Paige was trustworthy, but she was also a hot-headed, crime tv junkie. She'd have made this reality something fictional and exciting. But my life wasn't a game, or a show... my life wasn't a charade.

"You have to, Nina. I could hold it as evidence if it ever..." She paused and chewed on her bottom lip. "With his fetishes and sexuality, it could be some weird way he marks the women he's with, whether its consensual or non—"

"Non-consensual? Women?" I filled in as my stomach twisted, thinking about my children sharing the same roof as this man.

Pursing her lips, she leaned in and wrapped me in her arms. "Promise me you won't kill him," she murmured in my ear.

Crossing my fingers behind her back, I whispered, "Promise."

CHAPTER TWENTY-FIVE

I spent hours painting outside, wearing stained overalls and blasting songs from before I had met Warren. Lake Johan's annual fall festival was in a few weeks, and I had decided to buy a booth. It had been years since I participated in it, but I figured it would be a good distraction from the absolute shit-show my life had become.

Maybe selling a few pieces and putting myself out there would help me gain some confidence that I knew was long-lost.

Brushing my paintbrush against the smooth canvas, I started to paint the lake and the canopy of trees surrounding it. Perhaps a tourist would long to buy it as a way to remember their vacation full of the happiest of memories. They wouldn't know that the woman behind it was experiencing the worst times of her life, that her life was shattering into jagged shards.

"Mom." I pulled my brush off the canvas and turned around.

"Max?" Dropping the brush, I ran to him. The bags around his eyes were dark, his skin looked lifeless, and his lips were dry from a lack of caring for himself.

Tugging him into my arms, his head collapsed onto my shoulder, and he began to sob.

I ran my fingers along his back. "It's okay, son. Just tell me what happened," I forced out, praying his answer wasn't the one from my nightmares.

"Mom, I don't want to tell you."

My heart was shattering as I held my son.

"You can tell me anything. I want you to tell me because you don't need to carry any weight when you have me to do that for you, son." I patted his back before slowly moving his arms off me and gripping his face between my hands. Using my thumbs, I wiped away his tears.

"I saw Dad..." He choked on his own saliva as he tried to piece a coherent sentence together.

In some odd way, perhaps a mother's incomparable strength to protect her child at all cost, rampaged through me and held the internal broken pieces together.

"Mom, I saw Dad with some woman. I don't know who she was, but he was..." He tugged out of my arms and looked at me with so much pity. "He was kissing her, Mom."

I tilted my head and looked at my son.

I feigned shock and pain, but I wasn't feeling either of those things because I was married to a disgusting pig.

A disgusting pig and I only felt relief.

Relief knowing that our son hadn't seen him with a girl, and that girl being Scarlett. *Thank you, Warren, for cheating on me with another person instead of our son's girlfriend in that moment.*

Slapping my hand across my heart, I dropped my eyes to the ground and offered an Oscar-winning performance.

"Oh, sweetheart. Don't worry, it must be a misunderstanding. I'll speak to your father about it, but right now I don't want you to bring it up to him or anyone. Please. For me?" I rubbed his arms and nodded as he looked at me sadly.

He thought I was making this request because I needed time to process or maybe because I was completely humiliated by the fact that his father was cheating on me. The man he saw me married to his entire life.

"I won't, Mom, but are you okay? What the fuck is Dad thinking?" He brought me into his arms again and patted my back the way I had always consoled him.

"I'm…" I paused, but I never finished the sentence because when I closed my eyes, I just saw Warren Cooper covered in blood.

But that's not all I saw… I also saw myself with bloodied palms and a satisfied smile curling across my face. And all I knew was that my premonitions had never been wrong.

CHAPTER TWENTY-SIX

"Why are you asking me about prison time for murder?" Joss shrieked as we walked by the lake. We were hidden from the docks, the tourists, and lounging residents. Instead, we were hiking down the rocky path with hopes that this extremely shocking conversation wouldn't be heard.

"I'm just curious, is all." I looped my arm into hers and dug the tall stick into the dirt as we walked.

"Nina, I'm not kidding. I don't know what is spinning through your mind, but you're being emotional and irrational. Both mental states which cause a human to do mentally disruptive things. Not to mention, illegal. You'll end up in prison." Joss flung in front of me and pointed at my face. "Even as the best damn defense attorney in North Carolina, I wouldn't be able to get you out of it. Honey, you'd be in there forever."

"I'm not going to…"

"Don't even say it!" Joss widened her eyes and looked at the rustling trees. I leaned over into her and began to laugh. I laughed so hard that I had to grip her arms as my laughter echoed through the trees around us.

"Nina!" She started to shake me, but the more she scolded me, the more I laughed. Adjusting my straw hat, I grabbed my abdomen and wiped at the tears leaving my eyes.

There it was. Power. I wasn't crying over him ruining my life; I was now laughing to the point of tears over what I was about to do to him.

But first, I had to make a deal with the devil.

I sat at the small, vinyl booth for an hour and a half outside of Lake Johan in a nearby town in hopes I wouldn't be recognized.

Adjusting my oversized sunglasses, I fidgeted with the now cool mug handle.

The jingle of the door shook me as I looked up and met her eyes. The eyes that had watched me in my home, the ones that had made its mark on my son, and then, my husband. Eyes I wanted so badly to gauge out with the knife in my hand that I used to stir the burnt coffee with.

Scarlett's hair was tied up in a messy bun, and she was wearing a fitted crop top and even tighter shorts.

Waltzing over, and oozing with confidence, she thought she had won, but this was only the beginning in my plan.

"Mrs. Cooper," she taunted as she slid into the seat across from me.

"Scarlett." I handed her the sticky menu, but she waved it away.

"I don't do carbs."

"Do you not do fluids, either?" I rolled my eyes and sat it down.

Crossing her pale, thin arms across her body, she eyed me cautiously.

"Are you still sleeping with my husband?" I asked quickly, ignoring the pain that the words did, in fact, still sear into me.

Her glossy lips tipped upward in a dangerously, satisfied grin.

Sinking back into the outdated green booth, she brushed her hot pink nails against her chin. "What is this?" Scarlett purred out seductively.

I let out a dry laugh. I couldn't believe this girl. "Oh, you're good. What? My son and husband aren't enough, now you're trying to seduce me, too?"

"Is it working?" She licked her bottom lip before tugging the tube of light pink gloss out and reapplying it. Popping her lips, she smiled at me.

"I think you're repulsive, but I have a proposition for you."

Peering around and tugging my lukewarm coffee to my chest, I leaned into the table. "You're not in love with Max or Warren, you just thrive off the male attention they give you. In some sick way, you love the fact that two men from a family are smitten with you. But the truth is, my husband just thinks of you as a young piece of meat. He's sleeping with multiple women." I paused to study her reaction.

Just as I thought, her cheeks flushed, her jaw clenched, and suddenly, I knew she felt unworthy.

"Aw, you really thought you were special, didn't you, *sunshine*? No, even Max is already over you."

This wasn't who I was, but this is who I had to be. Warren made me into this woman. This bitter, revenge-seeking, hurt woman.

"What's the proposition?" she asked with irritation.

"Warren doesn't know that I know about you, nor

the others. I signed a prenup with him when I was…" I smirked, "nineteen."

"He took advantage of my innocence, and clearly, I was wearing the same rose-colored glasses you are now. So, I signed an iron-clad prenup, which states I wouldn't get any of our assets if I was the one to file for divorce—it doesn't matter the circumstances. When I was nineteen, I didn't think in a million years there'd be an end to us. Hell, I didn't think there would be an end up until *this week*."

"Well, you were an idiot," Scarlett taunted.

"Yeah, but at least I wasn't sleeping with a married man and his son." Rolling my eyes, I tugged out the small mini bottle I knew I'd need for this conversation.

Biting the lid off, I spat it to the side and poured it into my coffee. Scarlett's eyes widened as I chugged it down.

"I want you to continue to see him, date him, sleep with him, whatever you want, but I need you to start documenting it."

I decided to leave out the part that I also needed to buy time to figure out where Warren's first wife was. Considering there was only one reason someone could disappear completely.

Scarlett drew in closer. "Why would I do this for you?"

Opening my purse, I took out the stack of cash.

"You dropped out of school after your first semester because your financial aid didn't go through. Your parents are dead, and you live with some shady older woman that I'm absolutely sure you're drug dealing for, just to score a night's rest on her worn-out couch." Sliding the money toward her, I blew out a breath of air. "If you do what I say, I'll keep this coming."

Scarlett's sticky lips parted as her eyes dropped to the stack of cash. Brushing her finger against it, she looked up at me. "You've got yourself a deal, Mrs. Cooper. I'll fuck your husband." Reaching to move the cash into her purse, I slapped her hand onto it.

"No, no, no. One more thing." Digging my nails into her soft skin, I looked into her pale blue, eager eyes. "You will *never* go near my son, again. Except, you're going to call him in front of me. You're going to apologize for breaking his heart, and you're going to say you're not ready to be in a relationship because you need to work on yourself."

Cutting the money in half she slid it back to me.

"What are you doing?"

"You're going to need some money in case this doesn't work, and Warren takes it all."

I was completely taken aback. "Why do you care?"

"Because I wish I had a mom like you. Maybe if I had, I'd have been a better person."

My heart sank and the knots in my stomach tightened. I sighed and leaned back. What the hell was I doing? I was hiring my son's ex-girlfriend to catfish and lure my husband into a trap.

"You can be. And if you don't want to do this… you don't have to. You can keep that." The mother in me had to say it.

Laughing, Scarlett shook her head. "See, this is why you're the woman who gets cheated on." Fanning the cash in my face, she added, "I was still going to sleep with your husband, so you might as well get your information out of it." She shrugged and stood.

Tossing my head back, I sighed. "Save texts, take photos, make it clear that he's sleeping with you."

"Yes, ma'am." Scarlett saluted me before walking to my side. "By the way… you're the hottest one in the family; I just wish you'd have given me a try." Winking, she tightened the strap of her fake Chanel purse and walked out of the diner.

Blowing out a breath, I clenched my eyes shut. This isn't what I wanted to be doing in my forties. I spent my entire adulthood being a devoted wife and mother, and now, this is what I was doing? Setting my husband up so I could leave him, figure out more about his past and destroy our family?

Part of me understood why some women turn their head and ignore their husband's indiscretions because it is scary—it's terrifying to be the one who ultimately decides to watch your family break.

If I chose to turn my head, we'd be together and the only person full of pain would be me. Everyone else could live happily in their oblivious little bubbles.

But I was done prioritizing everyone's happiness over mine; I was done protecting everyone but myself.

Most of all, I was done letting Warren Cooper write the script of my life.

Getting into my car, I turned on The Chicks and blasted it.

Earl had to die.

Smiling, I clutched the hot leather steering wheel and fantasized about Earl being my husband.

CHAPTER TWENTY-SEVEN

The hardest part of my entire plan was knowing I'd have to pretend everything was perfect in front of the kids and Warren. I couldn't let him suspect, even in the slightest, that I was upset or plotting his demise.

"Something smells good." Warren came into the kitchen. What he didn't know was the black dress I was wearing was because I had sat in front of my vanity, practicing fake tears and sadness for when I'd be at his funeral.

"And someone looks good, too." His eyes lit up, which I hated, because it still elicited some kind of joy knowing I did that to him, still.

"Thanks, honey." I brushed my hands against my apron after pulling the lasagna out. I had a full face of makeup on, my hair was in shiny waves, and the bra I had on made my cleavage look incredible.

"I also made this." Bringing out the infamous Indigo blueberry pie, I set it next to the lasagna.

"What are we celebrating, babe?" Warren looked thrilled.

I placed my palms on both sides of his cheeks and stood on my tiptoes. "The empty-nesters. Us." I smiled and kissed his lips.

Sighing, he drew me in closer and parted my lips with his tongue.

"You taste so damn sweet…" he moaned into my mouth. I could feel him growing aroused as he pushed me backward into the counter, spreading my legs aggressively with his hands he tore my panties down my legs and quickly unzipped his pants.

Grabbing my waist, he lifted me up on the counter. I opened my legs for him, keeping my eyes on his while biting my lower lip.

"I've missed you. I wondered where my sexy, fun wife went."

It took every ounce of strength in my body to not take the steel pot behind me and smash his skull in.

Instead, I closed my eyes and pretended Warren was Chris Hemsworth as he pushed inside me and groaned in pleasure.

Opening my eyes, I saw he was already done, yet panted like he just completed an Olympic event.

"You're getting old, hubby," I joked as I slid off the counter.

His cheeks turned red as he zipped his pants up. "Did you…"

"Nope."

At least he had the decency to look humiliated. "Sorry, I just…"

"It's fine, sweetheart; I know men your age often need to get Viagra or something. I married a man so much older, and I knew this day would come. Don't worry; it's nothing my vibrator can't help me with tonight." I busied myself cutting the lasagna as Warren stood there in shock.

"Nina." He came around the kitchen island and held my arm. "Are you dissatisfied in bed with me?" The way he looked like a deer in headlights couldn't be more entertaining to me.

The male ego is a beautiful thing. When it's stroked, it offers society an over-confident, driven, and charismatic man. But when it's destroyed, it showcases a vulnerable, fragile, and docile man.

That's where women go wrong. We are raised to think we should be glorifying the man we love because then he'll love us, too. But I've realized, after twenty-plus years of stroking my husband's ego, that it was going to be far more pleasurable to annihilate it.

"No sweetie, I'm not dissatisfied. I just... I want to give you grace since I know you're aging." I wiggled my arm out of his.

If he could humiliate me by sleeping with women half my age, then I think it was time to remind him of his own.

"I can make you orgasm, Nina. I always do." He was beginning to grow angry. *Good.*

Placing our steaming plates onto the dining table, I offered him a tight-line smile. "Mm-hmm... you sure do." Peeling my apron off, I stuck it on the counter, and waved him over. "Grab a bottle of Prosecco, will you? I want us to enjoy this while it's hot, and then, of course, some pie."

Warren's jaw tightened as his ego crashed to the floor. "Yeah, of course, sweetheart." He dragged his way to the wine fridge before sitting beside me.

I sat at the head of the table—which was usually his seat. He opened the wine and poured my glass.

"You seem..." He tilted his head and observed me. I needed to tone the spice down; I knew I was acting out of character, which would make him overanalyze everything—and that was something I couldn't afford him to do. We all have roles to play in every story—it makes it more believable—and I just needed to stay in character before he figured out the major plot twist sitting right in between the lines.

Flipping the TV on, I knew he'd never be able to not indulge in the nightly news, even though it was something I hated. I dreaded hearing a highlight reel of everything bad happening in our city, state, or country. But just as I sliced into my lasagna, forking a bite into my mouth, Warren's eyes grew large as he watched the screen.

"Nineteen-year-old Collins James was spending the weekend with her friends at Lake Johan when she went missing. Her friends claim she went kayaking, and before they knew it, she was gone. Search parties have been pieced together. If you'd like to volunteer, the information is below. Any information can be directed to 888-138-1184." A photo of a young, gorgeous girl was plastered in the center of the screen. My fingers shook as I forced my eyes off the screen and onto Warren. His mouth was hung open, his eyes glued to the screen, and the way his Adam's apple bobbed as he choked on air had me convinced, without a shadow of a doubt, that my husband had something to do with that girl's disappearance.

Placing my fork down, I lifted my butter knife in the other hand, and dragged it down the smooth wood and into my lap as the story continued to unfold on our screen.

The way my heart pounded against my chest had me worried he'd hear it and know exactly what I was thinking. Clutching the knife in my palm, the grooves dug into my tender flesh as I watched Warren's face grow pale while the news flashed countless tips and images relating to the missing girl.

"Mom?" My heart sunk. Oh, no. Ava, my precious twenty-year old daughter, was home.

What kind of curse was I living where my child coming home now terrified me? Warren didn't budge. I slowly stood and walked around him, quickly cutting through the kitchen to Ava, who was kicking her shoes off in the foyer.

"Something smells good... Oh, wow. Mom, you look nice!" she said with her face covered in a light sheen from being out in the heat with friends all day.

"Hi, baby, do you want to go upstairs for a minute?" I said with urgency, flicking my eyes to the winding staircase. But Ava's eyes dropped to my hands.

"Mom..."

Looking down, I parted my lips. My palms were covered in streaks of blood from gripping the knife in my hand so tightly, yet I didn't feel any pain.

The fear surging throughout my body surpassed any ounce of pain I could feel. My daughter could have been on that screen tonight.

"Where's Max?" I released the hold around the knife and waved Ava over to the powder room. Nodding to the faucet, she turned it on for me.

"He's on campus." She shrugged. "He's fine now. We hung out with friends, and he's over his little break up."

Ava watched as the water turned red. "Are you okay, Mom?" She handed me the towel and looked over my shoulder, her eyes wide.

"Dad?"

CHAPTER TWENTY-EIGHT

*a*s soon as she said the word, I stumbled back and turned. Warren was standing in the doorframe, watching Ava and me, his face drained from the usual hint of pink that laid in his cheeks.

"I have to go."

"Where?" I managed to force out as I stood in front of Ava protectively.

"I'm going to join the search party for that girl," he said without a hitch. Running his hands through his hair, he looked at Ava behind me.

"Want to come with?" Warren asked her and my stomach flipped.

"No, I need her to help me with something tonight," I interjected before she had a chance to answer. "Besides, I don't want our daughter out there when who knows what happened to a girl the same age as her. Warren, how could you even think to put our daughter in harm's way?" Now I was angry. I was angry for so many reasons, but ultimately, that I was having to protect my daughter, *our* daughter, from the very man who was supposed to protect her fiercely.

"No, you're right. That was reckless of me. I think I'm nervous to leave you both here alone." Warren moved from the door, allowing us to all pour out into the foyer.

"I'll call Max on my drive and see if he could come stay here."

Warren's phone buzzed in his pocket.

He ignored it and kept talking to Ava and me, yet I didn't hear his words. The buzzing of his phone kept going on and on.

Then a text message alert.

Sliding his phone from his dark-washed jeans, his eyes lit up.

It had to be Scarlett.

I watched his lips curve upward as he read the message. The pink in his cheeks quickly returned and suddenly, I wanted to vomit.

He just saw the news of a missing girl—a girl he may have been involved with—and yet, one text from another girl and he was already back to an inflated ego.

"Who is it?" I barked at him.

Clearing his throat, his eyes drifted to Ava.

"Warren!" I shouted.

"A colleague." He grabbed a flashlight from the console table drawer before sliding his shoes on and turning the knob.

"Sure, it is." I squinted before slamming the door behind him.

I was letting my emotions get the best of me. I had told Scarlett to continue her affair with Warren; I had told her to document it all. Yet, here I was, still in agonizing pain, knowing I was married to a sociopath.

"What was that about?" I completely forgot Ava was standing right behind me.

"When are you going back to London for your study abroad? I don't want you falling behind." I was frazzled and my words were frantic.

Ava looked hurt, and I hated that she thought I was trying to get her out of the house.

"I know this was supposed to be your first year without Max and me... Sorry I came home." Ava knocked me in my shoulder before sprinting upstairs.

My heart shattered as I watched her. I didn't even try to call out to her. In a way, I wanted her to think that; I wanted her to feel the urgency to go back to a place that was far safer than being under the same roof as a monster.

Her dad.

After Warren left, I ran into the office and quickly opened my laptop. Plugging the charger in, I held my breath for a moment, hoping that it would turn on considering how old it was.

The blue screen lit up and relief washed over me as I frantically began searching about Collins James.

Furrowing my brows, my hands grew clammy as my breathing hitched.

"Oh my gosh," I breathed out as I scrolled and saw her social media pages linked. The news had shown an image of a blonde girl with light blue eyes, but this girl was originally a redhead, just like Scarlett. She must have recently dyed her hair.

Scrolling through, I clicked on her Instagram profile.

She was so young—only nineteen—and full of life. A maternal instinct kicked inside me as she reminded me of someone Ava could be friends with, or a girl Max could have fallen...

"What…"

My eyes grew fuzzy as I carefully clicked on a small square.

"Oh no… no, no…"

A photo of Collins, the girl that had just gone missing, was smiling while a jacket lingered in the kayak. Squinting and holding the screen even closer to my eyes in sheer hope that my eyes were deceiving me but I knew, there was a varsity jacket there.

My son, Max was with Collins on the boat.

Swallowing the small amount of saliva from my mouth to coat the excessive dryness, I shook as I dialed the only person who may be able to help me.

"Joss…" my voice trembled.

"Dear God, what did you do?"

"No, not me. Joss, I… I think Max has gotten himself into trouble." I began to cry as I covered my mouth, thinking of my precious, sweet son and what kind of terrible mother I had to be since I couldn't keep him on the right path.

"Turn the news on. Did you hear that some girl from UNC-Johan was out on the lake? She's missing…" I choked out.

The pause before Joss spoke felt like an eternity. "Adam's already out there helping the search party. What does this have to do with Max?"

"Adam? I thought you both weren't together." I brushed my hand over my tired scowl.

"I've told you that we're not. He's a friend who happens to keep inquiring about you."

"Joss, I think Max was on the boat with Collins."

Another pause. Walking over to the kitchen, I put Joss on speakerphone, and gripped the sink. Nausea was pooling inside me, and the acid trickled into my throat, choking me as I thought about my son.

"Did you talk to him?"

"No, I had to call you first." Tears trickled down my face as I puffed my cheeks, letting out a big breath. "I didn't know what I should tell him to do if he was there."

"There is a difference between thinking and knowing. Which one is it?" I could hear Joss move around, rummaging through things.

She was going to come over.

"Thinking, but at the same time, almost knowing."

"Don't say anything else." She ended the call, and I gasped out loud as I slid my finger to call Max.

The phone rang and rang. "Max, where are you?" I kept calling, even as my heartbeat grew more erratic.

"Hey, Mom," he answered. I could hear laughter and other boys screaming out in joy in the background.

"Max!" I screamed out. "Max, where are you?"

"Hey, Mom! I'm over at Jack's house."

Suddenly, my nerves began to settle. He wasn't there. But that jacket… Could that have been his?

Ava was upstairs, sound asleep, and Max was with friends.

Warren...

CHAPTER TWENTY-NINE

I sat on the floor, rocking back and forth, with my knees clutched to my chest.

The clicking of heels echoed as I pressed my face into my thighs.

"Oh, honey..." I lifted my head, but it wasn't Joss, it was Paige.

"Joss headed to the lake to help in the search, but she caught me up on everything." Paige was wearing a black jumpsuit and gold heels. Her hair sat in two shiny mermaid braids.

"It wasn't Max... It had to be Warren," I cried out as my face grew warm and I felt the knots in my stomach tighten.

"You know what I think? I think this year is such a

huge shift for you, babe. I think that you, Joss, and I should book a trip to the Bahamas, and just celebrate how much of a wonderful wife and mother you've spent the last two decades being." Paige slid down next to me and pulled my head onto her shoulder. Kissing the top of my head, she tried to offer comfort but I couldn't stop crying.

"Something is going on. Warren is doing something, P."

"Hey, it's going to be okay," she soothed with her voice low and calm. I knew that tone, the tone that says, 'I don't believe you at all, but I'm going to soothe you like a baby with colic.'

Pressing my head between my knees, I sucked in the air that felt stale. "I'm going to go."

Paige sighed. "Go where?"

"To look for that girl. The girl my husband probably killed." I swallowed the impeding lump in my throat and stood.

Paige knew there wasn't any point in fighting me on this; my mind was made up and I was hyper-fixated on this now. But who wouldn't be? The year we were supposed to rekindle who were, what we were to one another, and where we could see ourselves in five to twenty years from now, had all erupted into flames because apparently, my husband was so bored that he needed to blow up our entire life we had built together.

"Can you stay here with Ava?" I looked over my shoulder as I stuffed my feet into the bright pink rain-boots and tugged out a flashlight from the drawer.

"Of course, but..."

My hand shot up and I shook my head once.

The wailing sirens startled me as soon as I got outside. Lake Johan was a small, secluded town. This kind of thing never happened, and when it did, the entire town was shaking.

Sliding into my car, I felt completely numb. I felt like I was asleep, and this had to be a nightmare. A nightmare that was chopped up into bits and pieces where I couldn't stitch the scenes together. I wasn't lucid.

I drove in the direction of the sirens, and my jaw dropped once I arrived. Crowds frantically darted into different directions, women stood with their heads in their palms crying, and groups of teenagers whispering to one another.

"There are divers in the lake, but if you'd like to volunteer to search the water, there are canoes located two docks down. Just keep away from the divers!" a police officer shouted loudly.

"We've roped off the section they are working on."

A familiar voice echoed, and I turned my attention to her.

Joss. She was always the one who could step in and lead everything without even being asked to do so.

"Hey." A tap on my shoulder had me spinning around with my lips parting as I looked up at Adam.

"Oh, hey." Taking a step back, I instinctively wrapped my arms around myself. Adam was dressed in a fitted black V-neck and dark-washed denim jeans that hugged him perfectly.

"Want to ride with me?" He nodded over at the canoes the police had lined up for volunteers.

Looking behind me at the crowds, I couldn't see Warren.

My phone buzzed as I bit into my lower lip.

Hubby dearest is here.

Scarlett texted me a photo of Warren laying on his stomach, naked. The bedsheets were blush-pink with small flowers scattered across.

A nauseating pit grew in my stomach as our whole town searched for a missing girl who was exactly like Scarlett.

"You coming?" Adam tapped my arm gently.

Shaking my head, I sighed and followed him. Sliding the canoe halfway into the water, Adam waved his arm to it. "Ladies first." He held the canoe tightly in place as I walked into the softened, damp grass and my rain-boots squeaked. The canoe barely shook as I climbed in, took a seat, and lifted an oar. Adam pushed the canoe into the pitch-black still water and quickly climbed in behind me.

Grabbing a paddle, he turned the lantern on, immediately lighting his face up. His tattoos on his biceps peered out of the fitted shirt as he swiftly rowed us into the lake.

I began doing the same and looked around. The eerie shadows of the trees lined the lake, and the water slowly rippled around us.

"How did she just vanish from a kayak when her friends were with her?" I asked to fill the silence. Adam's eyes were darting around as he carefully rowed, as if he was nervous to hit something with the paddle.

Like a body.

"Apparently, the friends were all drinking at the dock, and whoever she was with had jumped in the water and must of swam away. Her friends don't know who she was with. Or if she was with someone to begin with."

"What do you mean?" I stopped rowing, but it didn't make a difference since Adam was doing most of the work anyway, and I felt the weight of the world around me collapse.

"I think someone saw her alone in the water, swam underwater, climbed in, and killed her." Adam paused and let the canoe move on its own for a moment.

The way his eyes were locked onto mine made me feel nervous. It's like that feeling you get when you're at the self-checkout at a grocery store, and you know you're not doing anything wrong, but the attendant's eyes are on you and you begin to second-guess it all. Did I steal something, unknowingly? Did I forget to scan an item?

I didn't do anything wrong. My daughter was safe in her bed, my son was with a friend he'd known for a long time. And my husband...

Well, I guess, technically, he was safe in a bed, too.

For now...

"We should keep rowing." My paddle sliced into the water as pellets splattered on me. Suddenly, a light rumble of thunder echoed in the sky that was mostly black, beyond highlights of navy blue.

"Of course, a storm would roll in." Adam began moving his arms faster as I lifted the oversized flashlight and shined it around.

Time went by and nothing. Rain pellets slammed down on us as lightning cut through the starless sky.

There wasn't any sign of the young girl who had vanished from her kayak mere hours ago. But Adam and I didn't discuss when we'd call it. The pit in my stomach wouldn't let me give up, even though when we looked into the distance we only saw a handful of flashlights glimmering compared to the countless flashes we saw when we had started.

I knew if it were my child, I'd pray that people would search and search, just in case they were still alive. A chill hung in the air, clinging to my arms as the water below us felt dangerously deep in the dark.

"Wait!" I called out to Adam and shined my flashlight toward the edge of the lake—the side most people didn't dare swim for it was far too deep.

"Oh my gosh." I plunged the paddle into the water, and Adam followed my lead as the canoe turned.

"Fuck," he breathed out as we grew closer, and he immediately pushed the canoe into the wet, red-clay mud.

Steadying the boat, I climbed out, dragging my feet through the wet mud and choked on the air around me. Tears built in my eyes as I looked at her.

The beautiful young girl whose photo was plastered all over the news, the daughter of the parents who cried and pleaded for strangers to bring their baby girl home, all flashed in front of me. Her hair was a mangled mess besides a small butterfly clip. Her clothes were ripped while leaves, small sticks, and debris coated her once shiny waves.

Kneeling next to her, I lifted her head into my lap as tears dribbled from my eyes and onto her soft cheeks. Sliding my fingers to her neck, I prayed I'd find a pulse. Anything...

"She's alive!" I turned toward Adam, who was attempting to make a call, but I knew there was no way he'd have signal out here. Before he came to us, I saw the shimmer of the compass in her damp palm. Tugging it out, I slid it into my pocket with shaking hands.

Adam shook as he kneeled beside me. He looked at her as if he were trying to figure out how to save her.

Just as I brushed my hands across her forehead, pushing the hair from her damp face, her eyes shot opened, causing both of us to gasp.

Piercing blue eyes locked onto mine as her shriveled pink lips quivered. Fear flooded her face as she looked between Adam and me.

"*Quae seminaverit homo haex et metet,*" she rasped. Each word seared into my soul harder than the previous.

The inscription on the compass.

And just as Adam began talking to her, she fell b

into my arms. I watched as the life left her eyes, and I could have sworn I felt her soul suffocate me.

Adam didn't stop, he kept speaking to her, pleading with her to stay awake.

He tried to save a dead girl.

CHAPTER THIRTY

Maybe I was crying because a young girl was dead in my arms, but most of all, I was crying because I knew that my husband had murdered her.

The simple Latin phrase was one he was obsessed with. Maybe this girl was my son's rebound and that's why she had his jacket? Maybe Warren couldn't handle it and had to take everything from our family.

What kind of sick father seeks out the girls his son is dating?

"No fucking signal!" Adam yelled out at the silent lake. "We've got to get her into the canoe."

"I think the jacket in the kayak… it was my son's," I whispered as I stroked her hair, adjusting the beautiful butterfly clip to keep the straggles out of her face.

"What?" Adam jerked around with sweat beads rolling down his temples.

Nodding, I looked at him with exhaustion. "But he didn't kill her. He was with his friends." My lips dipped downward as Adam looked up at the sky.

"You don't know that. They are going to find out it belongs to him, Nina." The light creases by his eyes deepened as he stared at me.

"Please don't say anything." My lips trembled as I brushed Collins' hair from her face and my tears dropped to her forehead.

"Nina..." Adam shook his head as he scooped up the girl crumpled in front of me.

He let out a soft groan as he tried to steady her. "I need you to hold the canoe still." He didn't look at me, and I knew he was going to tell the police. I forced myself up from the damp dirt where the small sticks and rocks had left marks across my soft palms. My legs were trembling as I selfishly walked slowly, knowing these minutes were the last few my son would have safe and warm in his bed. I knew it was wrong as another mother somewhere would soon learn her baby girl was left to die at the lake she was supposed to be having fun at. Yet, I knew my son wasn't a killer.

But don't all mothers think the best of their children?

The paddle cut through the murky water as Adam rowed us to the docks. I was as numb as the dead girl laying in my lap. She was truly beautiful. I stroked her hair, carefully readjusting the butterfly clip a few more times and keeping my eyes on her. I couldn't look at Adam. Because I knew if I did, I'd spiral and plead with him; I'd end up putting my family at a greater risk.

The red and blue lights lit up the sky as we grew closer to the north dock, and my heart sunk. There were officers still here, as well as a few straggling volunteers.

"Please, Adam. Don't..." I rasped as his motions grew more intense.

"They have her!" an officer screamed back to the others as the noise grew and floodlights blinded us almost instantaneously.

Everything was a blur. The swift movements and footsteps echoed around me. The delayed response to the lifeless woman laying on me. The shrill shrieks of...

"My baby! My baby girl!" I lifted my eyes as they began to fill with tears.

A woman with a similar appearance as Collins dropped to her knees on the dock as a man ran toward the officers and paramedics that lifted her onto the stretcher.

I sat there with tears falling down my flushed cheeks and the canoe shook halfway in the water and half jammed into the mud.

"Ma'am..."

I wiped my eyes against my forearm with a trail of black mascara smearing my skin.

Strong, calloused hands tugged me from the canoe as the world grew hazy around me and everything started to spin. Before I closed my eyes, I saw Adam talking to another officer as he glanced at me over his shoulder.

Everything went black.

"Mom?" A welcome voice tugged me out from a nightmare—a nightmare where I saw Max being cuffed and taken away. A nightmare where I saw my husband have sex with our son's ex-girlfriend after murdering another young girl.

"Mom?" I slowly opened my eyes and saw Ava. Relief washed over me as she opened her palm, and I slid mine into hers.

"It's going to be okay, Mommy."

The relief I momentarily felt dissipated even faster. Ava only called me 'mommy' when she was scared or nervous.

I flicked my eyes over her shoulder and saw Warren with a tired scowl.

"Where's Max?" I propped myself up, although my arms were weak.

"He's at Brian's. He's fine."

"I'm scared. Collins was my age," Ava whimpered as she dropped her head.

"They haven't caught anyone. Apparently, the jacket they found in the canoe went missing. It was a varsity jacket of some sorts..." Ava trailed.

"Ava! Enough. Let your mother rest."

My phone buzzed on the end table, where it had been plugged in. I had recently put a passcode on it after making a deal with Scarlett—a deal I desperately needed to call off. Warren crept closer to me as Ava kissed my forehead and whispered into my ear, "Be careful near him."

My eyes shot up and locked onto hers.

"I want you to go back to London," I breathed out.

217

She nodded slowly with a glisten in her beautiful brown eyes.

"I don't think I can run from the killer," she said under her breath just as Warren gripped her shoulders and gave them a light squeeze. Her back arched as she wiggled out from his touch and hurried away.

I watched my daughter rush away from the man she was supposed to trust.

The man I was supposed to trust.

CHAPTER THIRTY-ONE

*W*arren sat next to me and forcefully put my hand into his. "Nina, I know it's been rough for us. I hate how we are being toward each other, sunshine."

I would have laughed if my anxiety didn't have a chokehold on me and the sick pit in my stomach wasn't churning so quickly.

Closing my eyes. "It was Max's jacket. I know it was."

Warren let out a sigh. "What jacket?"

Blinking slowly, I looked at him. His blue eyes were fixed on my lips. "There was no jacket. And if there was, it's gone." His jaw tightened as he slowly nodded at me.

"What did you do, Warren? Did you kill her? Did

our son? I looked around frantically." I pursed my lips and tried to move to the opposite end of the bed, but Warren dug his fingers into my arm.

"You have to stop. Now." He gritted his teeth. "You have no idea how your big mouth can ruin this family."

My phone buzzed again, and I slapped Warren's hand off me.

"Get out of my room, Warren." I grabbed my phone and saw the endless missed calls and texts from Joss and Paige, but I didn't have the strength to listen to them panic or lecture me. Sinking my head back into my pillow, I took a deep breath and closed my eyes.

Warren had left the door opened and I could hear him ferociously typing away. *That damn book.* I rolled my eyes. He had been working on it for the past ten years. He'd write a chapter, delete it, write two more, re-write them. It made no sense. He said he was living each page in his mind and wanted it to feel real. Palpable.

He never let me read any of it. I tried to be supportive and tell him I'd love to give him feedback, but he always made me feel like he was in a different intelligence bracket than me.

Click, click, click. He was burning through the keys as I laid here, thinking about all the ways I had failed in this lifetime. Most of all, I had failed my children. I had chosen to keep them around a man who was dangerous. Ava would fly back to London and Max would be at school... they were safe. Now, if I could just figure out how to get a clean break from Warren, we'd all be fine. As a stay-at-home mom, I had no work experience, I didn't have a resume, let alone enough cash or money to support myself and the kids.

It's not easy to just leave. Warren had me sign an iron-clad prenuptial agreement, and essentially with the kids being over eighteen, I wasn't entitled to child support. Any alimony would be miniscule. I'd leave this gorgeous lake house with no place to go, and even my car was under his name. I hated how I had allowed myself to be this woman, the woman who trusted her husband more than herself.

I began to close my eyes, my head spinning.

"Mom?" Turning my head, Max looked at me with his brows lowered and the bags under his eyes sunken.

"Max, honey. Shut the door behind you." I waved him over as he carefully closed it.

He slowly walked over to me, as if he knew what he'd have to talk to me about next would be the hardest thing in his life.

Sitting on the foot of the bed, he dropped his head and fidgeted with his fingers.

"Max, I saw your jacket. Your varsity jacket."

He lifted his head and stared straight at the door.

"Baby, look at me please. Just tell me what is happening. What did you do…." My words cracked as I reached my hand out to him.

"I didn't mean to hurt her, Mom. I didn't." Tears began to stream down his cheeks as his skin flushed, and suddenly my college freshman turned back into a nervous, innocent toddler.

Suddenly, I felt like I couldn't breathe, but knew I had to. Because as mothers, even if our oxygen is depleting, we will do whatever it takes to make sure our child is breathing easy. I shoved the blanket off me and stood in front of Max.

"Tell me everything." I cupped his face in my palms as he shook his head. "Max, your jacket… They said it was gone. Did your dad…"

"I don't know, Mama." Max shrugged. "I don't know where it went. But I was with Collins that night, and…"

"Max, I'm only going to ask you once. Did you…"

"Yes."

Dropping to my knees as if the floor pulled me down into it, I burst into tears.

"Max… oh, Max… Why?" I cried out in a frenzy.

Putting my hands on his knees, I looked at my son. He was crying harder as he repeatedly shook his head.

"It was an accident. I swear. She… she fell over. She was drinking, she drowned. I couldn't… I didn't go in the water. I was drunk, too."

"Oh my gosh… You didn't mean to… kill her?" I clutched my chest as the tension built in it.

"No. No. But I… We were both drinking, and I didn't even try to save her, Mom."

I got back on my feet and clutched his shoulders, bringing him into an embrace as he cried harder. "I could have saved her…"

"It's going to be okay…" I pressed my chin into the top of his head as I stared out the window behind him. There it was again, the infamous sentence of reassuring someone something you very well know is a lie.

Maybe Adam had helped? He was the only one who knew…

"Listen, I want you to lay down here and don't leave. I'm going to run out and talk to Joss. She can help us. Don't worry, sweetie," I breathed out.

I sat curled in front of Joss and Paige for the next few hours as their mouths hung open. They couldn't believe everything I was pouring out.

"It's not his fault. Max did the right thing. Why would he jump into the lake in the dark, while he was drunk, and drown himself?" Paige justified.

Meanwhile, Joss was rubbing her temples, probably pissed that she was even associated with a neurotic friend whose family was damaged and deranged.

"I don't know what to do anymore." I leaned back and took another shot that Paige had poured as soon as I opened my mouth.

"For starters, you all just need to stop discussing anything with anyone. Just pretend everything is okay. Beyond that, if no one is questioning anything, then keep your mouths shut," Joss warned sternly.

"Okay." I closed my eyes and knew that all we had to do was get through this storm, and then I could finally leave Warren.

CHAPTER THIRTY-TWO

"We are gathered here today to honor the life that was taken from us too soon," the preacher from the small church said somberly.

I glanced around at the sea of black from where we were seated in the second row. The entire town of Johan was here. I crossed my legs and lifted my handkerchief to my eyes. The tears wouldn't stop. It was an open-casket ceremony, which I'd never understand. Ava was wearing oversized sunglasses and bawling. She had been staying with Paige until she left for London in a week. I had to keep her away from Warren. I had to keep her safe, and my mind was too hazy to be as alert as it should be.

Max was back on campus and chose to not attend

the funeral. Joss was furious, saying it would only make him look excessively guilty, but how could I force my son to sit here and watch Collins' family cry over the daughter they lost to an accident that Max couldn't have done anything about.

Adam came in and took a seat next to me during the speeches. He didn't look at me and he didn't say anything; he just stared ahead and listened as his eyes glistened.

Then Collins' mother began to speak, and I couldn't keep a strong front.

"My sweet baby girl was out on the lake—a lake she'd spent so many weekends floating on, learning to swim in, where she did cannon balls and laughed away her youth at. There is no way I believe that she drowned in those waters. No, Lake Johan wouldn't do that, Lake Johan wouldn't steal the beat of my heart from me. Lake Johan wouldn't break a family. Someone was with her… someone dumped her in the water and…" Collins' mother was hysterical. Her husband cut in and wrapped his arms around her as I sobbed along with her. Adam opened his palm and kept his eyes forward. Looking down through bleary eyes, I placed my hand into his, gripping it and feeling comfort for the first time in years.

"Adam Sutton and Nina Cooper, we'd like to thank

you both for saving our daughter from the depths of darkness and allowing us to properly say goodbye." Collins' father nodded at us.

The rest of the funeral was a blur. I didn't know who was speaking; I didn't hear the police officers discuss details and how they were certain it was an unfortunate accident involving a teenager and alcohol once the blood work came in.

I just sat there, numb, as the hushed whispers dissipated and everyone left. Ava left with Paige and Joss, but Adam and I stayed back. We sat with Collins' parents as they asked us for each and every detail of the moment we found her. The police had further questions since I fainted the first night, and Adam answered to the best of his ability.

How could I tell them that their daughter laid lifeless in my arms as Adam shook her, screaming for her to just breathe?

How could I tell them that I brushed her hair back and worried selfishly about my own son? Or terrified for my own daughter.

An hour came and went, and it was time to say goodbye to a stranger who spent time with me and didn't even know it.

Adam went first. He leaned down and patted her hand gently, before whispering against her ear.

I heard him.

"I'm so sorry. I wish I had found you just a few minutes before, maybe I could have saved you…"

The strength his voice was void as he backed away.

Clearing my throat, I took two small steps up to the beautiful cream coffin. Collins laid there on a bed of plush white, adorned in a white gown and…

The small butterfly clip I had fixed in her hair, but it had been moved. I drew closer to her. Brushing my hand against the lock it was clipping back, I sucked in a breath of air with realization.

Her eyes shot open and her pale pink lips parted. "You let this happen. You did this!"

I screamed and tumbled back, clutching my arms around my waist. Adam came rushing toward me. "Nina, what is it?"

Shaking, I blinked anxiously and looked back at her.

There she was, a beautiful angel, eternally asleep.

I was delirious.

But without a doubt, I knew Collins hadn't died accidentally. No, her hair was cut short in one spot, as if someone had clipped a lock of her hair.

Throwing my head back up, I knew.

My husband had murdered her.

My phone buzzed.

Your husband is boring. I'm over this. But he takes some pretty photos. He's in the bathroom right now. When are you sending my money?

My heart was racing as I saw the text bubbles. And then, a series of black and white images, just like the ones from his desk.

No, Scarlett couldn't do this anymore. I couldn't have her compile evidence for me that my husband was a cheater—I didn't need her to do that anymore. She was risking her life because I now knew that Warren Cooper was a killer.

Zooming into the photos, I saw the same thing.

A butterfly clip pining a single lock and a small silver compass necklace wrapped around her neck.

Scarlett, where did you get that butterfly clip from? Where'd you get that necklace from?

Scarlett, leave there now. It's not safe. He's not safe.

I waited and tapped my foot against the tarp.

The text bubble came back up...

"Come on, come on... shit," I whispered under my breath and quickly walked away from the canopy.

My finger shook as I found Warren's name in my contact list and called him. But it kept ringing.

Where were they? It looked like a hotel.

I had to find them...

Zooming into the photo, I saw a small logo. It was

the Lake Johan Inn, which was on the opposite side of the lake from us.

"Adam!" He was my only hope. I rushed over to his car and looked back at him. "Adam, I need a ride to the Lake Johan Inn."

"Why? What's going on?" He picked up his pace and unlocked his car doors.

"Please just take me there!"

We both got into the car, and I leaned back in the seat, closing my eyes.

We didn't move; instead, I could feel the warmth of his body hover over mine.

"What the..." I began, startled. He was reaching across, gripping the seatbelt and tugging it across me.

"Sorry, I forgot. Thank you, but please drive now." I waved at the window. Adam began to drive and sped through traffic to get to the inn. I kept calling Scarlett and Warren, but neither answered.

She was running out of time and didn't even know it. Things started to piece together as Adam pulled in the inn parking lot.

I unclipped the seatbelt and sprinted out of the car as Adam called out behind me.

The receptionist was filing her nails and had earbuds in, bopping her head to music as she blew a bright pink bubble.

I slammed my hands on the desk, causing her to spin and give me an attitude. "Which room is Warren Cooper in?" I looked at the wall full of vintage keys.

"Sorry, ma'am, we can't give that information out." She chomped obnoxiously on her gum as I frantically looked at the room keys that were missing.

"You don't understand, someone is in danger." My hands shook as Adam came up behind me. "Warren's my husband. Please..."

His hand rested on my lower back. "Her son is injured, and she needs her husband right away." His voice never shifted as I repeatedly called Warren and Scarlett. But just as the receptionist looked through her notebook full of names, I caught him in the corner of my eye.

Warren.

He was sipping a cup of coffee at a table, working on his laptop. His fingers were moving over the keys rapidly.

"Warren..." I forced myself to move toward him as his eyes stayed glued on the screen.

"Where is she?" I shouted as I looked around and called Scarlett again as the phone shook against my face.

"Nina? Adam?" Warren flicked his eyes behind me

and slowly stood while sliding his glasses down the bridge of his nose. "Where is who? Is Ava okay?"

"I'm talking about Scarlett. I know you're with her. I know you've been sleeping with her!" I screamed as Warren stayed completely calm as usual.

"You need to calm down," he warned. My eyes widened as I looked at him wildly, and I processed the five words a man should never say to a woman.

Walking forward, I leaned in and looked up into the pale, blue eyes I had once worshipped. I brushed my finger against the chiseled jawline I loved kissing. Taking a deep breath in, the gentle scent of sandalwood and cedar reminded me of the nights I'd be on his desk, teasing him as he worked.

"I am calm. But now, I'm angry. I can't be held accountable for what I do when I'm angry, honey. I might just..." I snapped my fingers and then dragged my index finger across his neck in a careful line.

"Where is she?" I hissed as Warren tilted his head slightly.

His eyes roamed behind me to Adam. "What are you doing at an inn with him?"

I glanced over my shoulder and looked at Adam, who had his tattooed, buff arms crossed over his chest.

"Seriously? How old are you? Twenty-five?" Warren taunted and let out a light laugh.

"Thirty," Adam said without a second doubt.

Oh, the irony. My husband could have a fetish for nineteen-year-old girls, but if his wife was with a man much younger than him, he had to play defense.

"Nina, you need to get under control. First of all, you need to stop being so anxious and secondly, you need to listen to me," Warren warned.

Adam walked closer and dropped his hand around my waist.

Chills darted up my spine as his fingers gently tapped into my lower back as if to say he had me. I wasn't alone against the monster in front of me.

Letting out a taunting laugh, Warren rolled his eyes. "So, you're fucking him? Nina, I hope you know what you're doing." He shook his head as Adam's free hand clenched into a fist.

"We aren't fucking. If we were, you'd know, because for once in your life, you'd see your wife satisfied."

My jaw dropped as I looked at Adam, and he flashed a smirk at me that had my heart racing.

"I'm not going to stand here and be disrespected. Let's go, Nina." Warren reached out and grabbed my arm assertively.

Adam immediately cut in and shoved Warren back,

to which my husband tumbled back and clenched his jaw in shock.

"Stop it!" I yelled out as I looked between them. My phone buzzed.

I'm leaving town. Sorry. I can't help you frame your husband. But feel free to use my messages and photos when you wipe his accounts clean. It was nice knowing you, Mrs. Cooper.

Moving away from the testosterone-filled air that was choking me, I quickly called Scarlett. It kept ringing. Why was she leaving town?

Sliding my finger down the screen, I quickly texted her back.

Why are you leaving? Can you please call me? I'm so sorry if I put you in a terrible situation. I'm ashamed of myself. I think Warren killed that girl Collins. I think... I think you might be next.

A text bubble appeared, and my breathing grew erratic.

Nothing.

I called again and when I did, I got an automated message saying the number was disconnected.

Looking back at Warren and Adam, I saw they were having a heated conversation.

Nothing was making sense. If she was texting me

and Warren was here, then maybe he didn't do anything to her?

Adam turned and walked back to me. "Need a ride?"

I nodded and looked over his shoulder at my husband.

He looked broken.

Just like my heart.

CHAPTER THIRTY-THREE

"What's going on, Nina?"

I stared out the window and watched as the dense trees blurred past us.

"Do you ever feel like the life you're living is the one you're watching and not really living? I wish I could just feel alive for once." I looked over at him as the veins in his muscular, tattooed forearms protruded while he drove me home.

"No." He glanced at me quickly before looking back at the road.

The sun was setting, and I felt so out of touch with everything. I was checking in on Ava and Max via random texts. Granted, Ava being with Joss made me feel better, but Max... he was just in his own world of friends and sports, with no care in the world about the catastrophic events that were budding around him.

Was I raising him to be just like his father? Had I failed my son?

"I live the life I want to live, but most of all, I live the life I know I need to live." He slowed down and took a left turn.

"My house is… right." I looked back as we drove in the opposite direction. The gravel crunched against Adam's tires as he drove and slowed the car without stopping.

"Adam?" A pit in my stomach grew as I watched his eyes stay fixed in front of him.

How well do I really know this man? How could I just get into a car with him without even thinking twice? My palms grew moist as I began to unbuckle my seatbelt. I could jump out and tumble roll before he could take me to this next destination where he'd probably kill me. Was Adam the killer? I thought about how we found Collins', and how we just so happened to paddle in that direction.

He began to pull over just as my fingers released my seatbelt. "Adam…"

"I just want to show you something." His eyes trailed to my hand and upward as the seatbelt spiraled back in place.

"You're making me nervous," I whispered as I looked into his gorgeous, mossy-green eyes and back to the dense trees in front of us.

"That means you like me." He flashed his signature smirk that deepened the dimples near his lips. "I'd never hurt you, Nina." He slid out of the car and walked around to my side of the door, opening it and reaching his hand down to me.

Sighing, I nodded in disbelief that this thirty-year-old gorgeous man was making my heart race in a way I couldn't even remember.

Climbing into the bed of his truck, he grabbed a blanket before jumping back down and lacing his fingers with mine.

A slight chill in the air rustled the trees, teasing us that fall would be here before we knew it.

I glanced down at our hands and walked next to him down the path before we saw the lake. I hadn't been to this part before. No houses were in sight, but a single, small, worn-down dock was nestled between the trees.

Cautiously strolling next to Adam, he let go of my hand and spread the blanket at the end of the dock. He looked at the sky and patted the spot next to him.

Pinching my lips to the side, I sat on the opposite

edge of the blanket. He looked at the space between us and smiled at me mischievously.

"I promise I don't always bite." He licked his bottom lip as my face grew warm, and I scooted closer to him.

"You don't *always* bite?" He was looking at my lips as I asked him the most confusing question of my life.

Leaning in, he tipped my chin up and brushed his lips against mine before carefully biting into my bottom lip. I moaned out as he ran his hands through my hair and he whispered against my lips, "I only bite when I know it's going to taste sweet." He rubbed his thumb against my bottom lip as I whimpered and he kissed my neck.

"Adam... I'm forty." I felt humiliated. It made no sense to me how we were conditioned to believe that a man could be with a woman less than half his age, but if a woman did the same, we should feel embarrassed or conflicted.

"You are the most gorgeous woman I've ever seen." He lips brushed against my collarbone before he lifted his eyes up at me. "Now, let me help you feel alive," he said without a sliver of uncertainty.

I looked at him curiously. "Is that why you brought me here?"

He shook his head. "No. I wanted to show you two

things. Here's the first thing." He gently turned me around to see the sun melting into the trees with orange and pink hues painting the entire sky.

"Oh, Adam…" I couldn't stop staring at how beautiful it was. I'd lived here for years, yet I'd never taken the time to truly soak up the sunsets. We were always chasing the sunrises for a new day, yet I never appreciated basically getting through one. And no one, not even my husband, had ever done something so simple and sweet for me.

Facing Adam, I ran my fingers down the center of his chest as my lips parted. He laid me down, and before I knew it, he had my legs spread and was between them. "You're so beautiful, Nina." Lifting the bottom of my dress up, he unzipped his pants and pressed inside of me. Gasping, my nails dug into the blanket he had laid down as he kept his movements steady. I couldn't handle how incredible he felt, but most of all, how incredible he made me feel.

My breathing shifted as tension built inside me. The chirping birds, the light ripple in the water, and the scent of early fall teasing us as I closed my eyes and let myself go. Adam pushed deeper inside me as I cried out in sheer euphoria.

My first orgasm in years that wasn't from the vibrator I had stashed away. When I said I wanted it hard, I didn't mean my life with him but apparently, my husband didn't get the memo. I knew he was probably overdosing on Viagra just to be the two-pump charming chump to all these impressionable young women who thought he'd give them a happily ever after.

I was that girl.

Adam laid next to me and brushed the hair from my face that the wind kept picking up.

"That was…" I sighed and turned my face to his with the tips of our noses touching, "surreal."

A small curve across his lips grew. "For me, too." He kissed me once more before we laid and watched the sun completely disappear and darkness take over.

I suppose my desire to get revenge on Warren and wipe him clean overtook my rationale. I was ashamed of myself for having Scarlett, a girl I should have hated essentially, catfish him just so I could have evidence to make my divorce stronger. But without it, I wouldn't get a dime. Our prenup would have left me with nothing. Warren ruined me. He ruined us.

I hated that I was still thinking about him, even during this beautiful moment. He had consumed me.

"What was the other thing you wanted to show me?" I sat up and turned my phone flashlight on as Adam followed my lead.

"I don't think tonight's the night to show you…" He stood and tugged his shorts back on before leaning down and grabbing his shirt.

Standing, I pulled my dress down and looked at him. "Please, Adam?" For some reason, I could sense it wasn't something good.

"Nina, this was amazing but…"

"Oh no, you regret it?" I felt a knot build in my lower abdomen.

Reaching out, he brushed his hands against my arms, drawing me in for a hug, and he planted a kiss on my head. "No, this was the best evening of my life with you. I just don't want to ruin it with what I need to show you."

"Is it about my kids? Max?" I began to panic, thinking something had changed in the case with Collins. Was the jacket found? Was Max going to be arrested?

"No. It's your husband. I think he killed his first wife, and I think you're next. You need to leave him. You need to get your kids out of the house and leave him, now." Adam held me steady as it felt like my blood was rushing out of my body and leaving me lifeless.

It's different when you have a thought about something, versus when someone else confirms a thought you never wanted to be true.

I didn't want this to be true.

I didn't want my husband and the father of my children to be a serial killer.

A cheater was hard enough, but a man who found pleasure in watching the life leave a human body…?

I chose to be with a monster, and worst of all, I was still standing by him.

CHAPTER THIRTY-FOUR

The drive back to my house was silent. Adam didn't explain anything to me, he didn't show me any proof of his accusations, and he didn't tell me why he thought my husband was a killer. How did he know anything about Warren's first wife?

Once we turned into the driveway, I unbuckled my seatbelt and looked at the gorgeous lake house in front of me. There was only one window illuminated and the rest of the house was dark. Max had texted me that he was back on campus, and I knew Ava was with Paige and hanging out with friends. Warren hadn't spoken to me since he saw us at the inn.

"I don't think you should stay here. You can stay with me." Adam cut through the silence and looked over at me with concern.

"Why do you think he killed his first wife? How do you even know anything about... him or me?"

"Your front door is open." Adam pointed at the door in front of us. I squinted and noticed the door was slightly ajar. I opened my door and looked around with the motion sensors flooding light into the driveway. Warren's car wasn't there.

Adam walked up beside me and gently gripped my hand. Shaking his head, he whispered, "Go back to the car."

Our footsteps felt even louder with nothing but crickets and creatures singing in the silent background.

Adam reached to his pocket and pulled out a gun. My heart stopped. What was happening? I stumbled back as he held it in a way that I knew was second-nature. Within a moment, he was inside my house and suddenly, all the lights turned on one by one. I didn't know what to do. Why did Adam have a gun? Why was my front door open?

Where was my husband? I texted Max, Ava, Paige, and Joss in a panic before Adam came back in and lowered his gun.

"Someone must have left it opened. No one's there. It doesn't seem like it's been a forced entry," he said calmly, and I stared at his hand clutching the gun. "I'll come in with you if you need to pack anything."

"Why do you have a gun?" My words trembled as I looked back at him.

"Safety. I'm a contractor, Nina. My job can get dangerous when I'm going to a stranger's house."

It did make sense, especially since we lived in the south and just about everyone had a gun. "Adam, I'm going to grab a bag and go to Paige's house. Ava is there, too, and I just... I need to be around..." Maybe the kids came home to grab something? Max had left the doors opened before. I asked Adam to wait on the patio; I didn't want him inside with me. Although he seemed completely safe, I didn't know who to trust at this point.

Walking inside, I looked around my home. Everything was tidy and in place. I made my way to Warren's office. His laptop was on his desk, sitting on scattered paper, meaning he had come home. He spent so many hours of the past six years writing this book and rewriting it. I'd hear him groan out of frustration, watch him crumple Post-It notes and tell me how it wasn't piecing together. He couldn't see his story the way he should. He wanted to be an author. He wanted people to fawn over his ability to craft a novel that hooked its claws into the reader. He spent hours giving up family events and memories to write it. Now, here he was, with a book deal and finishing final edits on it. He told me that he wanted me to read it when it was completely finished—he wanted me to be the first to hold the paperback in my hands.

Truthfully, I didn't care to read it. I didn't care to read the book that was more important to him than his own family. He'd stay late at work to write after teaching all day, and now I knew those long hours were really so he could have endless affairs.

Sitting in his desk chair, I opened the laptop. The password box came up, and I hesitated a moment before trying a series of random words that meant something to Warren.

Each time it was rejected. But then I sank back and thought of when we first started dating, and Warren made a joke when I had forgotten my email password. He said his was simple.

Ilovenina.

There was no way it was the same now, but I tried anyway. My lips dropped in shock when it went through and opened directly to his word document.

His password was still 'I love Nina'. I winced and closed my eyes for a moment as pain and sadness seared through me.

Every single day, multiple times a day, he typed

those three words in. I hated how my emotions were overtaking my logic; I hated how I wanted so desperately to forget all that is happening and move on with my family. My husband, my beautiful children, and spend the rest of my days at this lake house.

"Nina?" Adam called out.

"Give me five," I shouted back. I looked at the word document and scrolled up. The title wasn't there. I started to read chapter one.

This lake house was our safe haven, but it also became the walls that held blood.

Chills shot up my spine as I looked around the dark office with deep navy-blue walls and the old books filling the dark wooden shelves. Swallowing, I continued to read.

The screams that left their bodies never haunted me the way I always thought they would. The way their nails dug into the wooden floors my grandfather laid down decades ago, clawing away as wicked laughter cut through the silence. The way they begged as life left their eyes. It was poetic. I was God. I decided when they'd breathe their final breath of life.

"Nina?" Adam was standing in front of me as I slammed the laptop closed and looked at him while my body shook.

"Are you okay?" His brows knitted together as he looked around Warren's office.

"Yeah, I was... checking my email. I... I'm going to just lock up and grab a bag. I'm sorry. You can wait in the formal living room up front." I pointed in the direction.

He nodded with his forehead crinkled, as if he wanted to ask me more questions but knew I couldn't handle them.

Standing up, my legs felt weak as the words I had read haunted me. How could Warren write something so sinister and have our lake house be the setting? I walked to the back to check the lock before seeing shadows far by the kids' old playset. What was that? I cut the motion light switch off before carefully opening the sliding door and tiptoeing out.

There were two figures in the distance.

They were wearing baseball hats and something was swinging between them.

A body.

I held my breath as I walked to the rail and leaned in. Oh, no.

My son was wearing his varsity jacket, helping his father carry something that I knew had to be a dead body.

My baby boy. My heart shattered. I wanted to run

down there and kill Warren with my bare hands. What had he done? How could he bring our son into the sick, twisted game of death he was playing?

"Nina?" Adam said softly behind me. I flung around and quickly ran up to him, shoving him back inside the house.

Reaching up, I grabbed his face and slammed my lips to his.

He held my face in his palms as he kissed me back in shock.

"Mmm…" He sighed and smiled under our lips.

I couldn't let him see Max in his jacket. And I couldn't let him see my son carrying a body.

"We need to go." I grabbed his hand and quickly tugged him away. I felt like my soul was split in half and I had left it behind me. I wanted to go get my son —to help him, to save him—but it was too late. He was chasing darkness. But most of all, the darkness was chasing him.

CHAPTER THIRTY-FIVE

"Is everything okay?" Adam drove me to Paige's house. Joss was already heading over. I had panic texted them both. I couldn't handle this alone anymore. I couldn't just call the police, knowing my son wouldn't have wanted to do this. No, my husband dragged him into it with his overzealous misogynic personality and apparent passion for murder.

"Yes, it is. I'm sorry, Adam. I have to just... sort so much out, but thank you for everything." Nausea pooled in my stomach as I looked at him and we pulled into the driveway.

"I have to go," I added just before he opened his door and jogged out around to open my door for me.

Reaching his hand out, I took it and stood in front

of him for a moment as the world around me felt so hazy and full of fear.

Wrapping his arms around me in a tight embrace, I dropped my face into his chest and cried.

He rubbed my back as I sobbed while everything came crashing around me. As a mother, it's the innate need to protect your child. I knew what I saw was wrong, I knew I had to call the police, and I knew my son was now a criminal. But I also knew he was being influenced by the one man he should have counted on the most.

Was I making up excuses for him, and because of my love for him as his mother, letting him get away with…

Murder?

"It's going to be okay. I promise," Adam whispered in my ear before kissing my lips.

Using his thumbs, he swiped away the tears that kept falling just before kissing each eyelid softly.

"How can you be so sure?" I choked.

"Because you are good, and so many people aren't." I pulled away from him as Joss opened the front door.

"Hey Adam…" Joss called out from the door. She waved her fingers at him as he tipped his head in greeting before turning back toward me.

"You can run, but he can't. It's going to be okay. I've

got you." I didn't even know how to process anything Adam was saying. I slowly nodded and said goodbye before walking to my best friends. As soon as I got inside, I looked around and didn't see Ava.

"She's asleep. She's taking her meds and..." Paige reached around me and squeezed me tightly.

"Let's go out back." Joss grabbed two bottles of wine and two glasses.

Sitting around the fire-pit, she poured her and Paige some wine and handed me the full second bottle. "Girlfriend, you don't need a glass, you need the whole damn bottle."

I clutched the cold bottle of Prosecco and took a long swig. "I saw Max and Warren carrying a dead body near the old playset."

Paige started to cough violently as she choked on her wine while Joss looked at me in shock. "Nina," she started and quickly looked around. Grabbing a remote, she turned on music and looked at Paige to check the back door.

"Are you on drugs?" Paige put her glass down and looked at me carefully. "Let me see your arms."

"I'm not doing drugs, Paige." I shook my head and took another sip. "Max had his varsity jacket on. He was helping Warren carry a girl... who I think might be Scarlett."

It made sense. Scarlett "texted" me earlier in the day that she was leaving town. She had no family or friends who would be looking for her. Both my husband and son had been intimate with her, so they had a motive. Maybe Warren found out that I was using her to catfish him.

"Oh my..." Paige covered her mouth with her hands and looked over at Joss, who wasn't reacting. "You need to call the police." Paige reached for her phone but Joss quickly grabbed it from her hands.

"What are you doing?" Paige cried out as Joss shoved it into the sofa cushion.

"Do you want to see Max spend the rest of his life in jail when we don't know what Nina saw?" Joss fired at Paige.

Paige rolled her eyes and lifted her wineglass, taking a long swig before placing it down again. "No. You know I love those kids like my own, and I don't even like kids."

"Joss, I don't know what to do... What are my options?" I swallowed another mouthful of the sweet Prosecco and brushed my hand across my face, exhausted.

"Paige, I'm giving you one chance to leave now before I tell Nina what she's going to do," Joss said calmly.

Paige looked between us and cracked her neck from side to side.

"If one of us goes down, we all do. You know we're the best friends that get manicures, drink wine, slash husbands, and hide bodies together, right?" Paige offered a small smile. I rubbed my arms, feeling so cold and terrified of what Joss was about to say.

"Tomorrow, when the sun is up and people are out swimming in the lake, so there's noise and laughter, you're going to go out there and figure out what's been buried, but before that, I want you to go in the house and dig around. Find anything that could be evidence. We need to make sure your mind isn't playing tricks on you, and then, when or if, you see something that shouldn't be there, you're going to call me. Then… we will handle it." Joss didn't hesitate.

"How would we handle it?" My nerves were shot, and I couldn't stop the tremble in my hands.

"We're not going to handle it," Paige began and looked toward Joss, then back at me.

"We're going to handle him." Taking a tube of lipstick out, she handed it over to me.

"You're not just a stay-at-home mom he can wreck and destroy. You're a gorgeous, smart, and incredible woman who is going to rip this man to shreds for not only hurting you, but for also hurting your babies."

Taking the lipstick from her, I swiped it across my lips and smacked them together.

"We're going to handle him." I nodded in agreeance. I just needed to save my son first.

Could my mind have been playing tricks on me, after all?

CHAPTER THIRTY-SIX

I woke up with a pounding headache after drinking the entire bottle of wine and not sleeping for more than two hours. Holding the hot cup of coffee between my palms, I looked out at the lake.

The sun was rising and the birds were chirping, but my racing thoughts wouldn't stop.

"Mom, what are those?" Ava was wearing an over-sized shirt with her hair piled on top of her head. I followed her line of vision to my arms.

They were covered in deep, red scratches.

Shaking my head, I placed my coffee down and quickly stood. "I don't know..." I trailed my fingers against them. They looked like fingernails had dragged into my flesh. How did I not feel that? I placed my hand against my head and looked up at her.

"I think I was scratching at a bug bite," I lied. She tilted her head with concern but nodded.

"I'm leaving for London this weekend. I can't keep pushing it off," she said softly while hugging me tightly.

"I know, baby. I know. I want you to go, and please, don't come home until I figure this mess out."

She slowly pulled away and looked at me with fear in her eyes. "Is Max going to be okay?" The vulnerability in her voice reminded me of when she was a little girl, scared of the dark or when Max broke his wrist while playing football.

"Yes." I knew she didn't know the extent of the disaster brewing within our family, but she didn't need to. Ava couldn't wreck her life over the men in our family.

"Hey, will you paint me something pretty before you leave?" I brushed her hair out of her face, hoping this would be a welcome distraction for her. We always bonded over painting together, and I was hoping in some way she'd find peace in it while our life was about to be blown up.

"I will, Mama." She hugged me once more before wiping away straggling tears.

"I have to get some things done, but stay here and I'll see you in the evening. I love you so much, my Ava girl." I forced a smile for her and kissed her goodbye. I had to get going. Warren would probably be on campus.

Once I borrowed clothes from Paige, I got into my car and called Max.

The phone rang and rang, but then finally, he answered, "Hey, Mom."

"Max…" I started and tried to focus on driving. I was using Paige's brand-new Porsche and was one second away from a full mental breakdown and a car accident.

"Where are you?" I asked and pressed the gas pedal harder.

"I'm on campus, about to head into practice. Why?" I didn't like the way he was asking. I knew he thought I was over-stepping.

"Just wondering. I'll check in later. Max, you know I love you, right?" The emotion rocked each of those words as I turned into our driveway.

"Yeah. Love you, too, Mom." He ended the call abruptly, and that's when I knew what I had seen last night wasn't in my mind. I could tell he was off.

Warren's car was gone. I didn't care where he was, what he was doing, or rather, *who* he was doing. All I knew now was that I was racing against time to save Max and Ava—and myself.

Getting out of the car, I walked in and looked around quickly to make sure no one was actually home.

Tugging my hat, sunglasses, and dishwashing gloves on, I went out to the backyard, but I stopped. There were people out on the lake, boating. Glancing over at our deck, I grabbed a plant and decided I'd have to pretend to be gardening. Picking up my pace, I made my way down to my kids old rusted play set that Warren had kept swearing he'd eventually get rid of but never did. I always thought deep down he was emotional and didn't want to let go. I could hear our children's laughter echo as they shouted, "Push me higher, Mama! Dada, watch me!"

Now, here I was, standing over freshly dug dirt under the swings, knowing without a doubt that life as I knew it would be officially over in a few moments.

Sinking to my knees, I took one last look around at the beautiful lake, the gorgeous house behind me. Memories of a lifetime together flashed in front of my eyes as I gripped the moist ground and began to dig. At first, I was cautiously moving the dirt, but then fury rampaged throughout my body as I violently began to fling dirt in all directions. Some of it hit my mouth and face, and then, I felt it.

But it wasn't an 'it'. It was a her.

I felt her.

Letting out a scream, I fell backward and slapped my mouth closed. Long, red hair splayed around.

Scarlett? Her face was completely mauled. Her eyes were sunken in, her flesh destroyed with only a worm wiggling out of her mouth her skin looked even more drained of color.

"Oh my God," I cried as I looked at the young woman in the ground in front of me. Leaning toward her body, I gasped at the long cut in her arm where blood stained a gash that was meticulously carved into her flesh.

Tilting my head, I cinched my lips together.

It was a heart carved into her skin, with her arm discolored as if the blood was meticulously drained from it. Around her neck was the silver necklace with a small compass-style pendent around it.

I looked out to the lake. Luckily, everyone was in the distance, completely oblivious to what was happening outside of one of the lake houses that they probably assumed were filled with wealthy, lucky families.

Frantically, I began digging next to Scarlett until my blade hit something hard.

I didn't think my heart could take it; I didn't think I

could stay strong for long enough to see what was under the earth. Swiping at the dirt, I felt faint.

"No, no... no." I began sobbing at the hand that was starting to show. Who was she? Did Max help kill these innocent women? Why was Warren doing this?

A crack of thunder echoed in the sky, and I looked up. A storm was coming. I stood and raced back to the deck. I had to get tarp and my phone. I had to call the police. I knew that as much as I wanted to protect my son, if he was involved in this, I couldn't wait. He could be hurting someone else.

"Shit!" I had left my phone inside. Wiping the dirt off my hands, I ran inside and went toward Warren's office to get it.

Except, my feet dragged as I got closer.

"Hi, baby." Warren was sitting in his chair with his laptop open. His fingers hovered over the keys as a small, sinister smile grew on his face.

"Warren!" I cried out. "What have you done... What have you dragged our son into?" I broke down as my husband stood and carefully closed his laptop.

"Did you know I finished writing my book? The final edits were turned in, baby." He stretched his hands over his head and came around the desk.

"You killed Scarlett." I could see my phone on the corner of his desk, knowing I hadn't left it there.

He had known I was home.

"No, my love... *You* killed her." Warren came closer as I started to walk backward away from him.

"I didn't kill her. You did, and you had our son help you. But why, Warren? Why? Who is the woman buried next to her? How could you do this to them? To us? Our daughter is terrified of you. I'm..." I couldn't stop. My heart was racing and the breath in my lungs felt shallow and suffocating.

"We didn't kill her; William and Aaron did," Warren said calmly as his nails dug into my arms, pushing me into the wall behind us.

"Who?" I looked into his distant gaze as his hands traveled up to my neck, clutching it tightly.

"Warren, let go... You're hurting me." I clawed at his hands, which only constricted all that more. I tried to speak, but I couldn't. I was swallowing as much air as I could while his eyes pierced into mine.

"Oh, my beautiful wife." He lowered his lips to my neck, grazing his teeth into my skin as I held my breath. Fear had paralyzed my entire body.

"Warren—" I was choking while digging my nails into his fingertips.

"You just had to be a nosey bitch." He dipped his hand into his pocket and tugged out a white handkerchief.

"Warren..." But his eyes were filled with power, and I knew it was because he was about to see life leave the ones in front of him.

There was no human more powerful than the person who got to choose when someone would take their last breath, and it suddenly occurred to me that's why he'd been doing it all along.

My husband loved watching life leave innocent bodies because he felt powerful.

Lifting the white handkerchief to my nose, he smothered me with it. My eyes closed as I thought about Max and Ava.

"You pathetic asshole," is all that came out before everything went black.

CHAPTER THIRTY-SEVEN

*M*y head felt heavy as I slowly opened my eyes, yet I couldn't tell if they were actually opened considering it felt as if the darkness had swallowed me whole.

The scent of fresh dirt circulated around me as I blinked, but my eyes felt agitated with something inside them. I began coughing and brushing my hand around me until realization poured over me.

I was in the dirt.

I was buried alive.

I began clawing at the dirt around me in full terror while gasping for air, considering the panic attack I was now experiencing was probably using the limited oxygen I had left. I couldn't calm down. Clenching my eyes shut, they stung from the dirt trickling into my eyes.

"Help!" I yelled as I kicked my legs like a toddler throwing a tantrum. My neck started to itch as the air around me began to dissipate, and I knew I was depleting the oxygen by panicking and gulping down breaths.

I tried to cool myself down by placing my hands over my chest and shortening each inhale. "It's okay. It's okay..." I chanted. Opening my eyes, I looked to the side into the darkness but couldn't see anything. My eyes hadn't adjusted to the darkness and the panic was twisting in my gut as I tried to keep my breath steady.

I took one deep breath in and exhaled slowly while turning my head. There were specks of light flickering through the layers of fresh, wet dirt weighing down on my chest. I couldn't have been buried that far down.

My forehead touched something as soon as I turned. Lifting my hand slowly, I put it between my face and whatever object was now brushing against my flesh.

Padding my fingers across I assumed it had to be a rock? Dirt? An animal...

But then, as I dragged my fingertips down, I froze.

My lips parted and finally, I realized the scent I was smelling wasn't dirt.

It was death.

Rolling my lips together, tears burned my eyes as I felt a human mouth and insects crawling out of it. There was no moisture on what I assumed was a tongue, and when I traced their face, I could feel the deterioration.

"No, no, no..." I sniffled as my chest constricted with pain. I was going to die here. Underground, buried alive next to someone—probably another woman my husband had slaughtered. Dragging my fingers down, I felt what was probably once a neck and could feel a necklace wrapped around. Holding my breath, I traced the small compass pendant and began to cry.

I had thought about death before. I think once I became a wife and a mother, I thought about it all that more. I was terrified to die because I didn't want to miss a beat with the man I loved and the children I gave birth to.

The man I had entrusted with my heart, my life, and most of all, my children. The same man who had buried me in the dirt the way trash is compacted.

The stench of rot began to intensify in the already dense air clouding around me, considering I now knew where the odor was being emitted from. The sound of maggots and critters making their way out of the decomposing body had my skin crawling because as I swallowed the minimal saliva left in my mouth, I knew I too, would be covered in them as they chewed away at my eyes, flesh, and tongue.

But as I tried to make peace with the fact that I couldn't get out and how I'd die in under a day, I thought about my children.

I thought about Max, and how he was being pinned into a life of darkness by his own father. I knew he was completely lost because he'd never choose this life for himself. I thought about my daughter, and how she was terrified of the man she should have counted on the most. I thought about what would happen to them and all the other young, carefree women Warren would interact with and make his next victims.

Lifting my hands, I patted the dirt above me. It was damp. Once it dried, I knew it would only get harder to claw myself out of this burial. I had to try to get out. No, I would get out, and once I did, I was going to put my husband in a shallow grave and make sure he rotted.

I began peeling away at the dirt above me, frantically considering how the temperature was only rising, but I knew I couldn't have been too far deep. The way specks of light scattered meant there was hope that Warren had done a half-ass job burying me —just like he did with everything in his life.

Chunks of wet mud and rough rocks fell into my mouth and face. Clenching my eyes shut, I dug as fast as I could, shaking my face and brushing the dirt away from me. It felt like an eternity had passed as my nails chipped away and pain grew in each finger. I felt like I was burying myself deeper as the ground closed in on me. My skin was crawling with tiny insects, using my body as a way out.

I became frenzied and before I knew it, I was gasping for air again.

"Calm down, you need to get out. They won't stop until you stop them." I froze as chills shot up my spine, and I turned toward the body next to me. "Nina, they won't stop," the body rasped. Bony fingers grazed my cheek, and the heat my body once felt was now cold.

I was losing my mind, but still, I knew it was true. My fingers were sore, my arms were buried, and my legs couldn't move. I didn't have any physical strength left to do this alone. My heart rate quickened as I thought about my options.

I knew what I had to do next would haunt me for the rest of my days if I made it. I reached over with my right hand and felt the body next to me. First, tracing her face, I let my fingers drop to her shoulder and could feel that the skin was mostly gone. Poking my finger inward, I felt the smooth bone exposed in certain spots.

My stomach began to churn as nausea teased my esophagus. "I'm so sorry," I choked out as I garnered every ounce of strength I could muster and dug my nails deeper, peeling off as much flesh as I could before making one swift movement in order to break off what I assumed was a bone. My lips quivered as I held it in my hands, something crawling off it and onto my arm, but I kept my lips tightly closed to the best of my ability as I slammed it into the ground above me rapidly. I was running out of time. My head felt lighter by the minute.

I didn't know how many times I must have dug into the dirt; I don't know how many tears I shed, but eventually....

I saw a sliver of light. I screamed as loudly as I could until my voice went hoarse and the air in my lungs vanished.

I didn't have anything left in me, I was exhausted. "Help!" I closed my eyes with defeat swarming over my sweat- and insect-covered body. The small hole I managed to create was enough to let the evening air trickle in. At least I'd have a bit of fresh air before I eventually dehydrated to death. My mouth was coated in dirt, gravel, and thick saliva.

I kept my eyes closed and let myself cry. I couldn't stop. I missed my children. I missed Joss and Paige. I spent my life living in Warren's shadow, and now here I was, wishing so badly that I could have restarted my life.

But it was over.

He had won.

CHAPTER THIRTY-EIGHT

"Nina. Nina. Nina?" It felt like I was listening to my name through a speakerphone.

"Nina... please, open your eyes."

"Nina, it's me." I recognized his voice, but was scared this was some afterlife experience. I was scared if I opened my eyes, he wouldn't be there and instead, I'd fall straight back into darkness.

"Mom?"

Moisture grew under my eyelids as I slowly shook my head. My nose began to run as she repeated herself, "Mommy, please open your eyes."

"Ava, baby..." I looked at her. I was on the floor in the middle of a field. Turning my head slightly, I saw it was Adam who had me in his arms with fear and concern rampaging through his eyes.

"Mommy—" Ava broke down and dropped her head onto my abdomen.

"Nina, help is coming. We're just so fucking far out in the middle of nowhere." Adam looked around as I laid in his arms while Ava gently stroked my forehead.

"Mom, Dad is gone," she whispered as she opened a water bottle and pressed it against my dry lips.

I stared at her blankly as the wind rustled through the endless green grass surrounding us.

"He's gone, and Max... Max was arrested." Her hand trembled as she dripped water into my mouth. It hurt to swallow, and the taste of dirt and rocks lingered on my tongue. I forbade myself to think about what I did under the ground or look for the shallow grave and decomposed body next to me.

"Max..." My voice cracked as Adam held me tightly. Opening his phone, he waved it around as the signal notification chimed.

"We need to get you to the car." He looked down at me and brushed a straggling piece of hair from my mouth.

Lifting me in his strong, tattooed arms, he stood and said something to Ava, but I couldn't process the words or the light. I kept my eyes closed and wrapped my arms around Adam's neck. I reeked of urine, dirt, and most of all, death, but I didn't care. He didn't even flinch. Ava held my hand as we went through the endless fields.

"There's another woman... or person under..." I started to say as my voice went in and out.

"I know, baby. I saw." I shot a look at Adam in shock and didn't want to see Ava's reaction to the term of endearment he just called me.

"Where is he?" I forced out as I kept my eyes closed.

"Dad?" Ava asked.

"Mm-hmm..." My entire body hurt. I shivered as Adam picked up his pace.

"They found his body tonight," Adam answered.

Slowly opening my eyes, I blinked away the debris that had scratched them and was relieved when I saw the sky darkening.

"I don't understand..." I started, not wanting to have this kind of conversation in front of my daughter. Our daughter.

"He jumped off the Wimberly Pointe bridge."

My heart sank as I heard my daughter tell me that her father, my husband, had killed himself.

But I wasn't sad that he had killed himself; no, I

was sad that he didn't let me have the opportunity to kill him myself.

"Did they find his body?" I licked my dry, cracked lips as I leaned my head against Adam's chest.

"No. But they have video footage of him jumping in, and you know no one has ever survived the fall off of Wimberly Pointe," Adam said while sliding one hand into his pocket and quickly unlocking his truck. Ava opened the door and helped him gently place my body on the passenger seat. I looked at Ava as she tugged the seatbelt and buckled it in for me.

"Are you okay, honey?" Guilt shook me to my core as I watched her life be ripped apart in front of my eyes.

"I want Max to be okay, and for you to be okay." A tear ran down her cheek as she slid in next to me. Adam carefully shut the door and I let my head fall on her shoulder.

I thought about my son in prison. The kindest, funniest, and most lovable young man I had ever met. The child who was terrified of displeasing his father, mother, and coaches. He pushed himself so hard to be just like Warren.

A success.

But he, too, lived in the shadows. Just like me.

We pulled into the hospital, and everything was a daze. I fell in and out of sleep or consciousness as they rushed me through the stark white hospital hallways and staff shouted out to one another.

"There was a dead woman," I repeated as Adam held my hand just as the stretcher was torn away from him.

"Women," he said just as the door closed.

Women. *Plural.* I would have been included in that list.

I had a million questions and needed all the answers, but for now, I collapsed to the pillow and let my body rest and be taken care of. After this, I needed to make sure my husband was dead and then, I needed to get my son out of jail.

CHAPTER THIRTY-NINE

I spent six days in the hospital. Six days in silence. I don't know what happened to me, but suddenly, I couldn't speak. I'd wake up breaking out into a cold sweat, my heart rate would skyrocket to the point the machines would beep loudly, summoning a concerned nurse and doctor.

I was given anti-psychotics and then I'd close my eyes again. Every single time I closed my eyes, I saw death. I smelled dirt, and I couldn't handle what my simple life had turned into.

On my final day in the hospital, a detective came in, holding up his badge. "Mrs. Nina Cooper?"

Joss and Paige had visited countless times. They held my hands and prayed over me. They cried tears of heartbreak with me. They mothered Ava and visited Max. Joss was working on getting him out, but it was all a mess and completely complicated. He wasn't arrested for murder; he was arrested as the primary suspect in Scarlett's missing persons case. Apparently, she did have someone who cared enough about her to call in. No one knew who—whether it was a professor or friend—but someone did. And my son was the only connection to her. I knew she wasn't missing; she was dead and buried under the play-set in our backyard. How did no one find her body?

Joss knew about Warren's affair with Scarlett, but it was too hard to prove since there was no evidence. The texts had all been cleaned, and there were no pictures to be found anywhere. It was as if Warren knew he'd have to die a saint.

"Mrs. Nina Cooper?" the detective repeated himself.

"Yes." I felt sick to my stomach being called that name.

"Your husband, Professor Warren Cooper..." he started and stopped. Sinking down into a stool, he ran his hand through his hair and looked at me carefully. "Your husband was found dead, ma'am." He sighed. "I'm so sorry. He was an incredible man, and a pillar of our community."

My eyes widened in shock. I began laughing at the outlandish statement.

Was he serious?

"He's a murderer. He murdered countless women; they are buried in our backyard. They are buried in the field where I was found. He buried me alive! He's not dead!" I shouted in disbelief.

"Mrs. Cooper, your son hasn't been arrested for just the disappearance of Scarlett. He's also been arrested because he… he, well…"

The detective paused and cleared his throat as if the simple gesture would buy him time to make whatever he was going to say more bearable. But, really, it only made it worse.

"He was the one who buried you alive. He's also the primary suspect in the deaths of the women buried next to you."

I would think that many mothers could agree with the fact that once you have a child, you become fearful of all the things that could happen to your child. Is this the flu or is it a symptom of some malignant cancer? Is this new relationship going to hurt them? Are they eating enough vegetables? Have they checked in? All the questions and fears consume you as a mother. But ultimately, it's up to your child to decide the path they will go down with their own lives.

It's also every parent's wish that their children will be the ones to bury them and not the other way around. My child, my son—the baby boy I cradled for hours on end and raised mostly on my own—tried to bury me alive. Well, he did. My son buried me alive. He left me to die.

I looked into the detective's eyes. "I don't believe you." Without hesitation, I breathed out and said, "It was Warren."

The detective nodded slowly and lifted his tablet. "There's a difference in wanting an outcome to be a certain way and what it actually is. I know it's easier to hope that your husband was the one who had inflicted all this pain on you and your family. But, Mrs. Cooper, your son, Max, is the one behind it all."

My heart sank as I looked at the tablet screen he was holding up for me.

"This was the two pieces of evidence we found hidden in Max's dorm."

My head felt heavy, but not nearly as heavy as my heart. It was an image of Max's varsity jacket and a shovel covered in dirt.

"Warren. He had so many photos of young women in his desk drawer at work. He…" I became frantic.

"Mrs. Cooper, I need you to calm down."

Anger grew inside me. If a man tells a woman to calm down, he is tempting his fate.

"Don't tell me to calm down. I know that this is all a huge misunderstanding. My son is innocent." I attempted to yank the IV wires out of my arm, but the detective quickly called out for the nurse and tried to settle my hand.

"Listen, I know it's unfair, I know. I'm a father, myself. But your son isn't going to stop. He's showing no remorse. Him being locked away is in everyone's best interest, but also in his own best interest."

"I want proof that Warren is actually dead."

The detective pursed his lips as he scrolled through his tablet. "Are you sure?" he asked me stupidly.

"Why would I tell you I wanted proof if I didn't really want it?" I sat up and waited.

"Mrs. Cooper, this just came in."

Handing me his tablet, I clutched it and looked down.

My stomach flipped as I felt acid rise in my throat.

Handing it back to him, I looked away.

It was an image of Warren's left hand. It still had his wedding ring on it and the small tattoo he had of the letter 'N'.

My husband was dead.

"They found other body parts, but we haven't had a

chance to confirm with DNA. We are hoping to find the body for you. I'm so sorry, ma'am."

I hated how my eyes grew wet. I hated how sadness began to replace the irritation and rage I felt searing through my body.

I hated how I couldn't believe I'd never see him again.

I hated myself in this moment, but most of all, I hated him for making me have these internal battles.

Laying down on the pillow, I closed my eyes and hoped that sleep or medication would turn my brain off so I'd have a break from them and myself.

CHAPTER FORTY

*A*dam opened the door of my lake house and helped me inside. I stayed silent the entire drive back from the hospital. Paige and Joss told me Ava was grieving over the loss of her father and feeling distraught over Max being in prison. Joss was busy working on Max's case, so Paige took over taking care of Ava, who had now delayed her trip back to London for the apparent funeral everyone assumed I was planning.

But I was numb. I felt like a terrible mother for not visiting my daughter or even my son. But I felt bitter; I felt rage and sadness collide, and I didn't want to have to then show them this version of myself. My children couldn't see that I was a normal, fucking human with emotions. They'd only ever known the mother who slapped a smile on her face with pearls wrapped around her neck.

I wanted to feel something, anything, but Warren stole that from me.

"I already ordered food. Are you sure you don't want to just stay at my place?" Adam asked. I studied him carefully as he helped me lay down on the sofa closest to the windows that overlooked the entire lake.

The way his gaze held mine had my heart racing.

My moronic, dead husband had my heart race regularly from anxiety and feeling like I was less than him, so this was different. This was...

Feeling something I hadn't felt in years.

My life was in shambles, but I stared at Adam as he carefully tucked the blanket around me and was talking.

I didn't hear him. I just watched his lips move.

"Adam..." I began.

"Yeah?" He paused whatever he was saying and sat beside me.

"Tomorrow I'm going to the morgue to identify my dead husband's body parts, and then I'm going to go visit my son in prison. After that, I'm going to pick up my daughter's anti-anxiety medication so she can cope with the shit-show our life has become. But today..." I paused as his eyes drifted to my lips. The gorgeous thirty-year-old in front of me looked at me in a way that made me feel completely beautiful.

"Today, I need you to show me that I'm still alive and can feel." I didn't know what had come over me. Perhaps an intense urge to feel something for myself that wasn't pain-inflicted by the husband and children I'd done everything for.

Adam didn't even think twice; he leaned it, tilted my chin with his index finger, and kissed me hard. His tongue crept into my mouth as I moaned with the how my lips tingled as he brushed his other hand under my skirt and under my panties.

"You're so perfect, baby," he groaned as I arched my back and his fingers went inside me.

Moments later, our clothes were piled on the floor and Adam lifted me in his arms. I was sitting on his forearms as he pressed me against the windows over-looking the lake.

"Nina, you were always meant to be mine," he whispered against my ear as he bit at my earlobe. My entire body tensed as he slid me slightly lower so he could push himself inside me.

"Ah," I bit down into his neck as he pumped himself faster. My toes curled as chills grew and finally, my release overtook every ounce of my body.

"Fuck." Adam felt me clench and tighten around him, and he let go.

"Adam…" I sighed as he carefully took me to the sofa and laid us both down.

He kissed my eyelids, the tip of my nose, and then my lips.

I could feel something. I was alive. Opening my eyes, I looked into his and smiled sadly. "Thank you."

Breathing out, Adam brushed his thumb against my lips. "You only say thank you when it's one-sided. Baby, this isn't one-sided. You are perfect. You…" He pressed his forehead against mine.

"Adam, my life is a disaster." He held me in his arms as we looked out at the lake and the gloomy sky that hung low over it.

"We're going to fix it." He pressed his lips to the top of my head and for a moment, I believed him.

CHAPTER FORTY-ONE

*I*t's amazing what an orgasm and coffee can do for the soul. It can be the difference between letting your husband live an extra day or not. For me, I no longer had that option to choose if he'd get to live. My heels clicked against the yellow-tiled floor as I clutched my purse to my chest. I was going to see Max, and then I'd have to go identify body parts.

Only one of those two tasks had me feeling sadness.

"Hey, sweetie." Joss was standing by the door, wearing a pale-blue suit. She handed me a cup of coffee and sipped her own.

"He's going to be so happy to see you. But just remember, stay calm and let him talk. Don't…"

"I know. I won't be overbearing." I looked at her

and reached out to grab her arm for a moment. "Joss, is the case against him getting stronger?" The suffocating anxiety began to resurface and put a chokehold around me.

She nodded and dropped her eyes to the floor. "Yes. But... there's also something else building on the side that I can't talk to you about right now." She took another long sip of coffee before walking away. Following behind her, the clicking of my heels echoed as the stench of burnt coffee floated around us.

"What? For who? Did they ever find out who the dead bodies in the ground were? Did they ever find out who was buried in my backyard? By the play-set?" I started rambling and Joss slapped her hand over my mouth.

"You have to stop, Nina. Please. If you want to spiral, do it with Paige, but not with me right now. Right now, I have to be your attorney. But I love you." She was looking all around us and the clear panic in her eyes worried me even more.

"Okay, okay," I said under her palm, moving it off my lips.

Standing outside of the door, it buzzed and we walked in.

I had never visited someone in prison before. I didn't even know where the local prison was. Ever since marrying Warren, I lived in what I thought was a safe, suburban bubble, but it couldn't have been farther from the truth.

"Mom—" His voice broke me. What was it about the simple shift in how that one name was said that made every mother know exactly what place their child was in.

Max was afraid.

"Max." The frown on my face immediately flipped into a small smile. "Hi, sweetheart," I said under a hushed tone.

Joss choked back her own impending sobs as she stood in the corner and watched us. I pulled my chair out and sat across from the child I gave life to. Handcuffs were digging into his skin and attached to the table. With one glance, I saw his feet were also chained.

"Mom, I'm sorry. I'm so sorry, Mama. I didn't do that to you."

Another shift. Another shift in the way he said my name.

Max was apprehensive.

But most of all, I knew Max was innocent.

"I know you didn't." My son didn't bury me alive. I knew that, but I also knew, deep down, that there could be a small chance that everything I thought was wrong.

"Honey, Joss is going to get you out, but I need to ask you what happened to Scarlett?"

"I don't know. I swear, I... I didn't do anything to her. I didn't do anything to those other women, either." I looked back at Joss, who stood listening carefully as if she'd already heard it all before.

"Max, I love you. You're going to be okay," I lied to my anxious son, who was staring pleadingly into my eyes.

"Are you eating?"

Max looked at me, his eyes glistening. "No. The food is terrible, and I've been feeling sick." He paused. "Aunt Joss, how much longer until I'm out?"

Joss took a deep breath in and brushed her face with her hand. "Max, this is my most complicated case. There's a photo of you wearing your varsity jacket and baseball hat with Scarlett, and that was the last photo of her taken. You are the only one she was seen with."

"That's not true. There had to be video footage of her with..." I froze. My son didn't know that his father was sleeping with the girl he was dating.

Tears streamed down Max's face.

"I love her, Aunt Joss. I wouldn't have hurt her. I

want her to be found." Max looked back at me. "Mom, you know I didn't…"

I nodded, even though my heart was breaking as I watched my teenage son get tangled into a web of deception and pain his father had weaved.

"Time's up." The security guard reached for Max aggressively and I stood and tried to intervene, but Joss quickly grabbed my arm.

"Let's go." She widened her eyes at me. "Tell him you love him, and that everything is going to be okay." She nudged me. She knew I was a mess and would regret not saying those things to my son before I left.

"Max! I love you and everything is going to be okay. I promise." He looked over his shoulder at me and a blanket of peace wrapped around him before the door slammed shut.

I followed Joss outside the room and stopped in my tracks. Planting one hand against the wall, I shook as panic raced through me. Sliding down against the wall, I hugged my knees to my chest and began sobbing.

Warren had covered his tracks. He had cleared everything and thought of it all.

"The bodies in my backyard…" I whispered through the tears. "It was Scarlett. Her red hair…" I stared blankly at the ground.

"Honey, they searched everything. There were no bodies in the backyard. But yes, there were bodies uncovered where you were buried. The problem is, it's too soon for us to get all the DNA testing in, and until then... well, Max is going to be here. He's the primary, and worst of all, only suspect."

"They also found that some evidence was tampered with. Someone took the varsity jacket from the canoe Collins was in, and they think they gave it back to Max."

The only person who knew about the jacket being Max's was Adam and Warren. I didn't tell Joss this—I couldn't risk her being obligated to share a detail that could pin Max to Collins as well.

"Are you ready to go into the room to identify..." Joss trailed.

"Yeah." I followed her down the long, narrow hallways. The lights were flickering and buzzing as the temperature dropped the closer we got to the morgue.

Death hung around us as the medical examiner talked to me, but I didn't hear a word. I walked through the door, and in the middle was a shiny, steel operating table. But there wasn't a body covered by a sheet; instead, there were a few small lumps underneath smaller white sheets that looked more like pillowcases.

The stench of formaldehyde and bleach immediately twisted my stomach. Lifting one sheet, the medical examiner asked me if I recognized it.

My eyes stung as I saw a hand with the wedding band I had slid onto it over twenty years ago. The small tattooed 'N' was easily recognizable.

"Yes. That's his hand," I choked out as Joss turned away and clutched her abdomen.

A bag was lifted next, filled with dark brown hair with streaks of silver in it. "Yes. It looks like his hair," I confirmed, although it could have been anyone's.

"This is the last of what the police found, but it's a watch and clothing that was found in the water."

I looked through it all, then leaned in, flipped the watch over, and sighed. It was his watch. The inscription 'til the end of time. W + N' was still on it from our twentieth anniversary. A Rolex, the gift I was so excited to give him.

"Yes. It all belonged to him." I was asked to sign some documents, and the medical examiner offered a dry apology for my loss.

He's probably said the same line countless times and had no emotion attached to it anymore. It was okay, considering I had no emotion attached to it either, beyond rage.

I wanted to watch the life leave those pale, icy-blue

eyes that once captivated me. I wanted to watch him beg for his life with the same lips that once trailed over my entire body. I wanted to kill my husband. But instead, he took that pleasure away from me. It made sense, considering he never could pleasure me in any sense.

"Are you okay?" Joss laced her arm into mine as we walked out of the building and into the parking lot. It was chillier than usual. The leaves were falling with the gusts of wind cutting through the trees. The sun was hidden behind gloomy, thick clouds that teased rain showers.

"I need to save Max."

We slid into the car and Joss turned to me. "You started telling Max about video footage from somewhere linked to Scarlett? What were you talking about?" she asked me curiously.

"Adam and I went to the inn, and Warren was there. I think Scarlett was with him, too." I rubbed my temples as the pounding headache seared through my scalp.

"That's really good information. I'll text my guy and see if we can retrieve the information."

"But, Joss, there was a redhead buried in my backyard. It had to be her. I saw Warren and... Max burying her."

"Well, then Max is guilty for something, Nina. We have to be careful what we reveal. You need to remember to take emotion out of this."

"I just texted my guy, and he'll head over and check the footage. Until then, lay low and keep quiet," Joss warned me.

I knew she was right. I was going to go spend time with Paige and Ava and be forced to plan my husband's funeral.

CHAPTER FORTY-TWO

*A*va and I sat outside, looking at the darkened lake that rippled in front of us. The fire-pit was crackling as she lifted the burnt marshmallow, and I handed her graham crackers.

We were home. I picked her up from Paige's house and assured her that we needed some time, just the two of us, to finally unpack everything that had happened.

She cried over the loss of her father. Although she was certain he had done something to the missing and dead girls, she also loved him fiercely and the good memories were overtaking the ones filled with fear.

"He could have gotten help." She looked at me with tears dripping down her pink cheeks.

"Ava, baby, your dad killed those girls. There's no doubt in my mind."

"Then why is Max in jail? He helped Dad. What if… what if he asked Dad for help?" She wiped at her face before taking a bite of the gooey s'more.

"Why would your dad help Max kill innocent girls?"

"Because Max…" She quickly slammed her lips closed and looked away.

"Because Max, what? Ava?" I sat up and tugged the fuzzy blanket tighter around my body.

"Nothing. I shouldn't have—"

"Ava, if you know anything, you have to tell me. It's the only way we can help your brother." I watched as my daughter anxiously peeled the glittery blue polish off her fingers.

"He was obsessed with Collins back in high school. Then, he was obsessed with Scarlett in college."

"I saw your dad and Max…" I couldn't believe I was having this conversation with my nineteen-year-old daughter.

"What?" Ava shuddered as she tugged the strings of her hoodie tighter.

"I saw them bury a body in our backyard. But no one can find the body and no one believes me."

Ava looked at me with confusion. "Didn't they find

another two bodies next to you in the dirt out in the field?"

"Yes, but I swear I saw... I saw them. I went down there, and it was a red-headed girl."

Ava sank back into the chair and grew silent as the fire surged between us. The shadows danced all around us as she looked at the lake.

"I think Dad was helping Max because he didn't want him to get caught. I think Max is dangerous, and I think Dad died because of his stupidity."

"Ava, I thought you were scared of your dad? I think he might have even killed his first wife." Everything was becoming a blur and nothing made sense anymore.

"Mom... you really don't remember, do you?"

A shiver shot up my spine as the fire began to fizzle out and a glimmer reflected against Ava's face.

"We can't run from the killer, Mama. It's always following us. Chasing us. Stalking us." A rustle in the bushes had me jump as I looked back at Ava, who was now standing and walking toward the dock.

"Ava?" I threw the blanket off and followed her down. The chill in the air had my entire body shake as I followed her, but she picked up her pace.

"Ava! Stop!" I screamed after her as she lifted her arms to dive into the freezing water.

"How can you not remember, Mama? You started all of this," she cried out and turned toward me. Grabbing my arm, she tugged me closer to the edge.

"She's down there." Ava pointed into the opaque water.

I crept closer to the edge and stared down.

"Who?" I blew out.

"The killer and the victim."

"Ava…" I turned to my daughter, whose face was draining of blood. "Who is the killer?"

"Look at the water, Nina." Her tone was intense and my heart was rapidly beating against my chest as I turned back and looked into the water near her side. A single duck swam away as Ava spoke.

The only thing I could see was a girl in the reflection.

That girl being Ava.

"No, look forward!" Ava shouted, and I shifted my gaze to my own reflection.

"There! There she is!" Ava cried out.

"Ava…" I shook my head. "Baby, what is happening." Tears pooled in my eyes as I shook from the cold breeze that had picked up, causing ripples in the lake.

"You started all this, Nina. But Daddy loved it because you finally helped him find his story."

I began sobbing as Ava wrapped her arms around me. "No, no, I didn't…"

"You killed my dad's first wife, but you also killed my mother." Ava let go of me and walked away as I collapsed and the worn wooden dock pricked at my kneecaps.

I couldn't stop crying. I couldn't see anything in the darkness, and finally, I just closed my eyes.

CHAPTER FORTY-THREE

TWENTY-FOUR YEARS AGO

"Warren! How could you do this to me?" Her voice cracked through the heat of the moment like a leather whip, startling us both. I shoved him off my body as I frantically grabbed my dress and ducked behind his desk.

"We have children!" she screamed and guilt seared through me as I saw little black-and-white images of their family decorate his dark blue bookshelves.

"You said you were plotting your book. You said the kids were too loud, and I needed to take them out! This is what you were doing? Screwing what... a student?"

I clutched my knees to my naked body as I scooted back under Warren's desk. We usually never had sex at his house—just in his office on campus or an occasional night at a hotel.

"Jackie, I need you to calm down," Warren said in his low, unphased voice that I knew would cause his already distressed wife to lose it.

"You want me to *calm down?*" she screeched so loudly, I clasped my hands over my ears and closed my eyes.

Shame and guilt rampaged through me. I had never met her before; I had never seen her. All I knew about Jackie Cooper was that she was Warren's wife.

I was a nineteen-year-old college student who had terrible relationships with guys my own age and was tempted by the older, mature professor who smirked at me in a way that had my heart race. The way he'd talk to me about art and books with such zest and excitement, while the other guys I dated just wanted to go out to parties.

I fell in love with him hard and fast, even though I knew he'd eventually break my heart. This was the moment when I realized he wouldn't be the one breaking it... she would.

"Oh, get out from your hiding spot, you little tramp!" Jackie yelled as Warren quickly moved toward her to stop her from coming around the desk. I quickly fixed my dress, cringing at how my lace thong was too far away to reach.

Sliding out slowly and holding my breath, I wrapped my arms around myself and looked at her.

Jackie Cooper was beautiful; she was exactly who I had envisioned a man like Warren to be married to. Silky, straight brown hair, minimal makeup, and a simple white T-shirt tucked into a long maxi skirt.

Her face dropped when she looked at me. "How long?" She looked between Warren and me.

"How long have you been fucking my husband?" Jackie looked straight into my eyes.

They say youth is wasted on the young, and I suppose this was the moment when I realized why. I knew I shouldn't have been standing in between a married couple in their home with my lingerie strewn across the floor their children probably ran on.

I shouldn't have been sneaking around, believing Warren's lies that we'd be together one day.

But I did. I threw away my youth on a much older man who had already lived an entire lifetime. He saw me as disposable 'fun', and I saw him as a man I wanted to be with and create a future beside. "Why would he leave his wife for you when you're already giving him what he wants without any strings?" I remember my friend telling me when I cried over him.

"Since I was a freshman," I whispered full of shame as Warren slowly walked up to Jackie.

"Get the hell away from me, asshole," she shouted at him.

"Nina, will you please go out to the dock. I'll drive you home. I just need to talk to my wife privately."

My entire world felt fuzzy, and tears stung my eyes as embarrassment sucked me in.

Jackie pinched her lips as tears rolled down her cheeks.

I was too far from school to walk and, considering I had left my wallet back in my dorm, I had no money for a ride. So, I did as I was told and made my way to the back dock.

It felt like an eternity as I waited outside. I could see the outlines of Jackie and Warren through the seamless glass as they fought.

I walked to the edge of the dock and clutched myself tightly. This was it; I was never going to see Warren again. I was in love with him, and my heart ached as the pain of a break-up cut through me.

It was irrational, it was wrong, but it happened, and I couldn't change that.

Footsteps sounded behind me as I cried softly, knowing Warren was coming to end things for good with me.

Looking to the side, I saw the shadow. The thing about shadows is that they are deceiving—they let us feel larger and more powerful, and they follow us, reminding us that we can never escape one person... and that person is ourselves.

"How could you?" Her voice was hoarse as I flung around in shock. Her mascara was streaking down her cheeks as she looked at me with rage.

"I-I'm so s-sorry," I stammered, taking a step back, even though I was already teetering on the edge of the dock.

"You know we have two children, right? He loves me..." Jackie had a wild look in her eyes. "Warren loves me and is just confused.".

"Mrs. Cooper, I'm sorry." I felt humiliated calling her that. I felt humiliated just being here.

"Where is... Warren?" I looked behind her, not seeing him through the glass or outside.

She froze in her spot and tilted her head with a small smile growing on her face. One hand was tucked behind her back as she pursed her lips.

Slowly moving her hand from her back, she revealed a giant butcher knife covered in blood.

"Oh my gosh," I gasped.

"Warren!" I screamed loudly as I looked around and she walked closer.

"Please, I'm only nineteen. I'm sorry. I..."

She waved the blade in the air, slicing through it without a second doubt. I was screaming loudly as I tried to dodge her, but within seconds, she had sliced my arm.

The pain seared through me as I cried hysterically, knowing I had to jump into the blackened lake water.

She wouldn't stop, there wasn't an inch of space between us as she jammed the blade into my hand before pulling it out and laughing hysterically. I yelled as the pain burned into my body and slammed my eyes shut before jumping into the cold water.

I didn't know how to swim in water I couldn't reach the bottom of.

Jackie was shouting at me as I tried to float on my back and that's when I noticed the small canoe at the end of the dock.

I just had to get on it. I could do this.

"You little bitch! I'm going to kill you!" She looked around, and just as I reached my bloodied hand onto the wooden canoe, she tried to jump in but couldn't. I tugged it quickly, using it as a life raft and kicked my feet as hard as I could, gulping down large amounts of lake water.

Coughing and choking as the water grew around my chin and lips, I pulled myself into the canoe and grabbed the paddle, but I was too late. Jackie had jumped in and was swimming with ease toward me. I tried to jam the paddle into the water and put some distance between us, but between my nerves and the lack of knowledge of how to even swim or use a canoe, I knew I wasn't going to make it.

"Nina!" His voice shocked me as I looked at the dock.

Jackie stopped swimming and followed my line of vision as Warren clutched his bleeding abdomen.

"Jackie, stop it!" he shouted. But it only fueled more rage in her, and she kept swimming with her eyes locked on me.

"Hit her with the paddle, Nina!" he screamed. I was in a daze, completely soaked and freezing cold.

"Nina! Hit her with the paddle," Warren yelled again. Lifting the paddle, I looked at the frenzied woman in front of me, who was now climbing into the canoe, digging the blade into it, and I knew I'd be next.

Closing my eyes, I lifted the paddle and with all the force I had, I slammed the wooden paddle into her head and heard a crack.

I had hit her skull.

Blood immediately began pooling from her scalp, dribbling down her face as she looked at me with sadness.

"You'll never run from the killer." Letting go of the canoe, she sank into the lake, leaving nothing but blood behind.

I gasped and dropped the paddle with realization overtaking me.

Sobbing hysterically, I clasped my mouth and looked back at the dock.

But Warren wasn't alone; a little girl was standing in his shadows, looking at me curiously.

"Wow, that was amazing." She tilted her head and smiled. She began to clap softly with her small hands.

Warren looked down at her and brushed his hand across her head as blood continued to stain his shirt.

"Ava... you can never tell anyone about this." He shook his head.

"I'll miss mommy, but I have a new mommy now. She's prettier." She smiled as she wiggled her small fingers at me. Tucked under one arm was a doll with all the hair on her head completely shaved off.

My vision grew clouded as I cried harder.

What had we done?

CHAPTER FORTY-FOUR

gulped down air as I opened my eyes with the memories flooding back to me. All the years Warren would sit me down and put me through intensive therapy to help me forget. To make me replace what I knew with a false reality.

I was so young and terrified. He knew my darkest secret, and so did Ava. I killed her mother right in front of her eyes, and her reaction shook me to my core.

This was all my fault. Max was younger, so it was easier for me to replace his mother without much of a second thought.

At nineteen, I went from a carefree college student to a wife and mother. But not only that, I became a murderer.

I glanced over my shoulder and saw the light flicker inside. Standing, my legs trembled as I made my way up the dock. I had to get to Ava. I had wrecked her. I had to save her. I was her mother.

Sliding the glass door open, the light kept flashing and as soon as my feet hit the wood, it completely shut off.

The sudden darkness had me clutch the console table as I made my way to the light panel.

I flipped each switch, but no light would turn on. My heart-rate quickened as the scurrying of footsteps echoed nearby.

I swallowed the lump in my throat as my palms grew moist. "Ava?"

Making my way to the stairwell, I gripped the banister.

"Ava, sweetie? I'm so sorry for everything, but we need to talk," I called out with a clear quiver in my words.

I walked up to the hallway and froze in front of her door before placing my palm against the wood and slowly opening it.

Her small lamp was on and there she was, deep asleep.

Sighing, I wiped at the tears under my eyes and knew I needed to sleep. I was delirious. We'd deal with everything in the morning. I made my way back downstairs to lock the house up, but as I passed Warren's office, I stopped in front of the archway.

I hadn't processed his death yet, and part of me didn't want to. I didn't want to give him a second thought. He had manipulated me, made me repress one of the most traumatizing events in my life. But I also knew in some sick way, I appreciated that he hadn't turned me in. I would have been in jail for homicide. The life before Warren's affairs, Max being arrested, dead girls showing up all allowed me to live obliviously.

Walking into Warren's office, the scent of his cologne taunted me as I brushed my fingers against his desk.

Closing my eyes, I could see flashbacks of me on it, my legs spread wide as my head tossed back and his fingers gripping my hips, plunging deep inside me. How he made me feel beautiful and wanted, even as the girl who was on financial aid and had no family or real friends.

But it was all wrong. I was young and naïve, but he should have known better. We both should have.

Jackie didn't deserve to die. Ava and Max didn't deserve this life—a fake life that their father and his mistress had staged for them.

Karma was at play, ripping through this home. Sinking into Warren's desk chair, I stared down at the laptop he had spent a lifetime working on.

He never saw his dream come true as an author.

I opened his laptop and searched through the word documents for his manuscript. 'DBT' was the only one that was an acronym, so I clicked it.

'DBT by Warren Cooper'. I began reading, even though my body was desperate for sleep.

A husband, a wife, two teenage children, and a lake house. Every single description matched us—our lives, our secrets.

"What is this?" I breathed out as I quickly skimmed chapter by chapter as the hours ticked away. My mouth grew dry as my chest tightened.

DBT by Warren Cooper - Chapter 18

As men, we aren't destined to be monogamous. We are destined to explore, to relish, and to enjoy multiple women. My wife was no longer the young, beautiful, energetic woman she once was, and I craved the touch and feeling of someone who was less experienced and needed me to guide them.

Cora was perfect. She was young and vibrant, yet shy and nervous. She needed me to make her feel confident, and I did. I pinned her to the wall of my office, I laid her flat on my desk, and turned her around in my martial bed. But then, my daughter walked in on us in the worst possible position.

Anger flooded her soft eyes as she feared I'd replace her mother, again.

But I always knew Alex had demons inside her and needed to hunt and kill the way a wild animal needs to in the middle of the woods.

I found a solution. I couldn't have these young women fawning over me, asking me for more, threatening to tell my wife or the university.

That's what Cora did; she begged me to love her. *Stupid girl.* I didn't love her; I loved her tight body and the way she would drop everything and let me use her.

Now, it was time to dispose of her.

And best of all, I didn't have to do it myself. Alex, my sweet little girl, needed to cleanse her soul.

So, I told her to unleash the suffocating wrath and fury she felt since she was a small child witnessing a trauma so great.

She thought it was beautiful when her mother was beat to death by a paddle, and that's when I knew she was special.

I watched her from afar as she tricked Cora to go on a canoe ride with her. I watched my daughter slide into her brother's varsity jacket, tie her hair up, and put on his baseball cap. She was brilliant. Matt, my son, didn't have the intelligence or strength to be a true man. He was a pathetic excuse of a Carlton, much too sensitive and emotional.

I scoffed at the thought of him. My grandfather and father would be ashamed. We were raised to know women were inferior to us. Women were there for our pleasure, and they didn't deserve the same respect as men.

But my daughter... she was different. She was a stronger force. She had the violence and rage the Carlton men were embedded with.

Cora was laughing with Alex in the canoe. They were drinking seltzers, and I will never forget the way Alex turned over her shoulder and winked at me.

I shuddered with excitement knowing that she was mine, and she was about to witness the way life would flee the eyes of this girl in front of her.

Cora thought I wanted her to bond with Alex.

Stupid, stupid girl.

And just like that, I watched my daughter clutch the compass in her hand that my father had given me, and I had now given to Alex. She brushed her finger over it, feeling the same power I had felt. I had to make her promise me she wouldn't stab or leave marks. She was upset by it all, but we had to make it look like an accidental drowning.

Alex handed Cora the wine seltzer she had laced, and just like that, Cora became incoherent and once she did, Alex shoved her body over the boat and into the darkened waters. It was so simple.

She watched her drown, but unfortunately, Alex didn't stay long enough to make sure she didn't resurface. The stupid bitch came up and managed to get to shore.

But she didn't survive, and Alex was pleased—so was I. Together, we made the best team.

Alex didn't want to stop. Her next target was Sara, the gorgeous redhead I had actually developed feelings for. Sara was Matt's girlfriend, and sadly, my son didn't know how to fulfill her needs. The girl threw herself at me without a second thought.

But Alex hated Sara, hated the way she betrayed her brother. She hated the way I looked at her, and she knew I was in love with Sara. She knew it was only a matter of time before Sara replaced my wife, Nancy.

The only mother Alex had ever known. And Nancy was a good mother, but I was bored of her. I loved how Sara was so insecure and needy. I loved the way she looked at me as the intelligent, worthy man that I was.

My wife looked at me with annoyance and irritation. She let our marriage wither away—the same way she did with her body and appearance.

I didn't want to do what I had to. No, I wasn't a monster, but Alex was hunting Sara. She couldn't stop.

So, I found another redhead—a young woman who resembled her. I drugged her, pinned her down, and bashed her face in.

I presented her to Alex and let her stab her as many times as she wanted to. I watched my daughter laugh and shriek with excitement when blood splattered everywhere as she cut the girl's flesh.

We had to dig shallow graves under the play-set, just temporarily, until we could throw the bodies into our own graveyard out by Wimberly Pointe.

Sara knew my plan. She saw the same future with me that I had seen. Once she told me how my wife had hired her to deceive me in order to divorce me, I knew I had to outsmart her. I had to ruin her. I transferred all my money into the offshore accounts, I had Sara fly out first, and then…

Well, I had to stage my own death. It was painful, sure, chopping my hand off, but it needed to go. The tattoo of my wife's name and wedding band had tarnished it enough.

William Carlton was now dead and so was Sara. And now, we'd finally be together.

Matt, my worthless son, would be forced to man up in prison. Alex thought she could live her life and still be with the mother she loved dearly. She assumed Nancy was just like her.

A born killer.

I had to bury Nancy since she knew too much. I gave her company, though, with the other girls her daughter had already killed. But Alex was furious; she took her mother's lover and found her just in time.

That was disappointing. Though, I suppose children will always do that... become disappointments.

CHAPTER FORTY-FIVE

*M*y heart was crashing through my chest as my eyes and mind tried to process each word, each chapter, and every detail.

Warren had written every single murder out in detail; he had written out his affairs and everything that had been happening to our family.

He used our daughter as a character in his book? He had used her mental illness and criminal behavior as a plot for his thriller novel? Were Warren and Scarlett really alive? Somewhere out there, living a beautiful life on a tropical island, while he left me to die in the ground. Was Ava truly a sociopathic murderer?

I looked up at the ceiling and heard creaking.

Standing slowly, I lifted the mail cutter and began

walking back toward the stairs but stopped in my place.

"Mommy?"

I puffed out a breath and slowly turned, tucking the mail cutter into my pocket.

Ava was standing there in a short white gown, covered in red. Her voice changed into one that resembled a toddler.

"Mommy, I want to show you a painting I made for you…" She lifted a paintbrush up in the air and slowly smiled with her eyes completely desolate.

"Ava…" I covered my mouth and quivered as she grew closer.

"Please, Mommy?" She reached her hand out to me. I knew I had to go with her. This was all my fault. I had ruined her life and created a monster because of my sins.

"Okay, baby…" The fear was clear in my voice as I put my hand in hers. The slimy, red substance coated them as she clutched my hand tighter.

I begrudgingly walked behind her as the stairs creaked beneath my tired, bare feet.

"I've worked really hard on this for you." Ava turned toward my art room and opened the door. The doorknob was stained red and the chills that scoured my arms were growing all over my legs.

A small lamp was turned on and beside it, was a large canvas on my easel. Streaks of various shades of red and a deep burgundy were disordered all over it.

"Mommy, what do you think?" Ava opened her arms wide as if she were a game show model.

"It's... Ava, what paint did you use?" I rolled my lips together as her face lit up in a bright smile.

"From there." She pointed at the back corner behind me. I was terrified to turn around, so I just nodded.

"Turn around, Mommy!" Ava shouted, startling me and causing me to fling around.

"No!" I screamed so loudly, my voice started to taper out as I ran to her.

"Joss!" My best friend was crumpled in the corner, laying in a pool of her own blood.

I pulled her into my arms as my knees dipped into her blood.

"This one is from Collins. This one is from Scarlett." I cried into my best friend's lifeless body as I looked back at Ava. She was lifting jars full of blood wildly as the liquid splashed out.

"I've been storing each one carefully." She pointed at the small mini-fridge.

"Ava..." I threw my head back and cried as I ran my hands through Joselin's hair.

"She had to go, Mommy. She knew too much. She figured out it wasn't Max, but it was me..." Ava frowned over-dramatically and did a small twirl as she lifted the paintbrush and stroked the canvas. Paint... no, blood, splattering across the white carpet.

"Ava, I need to call for help." I began coughing as the saliva in my mouth thickened.

"She's dead." Ava paused and smiled at me.

My body was breaking, my heart was shattered, and my mind was frail.

"So, Mommy. I'm thinking we just go away together. You and me. Dad set an account for me in the Bahamas. We can go there and start fresh." She sat on the floor and pulled out a doll from a chest.

The doll. The doll Warren had a photo of on his computer. The doll Ava held the day I accidentally killed her mother. But the doll was no longer bald; she had multiple shades of braids taped on.

Looking at Joss, I realized a patch of her hair was cut off, and Ava was now braiding it and taping it onto the doll.

"Are those... locks of hair from..."

Ava looked at me happily and nodded excitedly. My stomach tumbled as fear shook through my body.

"Every single lock is from someone we killed. But I leave a butterfly clip in their hair so they can still feel pretty." She smiled as she stroked the strands. I looked down at Joss and saw the small, pink clip.

"It was beautiful, Mommy. Watching the life leave their eyes. Daddy even thought so." Ava smiled with satisfaction.

"Is your dad still alive?" I whispered.

Ava shook her head. "Nope. After he let me kill Scarlett, I think he felt regret or something, and he killed himself. Really sad though, because we got some really good scenes out of it," she added and spun in the chair.

"Scenes?"

"Mm-hmm... Daddy had writer's block and would sit by me as I killed the girls who tried to replace you, and he'd write out what I was doing. How I was killing them and torturing them. He called it a beautiful art-form." Ava beamed. "See? I'm an artist, just like you, Mommy."

"We just didn't have the final scene."

My head grew lighter as I looked at the teenager I had raised as my own. The little girl with pigtails who I swore I'd take care of.

"What was the final scene?" My lips trembled.

A loud knock on the door sounded downstairs. "Nina?" His voice was loud.

Adam.

"Nina?" he shouted again.

"Nina, open the door!" Adam banged on the front door, but Ava put her finger across her lips.

"Ava, baby… please. We can get help. We can get you help," I whimpered.

"No. He will go away and then we will leave, Mommy. We won't stay here." Ava sounded so young, her voice was just like it was all those years ago.

Moving closer to me, she brushed her sticky fingers across my cheeks. "My prettiest mommy."

"Nina?" His voice grew closer. He was inside the house.

Ava looked up angrily. "How did he get into our house?" She became frantic. "If you tell him anything, I'll kill myself." She lifted the sharp blade I didn't see from the easel and rested it against her throat.

My eyes widened. "No… no," I chanted quietly.

"Ava, listen to me. You have to hide. I'm going to go see him, and I'll get rid of him, okay?" I nodded and prayed she'd calm down.

"Pinky promise, Mommy?" She looked terrified. I had failed her in so many ways. I couldn't save Max, especially with Joss gone, and now, Ava…

"I pinky promise." I jolted up as Joss laid in her

own blood. My legs trembled as I stood and felt off-balanced.

"Adam?" I called out with my voice raspy.

"Nina! Where are you?" He seemed to be out back.

"I'm coming down! Just give me a minute." I raced to my bedroom and looked at myself in the mirror. I was covered in my best friend's blood. A woman who I considered a sister, and I couldn't even grieve. I had to be in survival mode.

"Is anyone else home? Nina, I know..." Adam shouted back.

"No, no, it's just me. Stay there. I'll be down."

Wildly, I rushed and washed my hands as the red drained into the sink. Flinging my clothes off, I took a wet towel and swiped at my skin before grabbing the thick robe and tugging it over my bare body. Sprinting down in a haze, I was out of breath by the time I got to the end of the stairs.

As soon as I turned the corner, I ran straight into him.

But it wasn't Adam.

It was Warren.

"Warren?" I jerked back from his hands. Or... hand.

One was missing and the other held a gun.

"Hi, sweetheart," he whispered with a grin.

"Where is Adam?" My voice cracked as I stared at the ghost of the man I once loved.

"Oh, baby, you're still thinking some thirty-year-old man is interested in you?" He let out a dry laugh as he shoved the gun into my abdomen.

"Adam left. I saw him leave just as I pulled in. Probably had a hot date with a younger, sexier woman."

"Warren, what have you done to our family? Our children?" I broke down into tears.

"No, Nina. No, no, no! *You* did this. *You* did this to us. *You* broke my family by killing my wife. You were supposed to be a slut I could fuck and forget." Warren's brows knitted together as he put his finger on the trigger.

"I hope you die a miserable death." I seethed as I bumped into the stairwell.

"I already died, baby. Wasn't it so sad that you got nothing?" He laughed. "You would never, ever get a dime from me. This house is one week away from being sold by my beneficiary."

"Ava?" I tilted my head. Exhaustion and fear made my body feel even weaker than it already was.

"No, my wife, Scarlett. Well, Sara... We had to change her name, which was fitting." He smiled proudly.

Scarlett was still alive. The redhead in the ground

was an innocent girl staged to show Scarlett was dead, too. No one would look for her or Warren.

"She's not your wife, you idiot. I am," I spat out.

"That's why I'm here. This is the end of your chapter, sweetheart."

"You're sick, Warren. This isn't your book and this isn't a fictional story, this is our lives. You are ruining Ava and Max's lives!"

"I needed the final scene. The ending." He cocked the gun. "I didn't know what I wanted it to be, but now this is perfect." He laughed loudly, shaking me to my core.

"Daddy?" We both flung around and saw Ava at the top of the stairs.

"Ava, honey…"

"You… you were supposed to be dead." Ava walked down the stairs and looked around at the mostly darkened house.

"Why are you pointing a gun to pretty mommy? You tried to bury her alive. You hurt her." She sounded childish with the anger and panic blending together.

Warren lifted the gun and pointed it at Ava. "Stop right there, you insane little girl," he said with spite.

Ava's mouth dropped before she sprinted down the rest of the stairs, and just as she was about to jump at him, Warren fired.

"No!" I screamed and tried to block her, but it was too late. Ava fell to the floor like a rag doll. Dropping to my knees, I began sobbing as I held her in my arms.

"FBI! Put your weapon down! Everyone down!" Voices roared through the once joyous lake house.

Warren started to run and wildly fired the gun, but not even a minute later, he was shot down.

The agent ran toward him while others held guns and came closer to us, while the rest stormed upstairs. The entire house was swarmed with FBI agents within seconds, and my mind was lagging, trying to process it all.

Lifting his helmet off of his face, he leaned down to me. I clutched Ava's wound as tightly as I could as she looked at me desolately.

I looked up in shock. "Adam?"

"Medic, medic!" he yelled before crouching to Ava and looking at her wounds. His eyes reached mine. "It's going to be okay, I promise." He nodded as medics raced in and lifted Ava from my arms. My ears were ringing from the gunshots.

"Joss is upstairs. She's gone," I cried as he held me in his arms.

"You're a cop?" I whimpered into his chest.

"FBI. I... I wanted to tell you, Nina. I didn't mean for us to..."

Shaking my head, I lifted my finger against his lips. "Don't." I sobbed into his chest and let him hold me as the home I once loved with all my heart became a morgue.

CHAPTER FORTY-SIX

ONE YEAR LATER

"Are you sure you want to read it?"

I tightened my cardigan around myself as the wind picked up.

"Yes." I offered a tight-line smile back at him.

He handed me the thick stack of papers that were neatly bound by a ring before sinking into the rocking chair beside me.

"Thank you, Adam." I looked into the soft, patient eyes of the man who helped me piece myself back together over the course of the worst year of my life. The man who slept beside me, even though I woke up multiple times screaming while living through nightmares. The man who touched me in the way that reminded me I was alive. The man who never made me feel less than.

He came into our lives to build a case against Warren after countless young women in the area were turning up dead. Every single year there was a different girl—whether she was a student from an online class he offered or a summer session or even a full-time student—but it was always the same. He'd have sex with them, captivate them, and make them believe they'd be loved by him, but in the end, he'd make sure Ava saw them and he'd trigger her. Trigger her to believe that he might fall for them and replace me.

I was Ava's security blanket. I didn't know why, considering I was a huge reason she was battling a never-ending demon inside her. I was the reason Max spent five months in jail before Adam finally was able to get him out with enough evidence.

Warren was in the same in-patient mental health facility that Ava was in, though they were on separate floors. The asshole plead insanity, and his lawyers made it seem that he became so consumed by his novel, that he began living it out.

But hadn't he?

He'd write out each violent scene Ava was creating while she was murdering innocent girls after being manipulated by her father.

He'd write a chapter and make sure we all played the right character.

Flipping to the final chapter, I took a deep breath and began to read.

DBT BY WARREN COOPER

DBT – Warren Cooper Chapter 47

It all started with my grandfather, then my father, and then me. It was a family tradition to rid the world of promiscuous whores—women who would spread their legs without a second thought. It was beneficial because we'd experience the pleasures of their company and then... save society by removing them. I knew my daughter wouldn't be one of those women because I had raised her right. When her mother tried to hurt Nancy, the woman who lost her virginity to me, I knew I had to protect her. She was pure, she was mine. I had to have her as my wife. Jackie wasn't pure, but I married her because she was pregnant with Matt. I couldn't let some other man raise my children. When she went to attack Nancy, I knew I had to end her. But

it wasn't so simple. Nancy was too sweet, too innocent. She was going to let Jackie kill her. So, I
screamed for her to beat Jackie with the paddle. Yet,
she wouldn't do it. I lifted the gun to sweet little Alex
and told her to aim it at her mother. And she did. Alex
began firing and to block herself, Nancy lifted the
paddle, but it hit Jackie's already bleeding head into
the water. Together, my girls had gotten rid of the
problem for me. And that's when Alex knew that she
and her new beautiful mother would be bonded
forever. Together, they killed the woman who would
have prevented us from being a family. Together, I
controlled them both.

So very beautiful. They'd learn that the shadows
we run from are the ones that haunt us the most.

I knew their very worst secret. I knew they killed a
woman. I owned them. A man couldn't be more
powerful than that.

But of course, things didn't end in a happily ever
after for me as I had wished. Sara, my gorgeous lover,
had aided me, but she vanished into thin air. I was
trapped in this hospital, unable to reach her. But one
day, I would. I'd find her and love her. I already had a
plan. I'd escape and find my way to her. I had the
money and charm to buy myself out of this... *misunderstanding*. Sara and I were meant to be, we belonged

together, and more than anything in this world, she was my soulmate. She was beautiful, unlike the woman I had spent my life with. She was vibrant and vivacious, while I was quiet and settled. She was everything to me.

Tears ran down my cheeks as my lips parted in shock. "Nina?" Adam gripped my trembling hands, removing the manuscript from them.

"Did you read it?" I looked at him with my eyes burning.

He slowly nodded. "Yes."

"I didn't… I didn't… kill…" I stammered.

"Nina, this is a work of fiction created by a demented, deranged man. When you're done reading…" He lifted a lighter out of his pocket and flicked the flame up. "It's the end of his story."

Warren had Ava kill her own mother, I didn't kill her. My paddle hitting her into the water may have been the true end of her life, but I wouldn't carry this guilt. It was all staged by the man who was writing our story this entire time.

"Scarlett is Sara. She's alive. She's out there." I rubbed my head as Adam slowly rocked in the chair.

"We couldn't find her."

"Nina, this is the end. It's all over. Ava is getting the help she needs. Warren is a lucky bastard to be institutionalized, but we will work to get him into a prison, no matter how long it takes. And you, well... you are free, beautiful."

"Adam... I'm not free. I'll never be free because you can't run from your own shadow."

Adam nodded slowly. "True, but you can choose to not look back." He leaned in and kissed me before standing.

"I'm going to make us something to eat." He left me with the manuscript and dropped the lighter on top of the stack. "I love you, Nina," he added before turning away and going inside our house.

Lifting the lighter, I stood and threw the manuscript into the fire-pit before lighting it. 'DBT' stood for *Don't Believe Them*. I laughed at the irony.

I watched it burn to ash, then walked back inside. What Adam didn't know is this wasn't the end... I planned on rewriting the ending.

NOW

I pulled into the parking lot of the Johan Psychiatric Facility. I had come here every single week for the past year, though I hadn't seen him. He was on the forensic floor of the psychiatric facility, and Ava was on the general psychiatric floor. There were moments I'd pause in front of the floor Warren was on and have to fight my curiosity.

We were divorced. He meant nothing to me. He wasn't my husband, and I had no blood relation to the Cooper's, nor any legal bindings. But I loved Ava and Max; they were my kids. I had raised them, but I was also the reason their mother was no longer alive... or at least, part of the reason.

Slowly turning the corner, I walked into her room.

She had decorated the walls with artwork and was sitting by the window seat, blankly staring out through the tiny, stained window.

"Hi, sweetie," I said quietly.

She waited before slowly turning around to look at me.

"Hi, pretty mommy." Ava's lips were dried out. I had fought with the nurses to let her have Chapstick, but it wasn't a priority.

She spoke like she was a small child, and the psychiatrist told me she had basically regressed into a childlike state to protect herself.

I smiled at her. "Wow, you've been busy." I walked

to all her artwork, which was all done in crayons and looked like a five-year old had drawn them, even though Ava was once a skilled artist.

At first, I quickly walked by the drawings, overdramatically fawning over them, but then, I stopped. It wasn't just a chaotic bunch of elementary-leveled art. No, it was a story being pieced together.

"Ava, what is this one?" I lifted a drawing of the lake and a canoe with two girls. A boy and another girl were on the dock, looking at them.

"It's Collins and the redhead Max and Daddy wanted to kill to make it look like Scarlett. We had to kill them both the same night because Daddy needed to finish that chapter in his book. He was struggling to write it out." She smiled and came toward me.

The redhead was buried with her face mauled in wasn't Scarlett. She was finally identified as a homeless girl from two towns over, with no friends and family. She was murdered to be a decoy for Scarlett. Collins was just collateral damage in a killing game that Warren wanted to make into a family bonding activity. He thought his book would be a best-seller if it felt real. If the scenes of murder and torture could be palpable, because while he claimed the book was fiction, it wasn't. He was acting out everything in that book.

Placing the photo down, I made my way to the small desk attached to the wall. A small notebook sat with photos peeking out.

Ava began humming and spinning around and around. Tugging the image out, my lips parted.

It was a postcard with Max and…

"Scarlett?" I brushed my finger across the side of her face. I couldn't make her out completely, but the smattering of freckles and thick, red waves flying behind her were spot on.

They were in wedding attire on some kind of Caribbean beach.

"Ava, when did you get this?"

She didn't answer me, so I frantically began digging through the small stack of papers and found the envelope.

It was dated eleven months ago.

I had hardly talked to Max because he told me he needed space, that he couldn't relive the trauma, and I respected that. He said he'd gone off to Florida and started a new life for himself. He asked me not to contact him.

I was heartbroken that he had quit school and worried how he'd ever make ends meet, but it wasn't my place to baby him. It wasn't my place to inquire about any of the money that I knew Warren still had control over. I had assumed maybe the children had gotten some. But the lawyer told me I had no rights to any of it, nor did I have the right to know since Ava and Max were no longer minors.

"Ava, do you remember being with Collins and the other girl?" I looked at her as she stopped spinning and fell onto her small bed.

"Yes. Daddy and Max told me to cut them once each so my fingerprints would be everywhere, but they were both there, too. They hurt those girls and buried them. And Max, he buried you, Mommy. But I couldn't let you die, so I told Adam where you were."

"What?" My body shook as I processed everything Ava was saying.

"Max wanted to show Daddy he was a true Cooper, but Max hated Daddy for making him do this stuff. He told me he'd get the ultimate payback."

"Max is still mad at you for killing the other mommy and making Scarlett do those bad things with Daddy."

He must have not known that Scarlett was sleeping with his dad before I had paid her. He knew my involvement in his mother's death? He thought I had coaxed Scarlett to be with my husband?

"I think he's going to kill you." Ava frowned and tugged the blanket up to her chin.

"No, Ava... Max... Max told me he loved me and was thankful for me and... I... I didn't mean to hurt your... other mommy." My head was spinning.

Ava shrugged and yawned. "He needs the final chapter." She closed her eyes and turned away.

"Who does? Warren?" I asked frenziedly. I walked to her but she wouldn't move. "Ava?"

She was asleep.

I tried to stay calm but deep down, I had a feeling I was still a puppet in some sick and twisted game of deception.

CHAPTER FORTY-SEVEN

*T*ime had come and gone. Seasons changed and for the most part, there was a new normal. Adam and I got married. We had moved away, leaving behind the lake and memories. I cried for weeks over leaving Ava in the psychiatric facility, but I had to live. And sometimes I think I never found time to be happy because I was too busy trying to be strong.

I was always trying to be strong for everyone. And now, I just needed to keep moving forward. Adam was down in Washington D.C. for work and busy with a new case. Apparently, the FBI had far more pressing matters than resolving every little detail of a homicide case in Lake Johan, North Carolina. Warren was pinned with everything, and Ava was the "insane" teenager who filled in any of the missing pieces. They were satisfied, but I wasn't. I don't think I'd ever be satisfied knowing something still felt wrong. The way I'd always looked over my shoulder and feel terrified, the way I'd triple-check the locks and still feel alarmed.

I tugged my coat tighter around me as the winter chill hung in the air and stung my cheeks. Passing a bookstore, I stopped in my tracks as snow flurries fell and danced around me.

A giant poster of an author book signing event was being advertised.

"The Broken Mother" by Mac Copper. My heart sank as nausea pooled in my throat with the author's photo next to a stack of books. Mac Copper? I leaned in closer to the date. It was happening tomorrow night. Running into the bookstore, I walked straight into the bookshelf and lifted a copy.

Flipping it to the back, I gasped. Mac Copper was my son, Max Cooper. Max wrote a book? Turning it around, I stared at the title.

My heart sprinted as perspiration built along my hairline, even though I had been walking in the freezing weather.

"It's a wild one." A bookseller looked at me as she restocked it. "He's going to be here tomorrow night," she added with a smile.

Pushing past her, I tugged out my credit card and slid the book to the cashier. Everything was a blur as I raced home and threw my jacket off. Sinking into the couch, I began flipping through the pages.

It was Warren's story. Max had taken it...

The hours flew by, and I noticed things had changed in the book. Descriptive scenes of the nineteen-year-old mistress bashing the beloved mother's skull in were written out. Everything in the book was focused on "the broken mother."

Me.

My body was covered in chills as the lamp flickered and my stomach rumbled. Skipping to the final chapter, I choked back my sobs.

But in the end, our family had been destroyed because of a woman who was supposed to be nothing more than a notch on my father's belt. She had weaseled her way into our lives as the whore who couldn't keep her legs together. She manipulated my kind-hearted father in believing she'd be the wife perhaps my mother had failed at being for him.

She was a broken mother. She was a broken woman. She had to die and pay for everything she had done to us.

She'd be our final kill, the final performance for me to finally prove to my father that I was worthy. I was a true Cooper son. I lifted the worn compass in my hand and...

A small creak sounded, and I looked away with my

eyes blurry and burning from binge reading for the past few hours.

My mouth was dry, and my head felt heavy. I was hungry and exhausted. Something dropped and echoed against the new, glossy hardwood floors Adam had installed. That wasn't a coincidence.

"Hello? Adam?" I slowly put the book down and stood. The house was dark beyond the small table-side lamp I had turned on in a rush to read.

I walked down the hall and my foot stepped on something.

Bending over, I squinted as I lifted it up.

"Oh no…" I whimpered, holding the compass in my hand.

"Max?" My voice cracked as I looked around in the darkness, backing away toward the front door.

"Max, please… just talk to me." I held my breath.

I felt like my pounding heartbeat and erratic breathing could be heard through the daunting silence.

As soon as I backed up, my body hit something, and it wasn't the door.

His arms reached around my waist as his hot breath grazed my neck.

I'd recognize the scent for the rest of my life. His fingers grazed the space between my shirt and shorts, but then I fought back tears as the other arm touched me, and there was no hand, no fingers… just a stub.

I began to cry as he kissed my collarbone from behind.

"Hello, sunshine," he whispered as fear suffocated me.

"Warren…" I breathed out.

I tried to pull out of his arms, but he tightened his grip.

"Warren, just let me go." I tried to stay calm through the tears and fear.

A light flicked on, and I sucked in a breath of air.

Max.

"Hi, Mother." He flashed a sinister smile at me. "I see you're reading my book." Max lifted the novel and grinned as he scanned the page I had left off on. "Ah, you didn't get to the final scene, did you?"

"What are you gaining from this, Max? Don't let him ruin your life. He's already dead." I dug my nails into Warren's hand until he finally released me.

Bad things happen to good people, but bad things never happen to bad people. They are always spared.

"What is this? You all are sick." I pulled away from Warren and pressed against the wall.

"Well, you see, Mother, Dad said he'd help me kill the bitch off, and in exchange, I'll let him have my wife. I'm pretty bored with her, anyway. But, shh… don't tell her. You remember Scarlett, don't you?"

"Why do you want to kill me? Max, I loved you. I love you. I've… Everything that happened to Jackie your dad had set it all up. I… I was protecting myself. I was nineteen and…" My face flushed.

"You ruined our family. You are a broken woman, and because of that, you seduced my father and destroyed our family. But then, it's been a good bonding experience, letting us release our natural urge to kill and to be able to document and sell it off as a fictional book. I mean, have you seen how successful this book has been?" Max laughed as he flung his novel to the side.

Warren was beaming as Max talked. For the first time in his entire life, he was proud of his son. That's what fueled Max—he wanted to prove to his sick, demented father that he was a true Cooper because he could kill innocent women without remorse?

"Come on, sunshine." Warren aggressively grabbed my arm and dragged me as Max erupted into laughter and followed us with the gun shoved into my back.

"Get on your knees." Warren smirked as he pushed me into the living room.

Shaking my head, I pleaded, "Warren, don't do this.

Please. I won't tell anyone." I cried out as they savored the fear emitting from my body.

"Get on your fucking knees," he said again through clenched teeth.

"You really were supposed to just be another notch on my belt." Warren sighed. "Come on son, let's finish this up. The final scene."

This was it. This was how their book ended, with me dying. They were acting it all out and playing a game with my life, Ava's life, and so many innocent women's lives.

"Does Scarlett know she's going to be given to you?" I rolled my eyes as Max came around and pushed the gun against my forehead.

"Oh, don't be jealous, sweetheart," Warren said callously.

Max dug the steel deeper into my skin. Slamming my eyes shut, I thought about, how as humans, we think we have full control over our stories. It's silly, isn't it? While also being completely heart-wrenching? We don't have much control over the story that we live through. I had made a terrible decision when I was nineteen years old to get involved with a married man. He should have known better and so should I, but I didn't.

Warren walked away and turned music on, loudly.

I knew he was doing it to cover the sound of the gunshot that would soon pierce my skull.

My heart was racing as I thought about how stupid I was all those years ago, and how Jackie, Warren's first wife, was so lucky.

She didn't have to watch her husband's darkness grow in the lives of her children. She didn't have to watch a family she loved shatter in front of her eyes.

"Max, I am sorry that I had to protect myself, and when I hit Jackie, your mother… she didn't have a chance."

Max began laughing again. "You think this is about my mother? No, this is about creating a legacy. Cooper men were destined to kill, to purge our communities of whores. Why do you think I don't mind letting my dad have Scarlett?" He leaned close to my ear and whispered, "Because one day, I'll purge her from this world, too."

"Bye, Nina. You were nothing more than a broken mother." He cocked the gun and I thought about the lake, I thought about Adam, I thought about Paige and Joss.

I thought about the good.

And just like that, the gun fired.

My eyes slammed shut as I screamed.

But I didn't feel anything; instead, a *thud* sounded next to me.

"Scarlett?" he yelled in shock.

Opening my eyes slowly, tears blurred my vision as my body felt paralyzed.

"Hi, sweetie." Scarlett was holding a gun in the air. Looking down, I gasped. She had shot Max, who now was lying in a pool of his own blood.

"Hey, Nins." She winked at me.

"Baby, it's been so long." Warren didn't even think twice about his son lying dead mere feet from him. Our son was dead. Shock washed over my entire body.

He looked like a dog running toward Scarlett, but she turned the gun on him. "Stop," she said without a hitch.

Warren instantly froze in his tracks. The gun Max was holding was now under his body. There was no way I'd be able to retrieve it without them knowing.

"Nina and Warren, we are going to the bedroom together. Any funny business, and I'll blow your brains out." She nodded in the direction of the bedroom I now shared with Adam.

Warren didn't hesitate and immediately walked to the bedroom. I stood slowly, glancing down at Max's body, then followed Warren while Scarlett walked behind us. My legs shook as I looked at the room, knowing there was no way out.

"Put these on him and attach both hands to the headboard." Scarlett pointed at the furry handcuffs.

What was she going to make us do? My stomach twisted into knots as Warren crawled onto the bed, his face lighting up.

"My girl was always the kinkiest." He licked his bottom lip as I attached his hand to the headboard.

"Take his pants off and take your clothes off, too, Nina." I looked at Scarlett and shook my head.

"No, Scarlett. Please don't do this."

"Do it now." Her jaw ticked as she waved her gun.

I did as I was told and dragged Warren's pants and briefs off of him.

He looked at Scarlett. "Sorry, baby." Glancing at his flaccid penis, his cheeks turned red. Then he slanted his eyes at me and looked at me with resentment. "You were always the reason I was limp," he fired at me.

Letting out a dry laugh, I looked at him and his pathetic excuse of a penis. "No, sweetheart. Your dick was always as useless as decaf coffee."

Scarlett yelped out, "Ooh, Nins, you're spicier than I remember. I love it." She turned to Warren. "But also, she's not lyin'."

"Nina, take this belt." Scarlett pointed at it.

I stood there in a lacy black bra and panty set, sliding my hand toward the end of the bed.

"Warren, what was it that you always said about Nina?"

Warren looked at Scarlett with heartbreak in his eyes. "Baby, let me fix us."

"Tell me! What did you always say about her?"

"She was always just supposed to be another notch on my belt." He shrugged and shot me a look of disgust. "I mean, look at her. Nothing more than a broken woman." His eyes dropped to my midsection and thighs. "I had to replace the old model with a new one," he scoffed.

Scarlett walked closer to me and brushed her fingers through my hair. "Warren, you are the biggest regret of my life. Your son was terrible in bed, and you were, too. I faked every orgasm. But Nina... oh how I wish she would have given me a chance." Scarlett turned my face toward her and locked her lips on mine. I could taste the cherry Chapstick lined on her lips.

"You're so beautiful." The warmth of her breath brushed against my lips as she dragged her fingertips along my collarbone and straight down my abdomen. Slowly, she pulled away. My body was tense as she whispered into my ear, "You're going to wrap this belt around his neck and watch the life leave his eyes."

I looked at her in shock.

"Do it. And just in case, here's this for some added fun." She placed a butcher knife on the nightstand as Warren's eyes grew wider.

I didn't even think about the way the gun was hanging by my chest. I didn't think about anything.

"We can fix this, sunshine. We can be a family, again," Warren pleaded. "You know I love you... I've always loved you." He whimpered like a small animal watching a predator stalk them.

My heart shattered. I had built an entire world with this man. I had spent most of my life with him. A movie reel of the happier times started to flood my mind, even though I begged myself not to trudge down that pathway.

Scarlett brushed her finger against my collarbone before she whispered into my ear, "He'll never change. He'll only hurt you. Don't believe him."

Suddenly, it was as if I was waking up for the first time in our twenty years of marriage. It felt like I had removed the blindfold from my eyes and saw every-thing clearly. Even the word 'believe' has the word lie embedded right in the middle of it. Yet, we still did. We still believed them.

I lifted the worn leather and wrapped it around Warren's neck as he bashed around wildly. Rage and memories flooded any ounce of clarity I held. I straddled Warren and tightening my grip as his legs kicked and he screamed, attempting to bite me.

"Down, dog," I spat at him as I tightened my grip and watched his face turn bright red.

"Nina, you were always a bad mother and a bad wife." He coughed out, knowing those words always broke me. There was nothing more I had wanted for decades than to prove to my husband and children that I was a good mother and wife.

"No, you pathetic piece of shit. You were always the bad husband." And just like that, I had changed the ending of Warren Cooper's story.

But as the life left his body, something overcame me. He looked too perfect; he was laying there, gasping for air. I slid my hand over to the knife and lifted it. Perhaps for the first time, I understood what an outer body experience was as I held it high and without a second thought, I slammed it repeatedly into my dying ex-husband's body. All I could see was red as splatters of blood painted across my arms, eyes, and face. Warren's shrill screams depleted just as quickly as the life left his body.

Dropping the knife and releasing the belt, I looked at Scarlett as her lips tipped into a smile.

"That's my girl." She winked at me.

I walked past her with nothing covering my body beyond my lace bra and panties. Reaching into my closet, I grabbed a long, silk emerald dress that I had never felt worthy of wearing. The day I put it on, Warren laughed and said I was too old to pull it off anymore. I slid into it over his blood staining my skin, then slid shoes on before leaving the house. Getting into my car, I gripped the cold steering wheel and kept driving until I found the closest lake.

Climbing out, I walked to the dock and looked into the still waters. One foot was aching and when I glanced down, I realized I had only put one shoe on. Closing my eyes, my body felt exhausted, but in my mind, it no longer belonged to me.

The lake house was so precious to me back in Lake Johan. I thought it was my safe place.

People think your forever home is four walls and a roof, but no, *he* was supposed to be my forever home. He was supposed to be my happily ever after. Staring blankly, relief spread through me as I realized I had a fresh new chapter right in front of me.

Lifting my hands above my head, I jumped into the frigid waters and let myself sink. I thought my husband would keep me from drowning, I thought he'd make sure to be my life raft, but instead, he was a weight wrapped around my ankles and pulling me into the darkness. Memories of our life flashed in front of me as my body crumpled under the water. I was washing myself of Warren, forever.

Just as the breath in my lungs began to dissipate, I pushed myself back to the surface and gasped for air.

It was over.

CHAPTER FORTY-EIGHT

ONE YEAR LATER

*A*dam and I were sitting together, chatting over steaming cups of coffee and carving pumpkins together.

"You are incredible, you know that." He leaned down and kissed me.

"Thank you for... everything." I sighed as his lips grazed my neck.

I was in therapy. The case against Warren and Max Cooper had resolved all the missing pieces the FBI needed. They uncovered even more bodies of young women buried in the field I was once in and almost came close to being one of those case files.

It was a killing game. A killing game that both father and son loved documenting. And all for what? A more realistic book?

Fame?

I didn't care anymore. I was no longer a Cooper. I no longer held on to the memories of my past.

"Paige is coming to visit next weekend." I smiled up at Adam.

"I'm so happy for you. I'll be sure to stay out of the way."

"You're never in the way, Adam." He wrapped his strong arm around me and drew me in closer.

My phone buzzed. Lifting it up, it was an unknown number.

Clicking it, my heart dropped.

It was a photo of Scarlett and…

Ava.

They were kissing under an altar. This girl really had a thing for Coopers. I slapped my hand on my head.

"Got my happily ever after. And now you do, too."

A notification pinged my phone.

It was a bank transfer.

Sliding my phone off, I looked out to the ocean.

I knew Ava had been released from the psychiatric facility. She was still under intense psychiatric care, but was, for the most part, rehabilitated enough to be out in the world and try to build a life of her own. That, and most of the psychiatric facilities were operating under budget and had no space left.

"Hey, babe, I need to make a quick call." I stood and brushed the sand off myself before walking to the ocean.

Lifting the phone to my ear, I called the number.

She answered on the first ring.

"Hey, Nins."

"Scarlett..."

We had agreed to never speak about what had happened. She lit a match, and we watched the house burn into flames.

The police didn't second guess it all. Max and Warren were predators and criminals.

Scarlett disappeared, and I was the victim who cried on the porch until Adam and everyone came.

"Ava?"

"I guess the Cooper men were such a letdown, but damn, the women are..."

"Scarlett." I shook my head. "The money?" I asked curiously.

"I promised you all that time ago that I would help you get away from him and get you the evidence you needed to get the money you always deserved to start over."

Tears stung my eyes as I looked out into the ocean in disbelief.

"Scarlett, I should have never asked you to catfish Warren."

"Nins, I should have never slept with your husband, or your son... and well, I won't apologize for Ava because she's actually good in—"

"No, no, no! I'm good," I quickly said.

Scarlett laughed. "Listen Nins, Adam seems great for you. But keep this money in your own secret account. Us, girls can't trust men. They always let us down, always.

Closing my eyes, I let the words sink in.

We don't choose the characters in our story, and we don't choose the way we get entrapped into their plot.

But what we can do is choose our own ending.

I chose mine and fuck, if it didn't feel good that I also chose Warren's. Most of all, it was something else of its own that 'the other woman' and the wife helped each other.

"You ready to go get some sushi, beautiful?"

I turned and walked back toward my sexy, younger husband.

"Absolutely." I paused and brushed my hand against

his jawline. "Adam, thank you for loving me, even though I was broken when you found me."

"Nina, you were never broken. You just got trapped within the broken family you never deserved." Tilting my chin up, he planted his lips against mine.

CHAPTER FORTY-NINE

There was a sliver of sunshine creeping in through the window, even though it was a cold day.

I glanced at the time and knew I needed to leave by nine a.m. to make the event. I had slept in after a late night with Paige, laughing over wine and charcuterie boards. Taking a long, hot shower, I tied my hair up in a towel and quickly applied my makeup. Turning around, I saw the gorgeous, curve-hugging black dress he had picked out for me and slid into it. Gliding on my bright red lipstick, I smacked my lips together and pulled my heels on. A quick spin in front of the mirror had me grinning. Reaching in my drawer, I grabbed the leather belt and slid it through the loops.

I felt beautiful. I checked my teeth quickly and raced downstairs, clutching the wooden banister.

The coffee was still hot and beside the empty mug was a note.

You're even hotter than this coffee. See you soon, baby.

My heart raced as I poured the coffee into my mug and clutched it between my palms.

I walked to the back door with my heels clicking against the floor.

The lake was still so beautiful even once the days grew colder. It had the unknown clinging to the fog that always hung over it. The usual lush green trees were all bare and hugged the darkened lake.

My phone buzzed.

I'm on in ten! His text had my eyes widen as I placed my coffee down and quickly rushed out.

I strummed my fingers against the cold, leather steering wheel and hummed along to the song.

Our first dance, John Legend's *All of Me* was playing, and it all felt so full circle.

I loved how excited I felt to see my husband. I would have never thought that being in my forties I'd still feel as giddy as I did when I was a teenager, but when you marry the love of your life, I suppose it isn't hard.

Sliding out of my car, I bit my bottom lip, seeing

how packed the parking lot was and made my way inside.

There he was, standing at the front of the podium with enormous banners behind him.

He caught me just as I sat down and instantly lit up.

I clutched the book in my hands and listened to him speak so eloquently as his fans eyed him with admiration and fascination.

My heart was so full of love and pride.

Our life was so beautiful.

After he was done speaking, he was guided to a table, and I quickly walked over to beat the line.

There were a few people who snuck in front of me, eagerly taking photos with him and having him sign their books.

"This book was so twisted! I swear, it felt completely real," one reader said in front of me.

"I agree, I felt like it all really happened," another chimed in.

His publicist smiled proudly. "That's what made this book an instant best-seller."

"Well, hello, sunshine." His sexy smirk could melt me all these years later.

"Can I get a picture with the author?" I giggled.

"Absolutely." Warren stood and smiled at me. "Max,

Ava! Come up here. I want to get a family photo." Our kids looked agitated as they dragged their feet to us.

"Thank you for believing in me and for helping me write the book I've always dreamt of, sweetheart. None of this would have been possible without you... my muse, my inspiration, my everything." Warren leaned in and kissed me.

"I'm so proud of you, Professor Cooper."

Whispering in my ear, he bit at my earlobe, "Thank you for writing the final chapter for me. I would have never finished this book without you. Just two empty-nester reconnecting, didn't we?"

Looking up at my husband, I scrunched my nose and kissed him. Who would have thought that writing and dreaming up a book together was what would reconnect us the first year of being empty nesters? But it was amazing to create a book together that felt real.

"You gave me a happily ever after... it was the least I could do."

"Most couples go on vacation or scrapbook; leave it to our parents to write a book full of murder as their hobby..." Ava sighed as we all laughed and took photos.

In the grand scheme of life, Warren and I were on our final chapter. We raised our babies, and Warren had retired from being a professor at the university we had fallen in love at. We lived in our dream lake house, and now we were reconnecting over a fun hobby that became his new career.

And there was no one else I'd rather do it with.

Warren took his seat again.

"Mom, Dad, I want you to meet my new girlfriend!" Max called out to us as he laced his hand with a gorgeous redhead.

My brows knitted together as I looked at her and forced a smile out.

"Hi," I breathed out in shock to the uncanny resemblance.

She looked at me blankly before dropping a copy of the book in front of Warren.

"Who would you like me to sign it to?" Warren asked our son's new girlfriend.

"Professor Cooper, I was in your Abnormal Psychology class last year. You can make it out to Sammie." She winked at him.

The smile on my face melted as I looked at the girl and the way my husband's cheeks turned red. The way his hands shook as he signed it and gave her a look of apprehension.

"I'm sorry I didn't remember. You both are together?" Warren stammered, pointing his pen between our son and Sammie.

Sammie's eyes filled with seduction as her tongue swiped her bottom lip while Warren's chest heaved faster.

Max was busy talking to a friend, and Sammie turned toward me as more readers pushed her out of line.

"This book... feels so very real. Don't you think, Nins?"

My heart raced as I looked between my husband and the young girl in front of us.

CHAPTER FIFTY

*J*olting up, I slammed my hand against my pounding heart. I stretched my hands over my head and turned to the handsome man beside me. Brushing my finger against his lips, I woke him up.

"Good morning, beautiful," he rasped with sleep embedded in his tone.

Grinning, I whispered back, "Good morning, handsome."

"How did you sleep?" He tugged me closer.

"Terribly. I had the worst nightmare." I closed my eyes as I shuddered.

"Warren?" he asked softly.

"Mm-hmm... he was alive. We were going to his

book event. You didn't exist. You were just a character in his book." I sighed.

"How about I prove to you that I'm definitely real, my love?"

I opened my eyes and looked at him, already feeling my cheeks flush. "I think that may make me feel better." I rolled my lips together.

Pulling my hair back tightly, he had one hand around my neck. Screams left my lips as the blindfold hindered my vision. My palms pressed against the glass as my breathing hitched.

He dragged his teeth across my collarbone as my entire body shook.

Dipping my head to the side, his lips pressed against my neck until they reached my earlobe and he whispered, "You're the most beautiful woman in the world."

I tightened around him as moans escaped my mouth and he gripped my hips higher.

"Adam." I sighed as a strong orgasm rippled through my entire body, and I folded in half over his tattooed arms.

"You are perfection." He shook his head and pressed his lips against mine.

Closing my eyes, I smiled under our kiss. I was smiling because I finally felt like I was living. I was smiling because I believed him. He was real. Warren was dead. Everything was right in the world.

In a world, where men only get better looking, more appealing with age, I was a forty-three-year-old woman with a turbulent past and trauma, having the hottest sex of my life with a gorgeous thirty-two-year-old man who worshipped the floor I walked on and made me feel like an absolute goddess.

"We've got to leave in an hour, baby," he said while brushing his thumb against my lower lip.

I swallowed the lump in my throat as nerves pooled in my lower abdomen. All I wanted to do was to stay in bed with Adam.

"You're going to be amazing. It's a sold-out event." He kissed my forehead before pulling away.

I watched as Adam walked away. I couldn't believe this was my new life, my new reality. I had never felt more content. Walking to my closet, I tugged out the stunning bright red dress I had saved for this special day. Stepping into it, I shimmied my body into the skin-tight dress that I once would have grabbed Spanx to wear under. Looking back at my reflection, I smiled. My hair was wild from a man, who adored me, running his fingers through. My eyes showed the confidence I felt internally. I was proud of myself. Adam was absolutely incredible, but I didn't allow him to be the reason I grew into the woman I now was. I did this.

I grabbed my purse and slid my stilettos on. "Damn, you are gorgeous." Adam was leaning against the doorframe with one arm higher. He was wearing gray slacks, a black belt, and a white button-down tucked in with the first few buttons undone.

Biting my lower lip, I walked up to him with my heels clicking against the smooth, wood floor.

"You're not so bad yourself, handsome." I planted a small red kiss on his cheek before looping my arm into his.

Walking into the bookstore, I couldn't believe it. A giant poster with my face on it and the book I had written was plastered right in the center of the lobby.

A crowd had already formed. Adam leaned down and whispered into my ear, "All for you, beautiful."

Letting go of me, he nodded as I made my way to the signing table. Stacks and stacks of my new, debut novel were lined up.

"The Broken Husband" a thriller novel I had spent endless hours and nights writing was now a best seller.

While I pushed it as a fiction novel, those who knew my story knew how truly real this book was.

"There's my girl!" My face lit up in a smile as I saw my best friend, Paige, shove past the lines and cut straight to the front.

"I didn't think you'd be able to fly out." I stood and wrapped my arms around her. I felt the painful emptiness missing from my arms since Joss wasn't there.

"I wouldn't miss this for the world. Soul sisters, babe." Paige squeezed me tightly. "Listen, book signing, alibi, murder, lunch, margaritas, whatever you need, you know I've got you forever." She tucked a strand of hair behind my ear.

Fighting back the tears in my eyes, I gave her a quick squeeze before turning back to sit as the bookstore manager introduced me.

Standing at the podium, I began reading a passage out of my book.

"It's amazing what coffee and orgasms can do for the soul. It can be the difference between letting your husband live an extra day or not." I paused as the crowds erupted into laughter.

Biting into my cheek, I grinned. "Unfortunately, my husband was terrible at both—making coffee and making me orgasm. I had learned in life that your coffee and orgasms should be equally as hot. But for us, my husband had failed me. He failed our marriage. He was having an affair. He said that we had a broken marriage, but really, I just had a broken husband." I sighed as I continued down the passage, occasionally lifting my eyes to the packed room of excited readers clutching my book in their hands.

I finished reading, signed stacks of books, and went out for dinner and drinks with Paige.

It was a night to remember. Making my way back home hours later, I turned my key in our door and walked in.

The scent of roses fluttered in the air as candles were lit all around the floor.

Following the trail of petals, I walked to our bedroom, kicking off my heels to one side and tossing my purse to the other.

Pushing open the door to our bedroom, I gasped at how beautiful it was. Adam was in the middle of the bed.

His clothes were off and the smirk that grew on his

face left me breathless. I walked to the side and turned, and he instantly unzipped my dress.

"Hi baby." He turned me around and sat propped up on his knees.

Pulling me down into bed with him, I laid in his arms and started to trace the tattoo on his forearm.

"You know, I don't think I've ever really studied these." I glanced up at him as the smile that was on his face began to fade.

Turning his arm, he tried to push away.

"Wait, Adam." My heart began to pound as I blinked quickly.

No. No. My eyes had to be playing a trick on me. Maybe I had one too many cocktails with Paige?

"Baby..." He relaxed his shoulders and sank back down.

My mouth grew dry as I traced my finger across the words.

Quae seminaverit homo haex et metet.

It blended into the intricate tattoos scattered all across his arms. A skull and then just beside it, a small compass.

"Adam..." Fear rose inside me as I trembled and began to move away from him.

Grabbing my arm, his forehead creased as his lips parted. "Nina, please..."

"Oh my god, what… Why do you have that?" My words shook as he pinned me down. "Let go, Adam." I felt cold, even though the warmth of his body was hovering between us as he pushed himself over me to keep me in place.

"Nina, baby, listen to me… This was never supposed to happen. We were never supposed to happen. But we did and I… I'm so in love with you."

"Adam, I need you to get off of me." I dug my nails into his flesh as he released his hold on me, and I tumbled out of the bed.

Grabbing my dress from the floor, I covered my body as I looked at him.

Standing quickly, he dropped to his knees in front of me. "Just one chance. Just give me one chance to explain myself."

"You have two minutes, and then I want you to get the fuck out of my house," I hissed.

"Warren Cooper was my father."

Five words that I would have never in an eternity guessed.

Five words that had my stomach twisting into knots and nausea rising into my throat as my vision blurred and I took a step back from the man in front of me.

"He was eighteen when he got my mom pregnant.

She was sixteen and never told him about me. She said he was always violent and would have hurt us. But he did find out about me, and he hurt her. He killed her when I was ten. He didn't want her to use me as black-mail one day." Adam clenched his eyes shut before opening them slowly as chills decorated my arms.

"He staged it like a suicide. I didn't know at the time; I didn't know for years. I lived with my grand-mother, and she had photos of him. She had a photo of my mom holding that compass. I got this fucking tattoo thinking it would be a way to feel connected to him." Adam shook his head and let out a dry laugh.

"But then, I found another polaroid. A polaroid of my mother the night she died. I found him posing with her dead body like a hunter with his prized deer. I knew no one would serve justice the way I would one day. For her." Adam stood slowly.

"You took the case because you always knew who he was. You got close to me... because you... wanted to get close to him?" I whimpered as tears fell from my eyes.

Shaking his head, he opened his palms. "Nina, you are the best thing that's happened to me. I didn't plan any of this. If there is one truth I know, it's that I love you endlessly."

Pressing my back and palms against the wall

behind me, I looked at Adam. "Why didn't you just tell me?"

He cupped my elbows and drew me in closer. "Because I was terrified you'd never believe me."

"Believe you?" I whispered back.

"I was terrified you'd never believe that I'm never going to be like him. I'm nothing like him." He closed his eyes and sucked in a breath as I stood there.

Brushing my fingers across Adam's jawline, I stood on my tiptoes and kissed the vulnerable man in front of me. "I believe you, Adam. But if you ever lie to me again or keep something from me... just know what I'm capable of." I reached down and lifted his black leather belt from the floor.

His eyes widened as he swallowed. "Never again."

CHAPTER FIFTY-ONE

I stood at the gravestone. Shaking my head, I couldn't help but laugh. Weeks had passed. I had needed some time to process and to think about everything I wanted versus what I needed. I loved Adam, I did. I made him tell me everything and give me factual evidence about his connection to Warren. I took time to stay with Paige and just have time to myself.

"Can you believe it, honey? I really upgraded the old model with the new one." I let out a laugh as I looked down at the weeds and unmaintained patch of dirt where Warren was buried.

In relationships, it was easy to wear a blindfold over our eyes. It was easy to see only what we wanted to in order to protect ourselves from the truth that was right there. I had a blindfold on my entire relationship with Warren, and it only tightened around my eyes once we got married—once we had built a life and family together.

But now, I knew the only time I'd ever wear a blindfold was when I was in bed with my wrists tied and a gorgeous man who was worthy of me. Now, I knew I'd never walk around believing just anything someone told me.

"Did you want a minute?" I turned over my shoulder and looked at Adam. He was leaning against the car with aviator sunglasses on and his arms crossed.

"Nah. I'm good, baby." He opened the door for me as I made my way up.

Sliding into the car, my phone vibrated, and I looked down at the screen.

Hi, my beautiful Nins.

Scarlett. I looked over my shoulder and through the window quickly rolling it down. Lifting my sunglasses to my head, I could have sworn I saw a figure in the distance with red hair billowing behind.

Are you here? I texted with my chest tightening.

I love that emerald dress on you. Just remember, the apple doesn't fall far from the tree...

Shaking my head, I rubbed my temples before sliding my sunglasses down the bridge of my nose.

Looking over at Adam, he smiled at me and laced his fingers into mine. "You know I'd never hurt you right, sunshine?"

My entire body went cold as I gritted my teeth. Nodding with my lips tight, I took a deep breath in. Why'd he call me sunshine?

Her voice echoed near me.

Don't believe him...

ACKNOWLEDGMENTS

To my children, Mila and Ari who gave me the strength to follow my heart and write books to keep a piece of my identity when I was in the thick of the newborn and toddler haze. Now, while in the toddler and kid haze, you both have made me remember I can still see clear enough to write and chase my dreams while being your biggest cheerleader. I love you both more than words could ever say.

To my husband, thank you for being nothing like the men I write and also listening to my many plot ideas where some reason the husband doesn't end up doing so well. I love you!

To my family who always cheers me on thank you for believing in me always.

Paige, my soul sister, you were a reason I finished writing this book even though I was in a chaotic place in life. You believed in me when I started to question believing in myself. I love you and you already know just how much you mean to me. Spiral soul sisters forever and always, my girl.

Joselin (Joss), you are the energy and positivity that brings me up and reminds me to stay true to myself and what I have always dreamt of. Thank you for being a dear friend I can trust, count on and tell anything to without judgment. You are beautiful inside and out. I promise to make book videos in my backyard with the tripod. Love you, my friend.

Marcie, my gorgeous friend, you took a chance on me with The Next Mrs. Wimberly and since then have showered me in friendship and support. The universe knew I needed you because you make my life brighter and celebrating these thrillers with you is something I'll forever be honored by. I love you!

My beta readers and book friends who read this book in its very first draft and helped me craft the final book, I adore each of you so much. Thank you so much for reading it in its most vulnerable state. Erin, Jessica, Gabby, Amanda, Caroline, Cristina and Kelly, and Kori you just know how special you are to me.

To my incredible ARC team who most have been with me since my first book, you all celebrate the books I pour myself into while being so precious, thoughtful and wonderful in this whirlwind. I am grateful for the gorgeous reviews, posts, kind words and everything in between.

And finally, my beloved readers, thank you for taking the time to read and review my books. It is an honor that you chose my words and novels to spend time with.

ABOUT THE AUTHOR

Monica Arya is a best-selling thriller and romance author. Her novels have been number one best sellers in countless categories and garnered praise along with awards at multiple conventions. Besides writing and reading, Monica loves spending time with her two young children, husband and family. She also enjoys chocolate, spontaneous dance parties, spreading joy and connecting with readers. You can find Monica through any of these social media outlets.

Monica Arya's Misfits (Facebook Reader Group)

Instagram / TikTok (@monicaaryaauthor)

www.monicaarya.com

Made in United States
Orlando, FL
28 November 2024

54593355R00243